ROBERT B. PARKER'S

BULL RIVER

THE SPENSER NOVELS

ROBERT B. PARKER'S

BULL RIVER

Robert Knott

G. P. PUTNAM'S SONS
New York

PUTNAM

G. P. PUTNAM'S SONS
Publishers Since 1838
Published by the Penguin Group
Penguin Group (USA) LLC
375 Hudson Street
New York, New York 10014

USA · Canada · UK · Ireland · Australia
New Zealand · India · South Africa · China

penguin.com
A Penguin Random House Company

Library of Congress Cataloging-in-Publication Data

Knott, Robert, date.
Robert B. Parker's Bull River / Robert Knott.
p.   cm. — (A Cole and Hitch novel)
ISBN 978-0-399-16526-9
1. Cole, Virgil (Fictitious character)—Fiction.   2. Hitch, Everett
(Fictitious character)—Fiction.   I. Title.   II. Title: Bull River.
PS3611.N685R38   2014   2013037162
813'.6—dc23

Printed in the United States of America
1   3   5   7   9   10   8   6   4   2

BOOK DESIGN BY EMILY S. HERRICK

For Julie

1

WE RODE HARD UP THE ROAD TO THE GOVERNOR'S mansion. Virgil was on his chestnut stud, Cortez, and I was riding Tornado, a big black gelding with a white lightning bolt–blazed face I'd won in a game of faro near Odessa.

When we got to the gated entrance, two sentries tried to stop us, but Virgil flashed his badge and we passed on through. The setting sun flickered behind tall pecan trees as we galloped up the drive to the mansion.

At the door, a butler met us, and we entered the stately manor just as the huge grandfather clock in the lobby sounded off six echoing chimes. Virgil's bone-handled Colt was on his hip, and I carried my double-barrel eight-gauge.

"I'll have to ask you for your weapons, gentlemen," the butler said.

"*No,*" the governor said, entering the lobby.

"Evening, Governor," Virgil said.

"These men are allowed to carry their guns wherever and whenever they please!"

Then I saw her, Emma, coming down the huge stairs, wearing a pale yellow dress. She smiled at me.

"Everett," Emma said. "So nice to see you again."

"What about me?" Virgil said.

"Oh, silly me," Emma said. "Of course it's wonderful to see the both of you."

~

At dinner, the governor stood and raised his glass.

"A toast! To you, Marshal Cole, and to you, Deputy Hitch."

The governor paused. He looked to his daughters, Abigail and Emma, and then his wife, before he looked back over the top of his glass held up in the direction of Virgil.

"I am so very grateful for what you, Marshal Cole, and you, Deputy Marshal Hitch, did for me, for my family."

The governor's tone of voice was solid, sincere, and it resonated with a dignified inflection that most likely helped get him elected.

I looked across the table, and behind the arrangement of daffodils, bluebells, and grape hyacinths, Emma sat stoically, gazing directly at me as her father continued his toast.

After dinner, Emma excused us and led me out of the dining room.

"Where are we going?"

"Oh, no place in particular," Emma said. "It's such a beautiful evening."

Emma kept her arm locked in mine as we made our way out the door and onto the back porch.

"Where is your fiancé?"

"He's away."

Emma stopped and turned to me. She placed her back to the post at the top of the railing that followed the steps down into the garden.

"Tell me something, Deputy Hitch," she said with a lift of volume in her voice.

"What would you like to know?" I said. "And it's Everett."

"Yes, Everett," Emma said.

She said my name like I'd never really heard it spoken before. She put emphasis on the last three letters, as if she were speaking French.

"If you could be anywhere in the world," Emma said, "where would that anywhere be?"

I thought about the question for a moment as she looked at me with an expectant, almost enthusiastic look on her face.

"Well, I don't know," I said. "I've never really thought about being anyplace other than where I am."

"Oh, indulge me, Everett."

"Well, okay, let's see . . . the Rocky Mountains are awful pretty."

Emma pulled me slightly closer to her and pleaded with me as if I didn't understand the essence of her question.

"Anywhere in the world," Emma said.

I looked down, studied the boards of the porch for a moment, and then looked back to Emma.

"Let me think about that."

Emma let go of my hands, turned, and walked down the steps like I had disappointed her.

"Where would you be?" I said.

"Follow me, I'll show you."

3

The rose garden behind the house was enormous, with rows and rows of yellow fragrant roses. The night was warm, with a gentle breeze. It was a clear evening, the moon was almost full, and there was not a cloud in the sky. Emma moved ahead of me some. She turned back to me, taking my hand, and led me toward a gazebo at the far end of the garden. When we were in the center of the gazebo, Emma twirled and twirled with her arms raised above her head like a ballerina.

"So . . . what? This is it?" I said. "Here? This gazebo?"

After her next revolution, she fell into my arms.

"Noooo," she said. "This is where I'd be, right here, with you, Everett, in your arms."

She reached up, sliding her hand behind my neck, and pulled my head down to meet hers. From somewhere I heard the faint sounds of a guitar.

"If I could be anywhere in the world," she said as she closed her eyes, "this is where I'd be."

I pulled her to me, and our lips met. We kissed, soft at first, and then we kissed deeply. Never in my life had I felt a kiss like this, never. I thought, *This must be what love is,* and then I heard Virgil.

"Everett . . ."

2

"Everett," Virgil said.

I opened my eyes from kissing Emma in the gazebo on a beautiful night in Austin City, Texas, to find myself where Virgil and I had been holed up for the better part of a week: the second-story room in an adobe hotel overlooking the plaza of the dusty village of El Encanto, on the border of Old Mexico.

"I believe we have us a rummy," Virgil said.

Virgil was sitting by the window, smoking a cigar and sipping on a glass of whiskey. Except for the light sifting within Virgil's cigar smoke from the plaza, the room was dark. I could hear guitar music drifting up, with the muffled voices of villagers moving about in the plaza.

The night was hot and humid. *Emma. That damn woman,* I thought as I sat up. *Another goddamn dream about Emma.* I stretched the ache from my back and moved to the window to see what Virgil was looking at.

"Captain Alejandro," Virgil said.

Across the plaza, seven men on horseback rode slowly into the plaza, and it was obvious Alejandro Miguel Vasquez led the pack.

Alejandro was much bigger than any of his seconds. He was at least six feet, handsome, with broad shoulders, long dark hair, and blue-green eyes. He rode a spirited tall tricolored medicine-hat geld with a thick, long blond mane and tail. Like the Sioux, Blackfoot, and Comanche, Alejandro claimed the medicine-hat protected him against harm.

The bandito was well known for his fancy Mexican attire: a large sombrero, tapered concho breeches, shiny spurs with huge rowels, and though it was hotter than hell out, he wore his trademark jacket—a silver-buttoned Mexican Naval Officers jacket with red velvet cuffs and a collar that he crossed with dual bandoliers. But he was no naval captain. Alejandro was nothing but a robber, a raider, an escaped killer, and now he was in El Encanto.

Alejandro was a wanted man. He was also a notorious gang leader and a mean sonofabitch. Virgil and I had tracked him down before and arrested him near Dead Man's Ford in the Pecos, but he managed to escape the custody of two deputies en route back to San Cristóbal.

They were taking him there, where he was to stand trial for the very thing Virgil and I had arrested him for in the first place: the murder of two men he'd shot dead in the streets of San Cristóbal on Christmas Day.

Three months after his escape, he was apprehended by a friend of ours, a deputy named "Newly" Ned Newcomb up in Butch's Bend. Within a few days of his capture, Alejandro got away yet again, and "Newly" Ned was found shot six times in the back.

It wasn't long after his escape in Butch's Bend that Alejandro got his gang back together and was instantly credited for a series of raids throughout the territories.

A week after robbing a Butterfield Stage between La Mesilla and Hatch, Alejandro and his desperadoes were said to have terrorized the border town of Santa Teresa, robbing every citizen and business in the place. The village was burnt to the ground before the looters set out for Mexico.

And now, here he was, at last.

We watched as Alejandro and his banditos circled around the stone water well in the center of the plaza.

"The captain and his crew," I said.

"Yep," Virgil said. "It goddamn sure is."

"He's returned to his port," I said.

Alejandro and his men passed slowly by our hotel and angled toward a cantina across the plaza.

He sat tall in the saddle as his bandits followed him through the plaza. He acted as if he had not a care in the world, but he was looking at everything, taking everything in. They dismounted and hitched up in front of the cantina.

"Looks like Alejandro's got a few less sailors," I said.

"Does."

"Maybe he killed 'em off himself," I said.

"Wouldn't put it past him," Virgil said.

Alejandro stopped from entering the cantina. He turned and looked around the plaza. Virgil and I eased back in the dark of the room just as Alejandro looked directly at us. He continued looking in our direction until one of his men said something that made him laugh. Alejandro gave the plaza one last look, then turned, and the seven outlaws made their way into the cantina.

"Here we go," I said.

Virgil nodded.

"High time," Virgil said.

"Is."

We had known it was only a matter of time before Alejandro would be coming to the village of El Encanto. We got a forewarning from one of his ruffians, a no-good named Javier who was arrested after the gang robbed the Butterfield Stage. A posse caught up to them and gave chase. Javier's horse got shot out from underneath him, but Alejandro kept on the run, so Javier didn't much care for Alejandro. He was more than *bueno* about providing us with the details of Alejandro's soon-to-be whereabouts, and, sure enough, he was right.

Virgil knew we could not trust the Federales, and a posse would be hard to conceal in the small village of El Encanto, so we were doing like we did most of the time: we were going at this alone.

Virgil set his cigar in an ashtray and got to his feet.

"What were you moaning about?" Virgil said.

"What?"

"In your sleep. You all right."

"Don't think I was moaning," I said, and pulled on my boot.

"You were."

"Just sleeping some."

Virgil shook his head slightly.

"No," Virgil said as he removed his holster from the back of the chair and strapped it on. "You were moaning. Thought you might be sick."

3

I PULLED ON MY SECOND BOOT AND MOVED OVER
to the washbasin atop a pinewood chest. I poured some water into
the basin, splashed my face, and changed the goddamn course of
the conversation to our business at hand.

"How you want to go about this?" I said.

I could see Virgil's reflection in the cracked mirror above the
basin. He picked up the cigar from the ashtray and took a pull.

"Figure I'll go down," Virgil said, with a point out the window.

"Position myself over there in the plaza corner, where I'll have a
good look at the cantina. Make sure they don't decide to go nowhere."

I moved to the window to see where Virgil was pointing.

"You get to our horses," Virgil said. "Get 'em ready to ride.
Bring 'em up the back side and meet me over there."

"Then?"

Virgil looked out the window a moment, thinking.

"Be a good idea we remove their transportation," he said.

The seven horses were in front of the cantina. Four were on one
hitch and three on the other.

"Walk 'em off," I said. "Or shoo 'em?"

"Get 'em gone," Virgil said. "Send 'em."

I thought about what Virgil was saying as I strapped on my Colt.

"Be quicker," I said. "Might get their attention, though."

Virgil nodded a little as he took a tug of the cigar and then blew out a roll of smoke.

"You been in that cantina since we been here, Everett?"

"Have. Bought our whiskey, beer there."

"Back door open?"

"Was," I said. "Both times."

"Was when I was in there, too."

"You want to go in each way," I said. "Mix things up a bit?"

Virgil nodded.

"Yep," Virgil said. "We'll see who's interested in going to jail and who ain't."

"Sounds right," I said.

I picked up my second Colt, loaded it, and put it behind my back, under my belt.

Virgil took a final pull on his cigar and loaded his second Colt. He secured it in the front of his belt, toward his hip.

I grabbed my eight-gauge and followed Virgil out the door and down the creaky stairs to the small hotel lobby. There was an old clerk sitting by a single lamp, reading a newspaper. He looked up at us, offered no smile, and went back to what he was reading. The door leading to the plaza was low. We dipped our heads some and walked out.

The plaza of El Encanto wasn't crowded, but it wasn't shy of people, either.

Since we'd been in the busy village we had stayed out of sight as much as we could. Two gringos residing in El Encanto for an extended period of time was conspicuous enough, so we avoided drawing attention to ourselves. When we did go out to get food, whiskey, or to check on our horses, we did so separately.

Our horses were stabled in a small corral with a lean-to shed a few hundred yards behind the plaza.

Virgil walked off down the boardwalk in the opposite direction of the cantina and I moved off between the hotel and the dilapidated mercantile building next to it and made my way out to the shed.

After getting our horses saddled up and ready to ride, I walked them around the back of the plaza and came up between the two buildings where Virgil was posted. I secured our animals there between the two structures and joined Virgil.

"You ready?" Virgil said.

I looked at Virgil. He met my eye.

"It's what we do," I said.

"It is," Virgil said.

I gave Virgil a nod and we started walking across the plaza. We passed the water well in the center and continued toward the cantina.

"I'll let go the four horses on the left hitch," Virgil said. "You take care of them three on the right, then get yourself to the back. I'll signal with an arm drop, and we go in with a five count."

We did just that. Virgil quickly untied the four on the left. I untied two of the three on the right, slapped their rumps, and sent them running.

I reached for the reins of the third horse and a shot rang out. The bullet zipped by my head so close I felt it.

11

A second shot was fired; it was from Virgil. A heavyset bandito stumbled backward, discharging his pistol.

The bullet splintered into the boardwalk a foot in front of him, then he dropped in the doorway of the cantina in a hazy waft of sawdust and gun smoke . . . *So much for plans.*

4

THREE OF THE OUTLAWS CAME OUT, FIRING AT Virgil and me. Virgil dropped two of them fast, and the other one came in my direction. I let go with both barrels of the eight-gauge, hitting him. The impact slammed him crashing through a storefront window. I moved quickly up across the boardwalk and put my back to the wall of the building next to the cantina.

Virgil had done the same. He was on the opposite side of the cantina from me, with his back to the wall. We both had a good look at the cantina door. Every person that had been out on the plaza was now nowhere in sight and the only movement at all was that of the drifting gun smoke.

I broke open the big gun, tipped out the spent shells, and slipped in two new double-aught buck.

Virgil opened the loading gate on his Colt, emptied his spent casings, and reloaded.

"*Buenas noches,* Capitán Alejandro! It's Marshal Virgil Cole and Deputy Marshal Everett Hitch! You need to give yourself up! We have a big posse out here! You're surrounded. Need you and your amigos to come on out!"

There was no answer from Alejandro, only silence.

"Alejandro!" Virgil called again. "I got a warrant for your arrest for killing two men in San Cristóbal . . . you remember that, don't you?"

Silence.

"You'll be caught or killed tonight!" Virgil said. "The choice is of course, by God, your choice!"

With a point, I signaled Virgil that I'd head to the rear of the building.

Virgil nodded and I slipped into the narrow alley between the cantina and the large structure next to it.

It was dark, but I could see light ahead of me between the two dwellings. Before I got to the end of the building I got down on my knee to have a peek around the corner of the cantina.

The back door was open because there was light spilling out onto crates and an outhouse without a door.

Up front, I heard Virgil again.

"Alejandro!" Virgil shouted. "You're surrounded. There is no place to go other than hell!"

Again, there was no reply from Alejandro, but I could hear Alejandro's men clamoring fretfully in Spanish.

The back side of the plaza was a narrow street lined with small homes and corrals. I stood and eased my way out some, keeping my eye on the cantina door. Then I moved swiftly behind the building next to the cantina, between rows of chicken coops. I stayed out of the spilling light from the cantina and ran quickly across the narrow street. I ducked into the shadows between two small adobe structures, where I had a good view of the back of the cantina. The outhouse obstructed my view of the door, but I could see if some-one tried to run, left or right.

"Alejandro!" I shouted. "You are no good front or back! You got nowhere to go!"

"That's right," I heard Virgil call. "You and them amigos of yours can give up or you get a grave!"

Two of the outlaws came out firing. One came around one side of the outhouse; one came around the other. They were shooting at everything and nothing.

I pulled the first trigger of the eight-gauge and hit the outlaw moving to my left. The impact from the double-aught blast was forceful enough it knocked him off his feet and slammed him into the chicken coops.

"*Alto!*" I shouted loudly to the second outlaw moving off.

He fired on me on the run. I pulled the second trigger of the eight-gauge. He buckled from the impact and hit the ground in a cloud of rolling dirt.

A slat on the outhouse kicked out. A rifle barrel came out and shots came my way. I ducked back into the dark as bullets rico-cheted off the adobe. Then I quickly went around the back side of the house and repositioned myself on the opposite side. I reloaded as the rifle continued to repeat. When it paused, I slid the eight-gauge around the edge of the adobe and let go both barrels, blow-ing a hole in the outhouse. A scream followed by the sight of a sombrero skittering out from behind the outhouse.

Six were dead, I thought, as I reloaded again. Then, out of the corner of my eye, I saw the silhouette of the final desperado: Cap-tain Alejandro himself on the roof. He was moving away at a pace.

I hurried quickly back in the alley next to the cantina, and just before I got to the boardwalk I said softly, "Virgil."

I looked around the corner and met Virgil's eye. I pointed to the roof and then pointed north, the direction Alejandro was running.

"One left," I said quietly. "The captain. He's on the run."

Virgil looked up, then looked back at me. I tilted my head toward the rear.

Virgil nodded and moved off quickly in the direction I pointed.

I moved down the alley to the rear again. When I got back to the street behind the cantina, I moved off quietly after Alejandro.

Just when I got toward the end of a row of buildings I heard two shots followed by:

"Hands above your head! Heaven high, Alejandro!" Virgil said. "The next shot will be in your head!"

When I came to the corner, I stopped. Then I peeked around the edge of the building and I was face-to-face with Alejandro. His hands were where Virgil had asked them to be. Up in the air. Virgil was behind him, with his Colt pointing at Alejandro's head.

"Everett," Alejandro said, almost friendly-like. "Good to see you."

Alejandro's English was good, but his accent was Latino heavy.

"Couldn't you find anyone better to visit beautiful Mexico with other than fucking Virgil Cole?"

5

By trail and train it took us five days to travel Alejandro back to San Cristóbal. Alejandro slept a great deal and didn't have much to say on our journey other than an occasional comment about Virgil not being very good company. He did hum or sing a string of Mexican ballads now and then, which annoyed the hell out of Virgil. We provided him with the minimal amount of food and water on the trip, and on a Sunday, just before noon on a blazing-hot day in June, we arrived in San Cristóbal by way of the Transcontinental.

We unloaded our horses, got directions, and made our way through town for the sheriff's office. Churchgoers on the streets dressed for service watched us as we rode slowly, with Alejandro wearing his Naval Officers jacket and a pair of shackles.

We'd heard about this place, but Virgil and I had never visited San Cristóbal. It was a big community, an old, well-established township with many manufacturing industries, including mining and cattle.

Church bells clanged loudly as we rode through at least ten

densely packed blocks of well-built buildings. Many of them were brick buildings, and some of the streets were brick, too.

San Cristóbal was a stately community built on rolling hills nestled in the San Cristóbal River Valley between two mountain ranges, the Angeles Altos and the Blue Ridge.

We located the San Cristóbal sheriff's office and went about the business of getting Alejandro locked up behind bars.

When we arrived, there was only one deputy in charge of the office. He was a skinny old man, and though he was long in the tooth, he still had some spit to him. He didn't move like an old fella. He got up from the desk quick-like when we walked in the door, and after we introduced ourselves he did the same.

"I'm the jailer here. Name's Cross," he said. "Ira Cross."

"Where's your sheriff?" I asked.

"Not in," Cross said.

"Well, we need to get this man here locked up," I said.

Cross looked our prisoner up and then down.

"This is Captain Alejandro Vasquez," Virgil said. "He shot dead a few fellas here in San Cristóbal a while back and somehow managed not to be here for his arraignment and trial, but he's back now."

"Well, I'll be goddamned," Cross said, looking at Alejandro and shaking his head. "Got your ass snagged."

"Temporarily," Alejandro said with a smirk.

"That was no goddamn question," Cross snapped. "When I ask you a question you will know it!"

Cross unlocked the desk drawer, pulled the cell keys out, and moved to the hall leading to the cells.

The jail was a secure one, and for the moment it was empty. There was nobody locked up. The cells had very small windows with heavy bars, and they were separated from the office by a metal door.

Cross carried a police club as we led Alejandro into one of the cells. After we got the cuffs off Alejandro and locked him in the cell, Alejandro smiled at Virgil.

"You know," Alejandro said, "Alejandro is never long for confinement."

Cross slammed the club on the bars just in front of Alejandro's face.

"Shut the fuck up, Captain Alejandro," Cross said. "You're my prisoner now, and from now on, you will be on good behavior or I will make what is left of your miserable life on earth hell."

Cross ushered us out of the hall and closed the metal door behind him. Virgil looked at me and smiled as Cross locked the door.

"I don't need to tell you," Virgil said, "but I will tell you anyway. Watch him like a hawk. He might seem sleepy, but he's sleepy like a goddamn mountain lion. Do not feed him until you got others back here to give you a hand."

"I rode shotgun on the Antone and Diego Stage route for eighteen by-God years," Cross said. "After that, I policed in Silver City for ten piss years and as of February of this year I been manning this office for the sheriff for seven years and I don't need you or nobody else to tell me how to do my job."

I looked at Virgil and smiled a bit as Cross walked to the desk by the door. He locked the cell keys in the top drawer of the desk.

"When do you expect your sheriff back?" I said.

"Don't know."

"Where is he?" Virgil said.

"On posse."

"What for?" Virgil said.

"Robbery," Cross said sharply.

"What kind of robbery?" I said.

"Not s'posed to say."

"Why not?" Virgil asked.

"My orders."

"Orders?" I said. "What is it, some kind of secret posse?"

"You'll have to ask the sheriff about that. I was told to keep my mouth shut, so that's what I'm doing."

"Fair enough," Virgil said.

I pulled the warrant for Alejandro from my pocket and set it on the desk.

"I'll need you to sign here," I said.

Cross took a seat behind the desk like he was sitting to write a proper letter. He pulled out a pair of spectacles from his pocket, put them on, and started reading the warrant. His lips moved, mouthing each word he read, and his eyes went slowly from left to right as he read each line.

I looked to Virgil and took a seat next to the desk. Virgil looked around. I pointed to the chair behind him, and he took a seat.

It took a while. Cross read every word of the document. When he got to the end, he pulled a pen from its inkwell, and with his tongue clamped between his teeth he signed his signature. He blew on his autograph until it was dry and then handed the warrant back to me.

Virgil stood, and I stood.

"Need to see Judge Bing," I said as I put the warrant back inside my coat pocket. "You tell us where to find the courthouse?"

"I can. It's just up the street a ways. Can't miss it. Big stone building on your left, says *Courthouse* above the doors."

"Appreciate it," I said, and we turned for the door.

"Course, there's nobody there, though, on Sunday," Cross said. "Judge Bing is most likely fishing. Tomorrow you might find him. Course, he might be fishing tomorrow, too. Hard to say about the judge. He's on his own clock."

I nodded and opened the door.

"He is busy, I'll grant you that. Big landowner-versus-mining-companies trial happening."

"All right, then," I said.

"Question," Cross said, stopping us before we left. "Captain Alejandro? What is he the captain of?"

"His own mind," Virgil said.

6

VIRGIL AND I WALKED OUT OF THE SHERIFF'S
office and down the steps to the boardwalk. The streets had some
after-church traffic moving about. Two ladies with parasols, dressed
in their Sunday dresses, passed Virgil and me. We tipped our hats.
They nodded a little. We watched them as they moved on down the
boardwalk. One of them, a blond woman with bright blue eyes,
turned back and smiled.

I tipped my hat again and smiled. She looked to her friend and
said something that made the two of them giggle some as they
continued on.

"Nice place," I said.

"Is."

"Refined."

"Seems to be," Virgil said.

Virgil pulled a cigar from his pocket. He fished out a stick
match, dragged the tip across the iron of the stair banister, and got
his cigar going good just as a short, stocky fella with round cheeks
and wearing a dark suit walked up. He had a small badge pinned
on his suit jacket.

"You the sheriff?" Virgil said.

The man looked back and forth between Virgil and me.

"No," he said. "I'm the constable, Winfield Holly . . . and you are?"

Virgil pulled back his lapel, showed the star.

"Territorial Marshal Virgil Cole. This here is my deputy marshal, Everett Hitch."

"My God," Holly said as he removed his hat. "You're here."

Virgil looked at me.

"We are," Virgil said.

"Why . . . I just tried to wire you in Appaloosa!"

"We ain't there," Virgil said.

"No," Holly said. "Of course . . . What, what is the nature of you being in San Cristóbal?"

"Inside your jail there is Captain Alejandro Miguel Vasquez," Virgil said.

Holly looked to the door of the office and back to Virgil with a shocked face.

"My God!" Holly said. "My God."

"Yep," Virgil said. "Not sure how much God's got to do with Alejandro, but he's locked up."

"You met Ira, I presume?" Holly said, nodding toward the office.

"Did," Virgil said.

"I apologize in post for his lack of good manner," Holly said, "but he is a fine jailer."

"No post necessary," Virgil said.

"Well, this is just serendipitous," Holly said.

Virgil looked at me. A questioning look.

"Good luck, like," I said.

Virgil nodded.

"Thank God . . . and now here you are!"

"We are," Virgil said.

"What were you wiring us about?" I said.

"Well," Holly said. "We need your help."

"What sort of help?" Virgil said.

"We have a very serious situation on our hands," Holly said as he nervously turned his hat by its brim.

"Situation being?" Virgil said.

Holly looked around, making sure no one was listening.

"This have to do with the robbery?" I said.

"You know about that?" Holly said, dropping both of his hands to his sides.

"Know some," I said.

"Ira mentioned it?" Holly said.

"He did," I said.

"What do you know?" Holly said.

"That there is a posse out," I said.

Holly nodded.

"Yes," Holly said. "I just stopped by to see if there had been any discovery I needed to hear about."

"We wouldn't know about that," I said. "But I suspect not, seeing how there's nobody here but your jailer."

"You want to tell us about this?" Virgil said.

"I do," Holly said. "Tell you what. Now that you are here. Let me gather the parties involved. It would be better if you got the details firsthand. It will take me a little time. Where are you staying?"

Virgil looked at me.

"No place," I said. "Not as of yet, anyway."

"Tell you what," Holly said. "My brother Lewis owns a nice little hotel just around the corner called Holly's House Hotel. He's got a stable in back and he serves good food. Let me get those involved together and I will let you know when and where."

Virgil looked at me.

"I could eat," I said.

7

HOLLY WAS RIGHT. HIS BROTHER HAD A GOOD place for us to stay. Virgil and I got a room and freshened up a bit. We ate some good corn-potato soup before Holly stopped by and told us when and where we were to meet.

Thirty minutes later Virgil and I rode down Main Street. We located the large brick-and-limestone building we were looking for on the corner of Sixth Street and Main. It had tall windows and double doors with COMSTOCK NATIONAL BANK etched across ribbed glass panels on the top half of both doors. A CLOSED sign hung crooked on one of the doors. We left our horses on a hitch across the street in front of an upholstery shop, waited for a few buggies to pass, then walked across the street and entered the bank.

Inside it was cool and a relief from the hot day. The bank was big and fancy. The ceiling was high, with wide, ornate iron chandeliers that nested frosted globes casting a honey-colored glow. The walls were raised wood panels with gilded framed paintings of ships. The floor was shiny hardwood with a band of green marble that bordered the perimeter of the lobby. There were two young men busy shuffling papers behind the brass bars of the polished tellers' counter, and seated in a large carpeted seating area to the left of the entrance were four men, including Constable Holly. They were looking at us. Holly and one of the three other men got to their feet. They moved quickly to greet us. The man with Holly held out his hand.

"Marshal Cole, I presume."

Virgil didn't shake his hand but nodded toward me instead.

"This is my deputy, Everett Hitch."

"This is Mitchell," Holly said.

"It's a pleasure to meet you. Mitchell Brisbane. I'm the Comstock Bank manager."

Brisbane was a smallish man, clean-shaven, with close-cropped dark curly hair.

A very large and imposing man wearing a Panama hat called to us from where he remained seated in a corner chair.

"Do you know who I am?" he said loudly.

His voice was gruff, and it echoed in the bank's cavernous lobby.

Virgil glanced at me, smiled a little, and I followed him as he walked toward the big man in the corner chair.

"Don't," Virgil said. "I suspect you're going to tell me."

"I am," the heavyset man said as he puffed and chewed nervously on a fat cigar. "I'm Walter C. Comstock, and this is my bank."

Virgil nodded, glanced up to the massive chandelier and back to the glossy tellers' counter.

"Looks like a fine bank," Virgil said.

"This is the biggest, most secure bank between New York City and San Francisco, but we got robbed, Mr. Cole. The whole vault was cleaned out two days ago, and now it's not so goddamn fine."

Comstock was sitting on the edge of the armchair. He was doing

27

so because he would not fit in the chair if he tried to rest himself back into the seat properly—he was too wide. He wore an expensive suit and had a gold watch chain that looked to be about two feet long draped across his button-stretched vest.

"This is Truitt Ellsworth, the vice president of the bank," Comstock said as he motioned to the older man to his left.

Ellsworth was a long and slender-looking man with a nervous energy about him. He nodded sharply and offered a crooked smile but did not get out of his chair.

"Please sit, gentlemen," Comstock said. "Please."

Virgil and I took a seat facing Comstock in a pair of straight-backed chairs that were separated by an oval-shaped cherrywood table.

Holly and Brisbane sat on a sofa to my right.

"We appreciate you, Marshal Cole," Ellsworth said, "and your deputy, for being here."

Virgil nodded a bit.

Ellsworth leaned forward, quickly putting his hands together in a manner that resembled praying, and started to speak, but Comstock beat him to the draw.

"This is the goddamnedest situation," Comstock said, shaking his big head back and forth.

"Why don't you fill us in on the situation, Mr. Comstock?" I said.

Comstock looked to Brisbane and nodded to Virgil and me.

"Tell them," Comstock said, as if he didn't have the patience for what needed to be imparted.

"Well, I opened up with two tellers," Brisbane said, pointing to the two young men behind the teller windows. "It was Friday, and Fridays are busy days, so there are three of us—"

"And that goddamn Henry Strode!" Comstock said, interrupting. "He did it!"

"Yes," Ellsworth snapped quickly, "he damn sure did."

"Mr. Strode," Brisbane continued, "came in and told us we wouldn't be opening for business. He said Mr. Comstock ordered for us to remove the contents from the vault and load it into a buckboard."

"Horseshit!" Comstock said.

"Who is Henry Strode?" I said.

"The goddamn president of this bank," Comstock said with a huff.

8

"YOUR BANK PRESIDENT ROBBED YOUR BANK?" I
said.

"He damn sure did!" Comstock said. "It'd be funny if I read about it in the newspaper and it was someone else's bank, but it's not. He robbed *my* bank and now he's vanished, gone. Him and that wife of his . . . makes no sense."

"His wife," Ellsworth said, "was quite well off. Henry had a good salary here, too. Money certainly was not an issue with them, so it is all perplexing."

"What about your police?" I said. "What have they found out?"

Holly shook his head.

"Far as we know, nothing," he said.

"It seems," Comstock said, "they just goddamn disappeared. Our illustrious sheriff, Webster Hawkins, put together a posse but has found no sign of him."

"Webb Hawkins?" Virgil said.

"Yes," Comstock said. "Do you know him?"

Virgil nodded.

"I do," Virgil said.

Comstock nodded some.

"Well, he's come up empty-handed," Comstock said, "so I told Constable Holly to contact you!"

"Where does Strode live?" Virgil said.

"Just on the edge of town," Holly said. "A nice home."

"I imagine that was the first place you boys had a look-see?" Virgil said.

"We did," Holly said.

"You find anything there?" Virgil said.

"No," Holly said. "Nothing out of place, no, just vacant. We asked the neighbors if they'd seen anything out of the ordinary, too. Turned up nothing."

Virgil didn't say anything.

"You said Strode had a buckboard?" I said.

"He did," Brisbane said.

"The vault had that much money," I said, "it took a buckboard?"

Brisbane looked to Comstock and then to Ellsworth.

"There was a good deal of money in the vault," Ellsworth said.

"Good deal being?" Virgil said.

"Near two hundred thousand," Ellsworth said. "A little less than a hundred in currency, smaller denominations, so there was some bulk, and another hundred in gold."

"You always have that much money in the vault?" Virgil said.

"Not always," Ellsworth said. "No."

"Why so much now?" Virgil said.

"Well, it's not that uncommon—the amount fluctuates, you see," Ellsworth said. "We service many large organizations, including two military operations, the BIA reservations departments, as well as three major investment firms here in the city. We handle large volumes."

"The fact this happened on Friday," Comstock said, "bought us a few days of avoiding chaos."

Ellsworth nodded.

"But it's only a matter of time," Ellsworth said.

"It is," Comstock said. "The hell of it is, up until this happened, I would not have thought Henry Strode was capable of something like this."

"Me, neither," Ellsworth said. "I appointed him myself."

"I thought you were the vice president?" Virgil said.

Ellsworth nodded.

"I was president of this bank for sixteen years. I stepped down, and we put Mr. Strode in the position," Ellsworth said. "Strode was an exceptional banker, highly intelligent. His thoroughness and thoughtfulness made our customers comfortable. He's much younger, and frankly better suited for the job than I ever was. My vice position is nothing more than handling the occasional loan. It's now a board position, really."

"Truitt and I started this bank together," Comstock said. "We built this goddamn thing from the ground up."

Ellsworth nodded.

Virgil nodded a bit, looking down to the elaborate red-and-gold patterns in the rug splayed out under the seating area, then looked to Constable Holly.

"What about guards?"

Comstock shook his head with a disgusted look and pointed toward the front doors with his cigar wedged between his first and second finger, as if he were damning the existence of something unseen.

"We have two armed security men on guard every time the bank is opened, but they were told by goddamn Strode the bank would not be in operation on Friday. Goddamn nonsense. They went home."

"Yes," Brisbane said. "Mr. Strode had driven to the bank in a buckboard. He said it was Mr. Comstock's orders to temporarily close and transfer the money. Said it was a safety precaution."

"A safety precaution my ass," Comstock said with a scoff. "Horseshit!"

"And you did that?" I said. "You loaded the buckboard?"

"We did," Brisbane said with a slight shake of his head. "Mr. Strode is . . . well, was, after all, the president. He had both keys, and we did as we were told."

"Both keys?" Virgil said.

9

BRISBANE NODDED. HE LOOKED TO ELLSWORTH
and then to Holly and then to us.

"It takes two keys to get into the vault."

"Yes," Brisbane said.

"Then what?" Virgil said.

"Mr. Strode locked up the bank and told us he would get in
touch with us when he wanted us to return to work."

"Don't seem like much security," Virgil said.

I nodded.

"It doesn't," I said. "Not for that amount of money."

Brisbane looked to Comstock and Ellsworth.

"Well," Ellsworth said with a sigh, "as Mitch said, Strode had
two keys. The opening of the vault requires one key from the president and one key from me or Walt."

"But Strode had both keys?" I said.

Ellsworth nodded.

"Who all has a key?" Virgil said.

"Myself," Ellsworth said, then he looked to Comstock. "And
Walt here and Strode."

"Walt and I," Ellsworth said, "we took our wives up to the Montezuma Hotel hot springs for what was meant to be a therapeutic few days. We go up periodically."

"You left your key with Strode?" Virgil said.

Ellsworth nodded sheepishly.

"Yes," he said.

"The sonofabitch," Comstock said. "He waited for us to be away, came up with this ruse, cleaned us out, then . . . poof, vanished."

The front door opened, and two young men entered. They looked in our direction, then walked toward us. They both had good-sized bellies and shiny stars pinned on their vests. One was taller than the other, but they looked enough alike that they most assuredly were twins.

"Deputies," Comstock said. "Tell me some good news. Tell me you found Strode! Tell me you have recovered the money!"

They moved a little closer. Before they spoke, they sized up Virgil and me.

"This is Marshal Cole," Holly said, "and his deputy, Everett Hitch."

The taller of the two men removed his hat and spoke.

"We've heard about you two," he said with a respectful tone of voice. "We heard you was coming. I'm Deputy Danny Rangfield, and this is my brother, Davy."

"What is it, boys?" Holly said.

"Yes!" Comstock said impatiently. "Goddamn!"

"We come to let you know we found Mr. Strode."

"Where?" Comstock blurted out as he sprang to his feet like he'd been stung by a scorpion. "Where is the sonofabitch?"

"He's near dead, sir," Davy said.

"What?"

"Yes, sir," Danny said.

"What happened to him?" Virgil said.

"Don't know," Davy said. "Sheriff Hawkins told us he had been beat up real bad and was . . . un—"

Davy looked to Danny.

"Unconscious," Danny said.

"That's right," Davy said. "Slingshot Clark found him. He's at the Cottonwood Springs."

"Slingshot Clark?" Comstock said.

"Yes, sir."

"And the money?" Comstock said.

The brothers shook their heads.

"Don't know anything about the money, sir," Danny said.

"What about the wife?" Ellsworth said.

Danny and Davy shook their heads.

"Don't know nothing else," Danny said. "Other than that Doc Mayfair is on his way out to the Cottonwood Springs."

"Slingshot Clark," Comstock said, shaking his head, "and the goddamn Cottonwood Springs!"

"Who is Slingshot Clark," I said, "and where is this Cottonwood Springs?"

"Slingshot Clark is the madam of the Cottonwood Springs," Davy said. "A high-class whoring outfit south of town."

10

VIRGIL AND I RODE SIDE BY SIDE FOLLOWING
the Rangfield brothers south toward the Cottonwood Springs
whorehouse where Henry Strode was said to be found. Comstock,
Ellsworth, and Holly followed in a covered two-seater driven by
Brisbane.

"Don't look like we're gonna be going back to Appaloosa anytime soon," I said.

"Don't," Virgil said.

I turned in my saddle some and looked back at Holly and the
bankers.

"Ol' Comstock's sure enough a state fair hog," I said.

"Blue ribbon," Virgil said.

"I wonder if he's the same Comstock of the Virginia City silver
mines," I said. "That Comstock, the Comstock Load?"

"Might well be," Virgil said. "He's a hell of a load himself."

"He is," I said. "This robbery's a hell of a load, too."

"Comstock and Ellsworth fucked up."

"Giving Strode the key?"

"Yep."

"That they did."

"That money don't belong to them," Virgil said.

"They're gonna have hell to pay," I said.

"What do you figure happened to Strode's wife?"

"At this point I can only surmise nothing good."

"Comstock referred to her like she was a barn cat or something."

"He did," Virgil said.

The road we were traveling came to a long line of spruce trees that followed a creek. The Rangfield brothers splashed on through the low crossing, but our horses took the opportunity for a good drink from the clear brook water.

"Figure Strode got himself in a cross-thread of some kind," I said.

Virgil nodded.

"Somebody was more than likely in on this with him," Virgil said.

"Good chance it's the same somebody left him for dead," I said.

"That'd be my thinking," Virgil said.

"Maybe this Slingshot knows something," I said.

We watched our horses drink for a moment.

"More to this," Virgil said. "That's for certain."

I nodded and thought about that. I looked as the buggy driven by Brisbane approached the water.

"Wonder what keeps more bankers from stealing?"

"He's damn sure not the first," Virgil said.

Virgil and I moved our horses on through the low water crossing and continued up the road following Davy and Danny.

"Big damn town," I said. "San Cristóbal."

"Is," Virgil said. "Six thousand plus."

"Hard to believe the police didn't find anybody that saw Strode and the buckboard?"

"Is," Virgil said.

"This sheriff, Webster Hawkins?" I said. "He a good hand?"

"Don't know what kind of lawman he is. He was a friendly fella, I remember," Virgil said. "Last time I saw him he was young— behind bars, though."

"What for?"

"Stealing?"

"What'd he steal?"

"Cattle."

"You arrest him?"

"I did."

"And now he's a lawman."

"So it appears."

"He a gun hand?"

"Was."

"Any good?"

Virgil shook his head some.

"I only saw him go at it one time."

"He pull on you?"

"Matter of fact, he did."

"What happened?"

"I shot him."

"He shoot back?"

"Nope."

"He clear leather?"

"Nope," Virgil said.

"Obviously, he lived."

"He did."

"Where'd you shoot him?"

"Panhandle."

"No. Where?"

"Shoulder."

"Don't imagine he much cares for you."

"He should," Virgil said. "I was kind to him."

"Kind?"

Virgil nodded.

"I could have put the bullet in a more vital spot, but I did not. Him being a likable fella and all," Virgil said. "I was being kind."

11

⤳⤲

WHEN WE ARRIVED AT THE COTTONWOOD
Springs, Sheriff Hawkins, a third deputy named Brooks, and a
small, attractive redhead wearing a black dress with red trim were
waiting for us. They were sitting on folding chairs under the shade
of a sprawling cottonwood tree. Behind the tree sat the whoring
establishment. It was a well-built two-story house with a wide front
porch. In front of the house was a buckboard hitched to an old
dark bay.

The men got to their feet when we arrived, but the woman
remained seated.

A big man stepped out a ways as we rode up. He had a star on
his chest.

"That's Hawkins there," Virgil said as we got closer.

Hawkins shook his head back and forth as we came to a stop.

"Virgil Cole," Hawkins said.

"Webb," Virgil said.

"It's been a very long time," Hawkins said.

"Has."

"What has it been? Like twenty years?"

"Seems about right."

"I'll be damned," Hawkins said. "Holly said he was contacting you and . . . well, I suppose we appreciate the help."

"Suppose?" Virgil said.

"We do, Cole," Hawkins said. "You got here damn quick."

"Just so happened we come to San Cristóbal on other business," Virgil said.

"Such as?" Hawkins said.

"Alejandro Vasquez," Virgil said.

"What about him?"

"He's locked up in your jail," Virgil said.

"No shit?"

"No shit," Virgil said.

"I'll be damned," Hawkins said. "Bet he's none too happy 'bout that."

"Nope," Virgil said. "He ain't . . . So what's the situation here? This Strode fella alive?"

"He is," Hawkins said. "His lights are out, but he's breathing. Doc's in with him now."

Virgil looked to the house, then nodded to me.

"This is my deputy, Everett Hitch."

I moved my horse up some, then dismounted and shook hands with the men. Virgil was right about Webster Hawkins. He was a friendly fella. He didn't much look like an ex-thief or a gunman. He was a big easy-moving bear of a man with a friendly face. He seemed more akin to a Baptist minister than a lawman. Deputy Brooks was short, with a thick, drooping mustache.

I turned, looking to the woman, who was still seated. She was sitting sideways in the chair with her slim legs crossed and one arm resting on the chair back. She smiled.

"This is Slingshot Clark," Hawkins said. "She owns the place."

"Ma'am," I said.

"Deputy," Slingshot said with a deep, sultry voice, then looked to Virgil. "Marshal."

Virgil nodded toward her a bit, then rode his horse to the far side of the tree. He stepped out of the saddle, looped his reins on a thick, low-hanging branch, then came back to where the rest of us gathered.

"How long you been wearing that badge, Webb?" Virgil said.

"Twelve years, Cole."

Virgil nodded some, smiled a bit.

"Good," Virgil said.

Hawkins looked to Brisbane coming to a stop in the buggy with the bankers.

"You got the whole of it spelled out to you, Cole?" Hawkins said. "About this situation with Henry Strode robbing Comstock's bank?"

"We did," Virgil said.

"Speak of the devil," Slingshot said, looking at Comstock.

He was working with great effort to get his huge body out of the buggy.

Virgil looked to Slingshot.

She hadn't changed her position on the chair. She sat straight-backed as though she were an aristocrat posing for a portrait.

She smiled at Virgil.

"You found Strode?" Virgil said.

Slingshot nodded smoothly.

"I did."

"Where."

"He was on the porch this morning."

Virgil just looked at her for a moment.

"The damnedest thing," Slingshot said. "I opened the door and there he was."

12

❦

BRISBANE HELPED COMSTOCK AND ELLSWORTH out of the two-seater. Comstock was talking loudly before he got both feet on the ground.

"Sheriff Hawkins! Where is he? Has he talked? What does he know?" Comstock said without hesitation or concern for Strode's well-being.

Hawkins looked to Virgil and shook his head a little.

"He's not talked," Hawkins said. "Doc Mayfair said if he came to, he'd holler at us."

"Well, goddamn," Comstock said. "Just how long can a man be unconscious?"

"Doc said from a nick a time," Hawkins said, "to forever . . . Depends."

"Oh, good Lord," Comstock said.

Comstock was sweating and gasping for air from the talking, climbing out of the buggy, and the five steps he'd walked. He rested his hand on the neck of the buggy horse and caught a few breaths.

"I heard about your bank, Walt," Slingshot said flatly. "That's a crying shame."

Comstock shook his head like he was trying to keep flies off. It was obvious the head shake was not just the thought of the robbery but also the sappy inclusion of his given name so easily uttered by a woman of ill repute.

"The boys here," Ellsworth said, gesturing to Davy and Danny, "said there was no sign of the money."

"Of course not!" Comstock said with a sarcastic gasp.

Hawkins shook his head.

"No, sir," Hawkins said as he looked to Slingshot. "Don't have any idea. More than likely, whoever did this to Strode made off with the money."

Slingshot nodded.

"Believe me, Walt, I don't have it," Slingshot said with a smoldering look. "I've been scratching a poor woman's ass my whole life and I wouldn't even know what to do with a bunch of money like that."

"Oh, I'm sure you would," Comstock said.

"Well, you are probably right there," Slingshot said. "But I have to say I don't know this Strode from Adam. Fact, he's the only banker in all of San Cristóbal I don't know."

Comstock shook his head again and turned his attention to Hawkins.

"Well, who did this to him?" Comstock said angrily. "Who took the money?"

"Good question," Hawkins said. "If we knew that, we'd not be under this cottonwood tree."

Comstock wiped sweat from his face with a handkerchief as he looked to the old house.

"We've scoured all around this area," Hawkins said with a sweep of his hand, "and we don't really have any idea about much of anything."

"The sonofabitch," Comstock said.

"If you're lucky, Mr. Comstock," Hawkins said, "the sonofabitch you're talking about will survive and come to. He don't, well, then we're back to the start of the trail."

"Webb," Virgil said. "Let's have a look-see."

"Good idea," Comstock said.

Virgil stopped and looked to Comstock.

"Just rest yourself, Mr. Comstock," Virgil said.

"But?" Comstock said.

"Let us do our business," Virgil said. "No reason to get yourself any more worked up than you already are."

"I suppose you're right, Marshal," Comstock said. "I suppose you are right."

"Good," Virgil said.

Comstock put two of the folding chairs side by side and took a seat.

"You want to lead us the way there, Miz Clark?" Virgil said.

"Certainly, Marshal," she said, "and, please, call me Slingshot."

13

⁓

LITTLE GREEN GRASSHOPPERS SPRANG UP OUT of the weeded scrub grass and skittered about in the slanting rays of afternoon light as Webb, Holly, Virgil, and I followed Slingshot to the Cottonwood Springs. When we climbed the steps, Doc Mayfair stepped out the door, smoking a cigarette. He was a frail man, balding, with wispy gray hair and an instant no-nonsense disposition. He wedged the cigarette between his teeth, removed his spectacles, and wiped them with his shirttail.

"Doc," Webb said, "this is Territorial Marshal Virgil Cole and his deputy, Everett Hitch."

Mayfair looked back and forth between Virgil and me as he continued to clean his spectacles.

"He still with us?" Webb said.

Mayfair nodded some, then removed the cigarette from between his teeth.

"He's breathing, stable," Mayfair said with a raspy and weak voice. "Stable, but he's still unconscious."

Mayfair replaced his spectacles on the bridge of his nose, then turned and tilted his head toward the door.

"Come in," Mayfair said.

He stepped back inside the house, and we followed after him.

The Cottonwood Springs was a nice establishment for a whorehouse. It was clean, with lace curtains on the windows and nice furniture—sofas, tables, and lamps—and it smelled of lavender perfume. There was a stairway just inside the front door that led up to the working rooms and a hall next to it that led to a rear kitchen. Two ladies sitting on the back porch looked at us when we entered.

Strode was in the parlor to our left. He was on a carpet with a blanket underneath him. He was laid out flat on his back with a pillow under his head. His shirt was open and his trousers were unbuttoned. His face was badly beaten, bloody, bruised, and swollen. There was dried blood all over his suit. Virgil moved closer to him.

"You undo him like this, shirt, trousers?" Virgil said to Mayfair.

"I did," Mayfair said.

"He's not been shot?" Virgil said.

"No," Mayfair said.

"Stabbed?"

"I've not found punctures, bullet or knife."

"Poor dear," Slingshot said.

"It seems he's just been beaten, beaten bad," Doc said. "He has broken ribs, and his groin's swollen badly. He's been kicked. He has some internal bleeding. Someone worked him over good."

Even though Strode was battered, he appeared to be a handsome man. He was strong-looking and tall, with thick, dark hair.

Virgil got down on one knee and looked at Strode more closely. He lifted a lapel on Strode's jacket a little and searched his pocket, then looked back to Hawkins.

"You search his pockets, Webb?" Virgil said.

"I did," Webb said. "He had nothing."

"No keys," Virgil said.

"Nope," Webb said. "No keys, no nothing."

Virgil looked at Strode's hands, first his left, then his right. He stayed on one knee, looking at Strode for a moment, then stood and looked around the room at nothing in particular.

"Could have shot him," I said.

Virgil nodded.

"Didn't want to, though," I said.

"Nope," Virgil said. "Did not."

"They were enjoying this," I said.

Virgil nodded.

"Seems so," Virgil said.

Virgil looked to Slingshot.

"How'd you get him in here?" Virgil said.

"The girls and me. We picked him up and brought him in," Slingshot said. "Took four of us."

"Who found him on the porch?" Virgil said.

"I did," Slingshot said. "I told you I did!"

"What time?"

"Not early, really," she said. "I was piddling around, cleaning this morning. I'd been in and out of the back door a few times but not the front. I opened the front door about, oh, nine, nine-thirty, and there he was. Scared the hell outta me."

Virgil looked at Slingshot for a moment, then looked to Doc Mayfair.

"Be dark in a bit," Virgil said. "Want and try moving him?"

"Yes," Mayfair said. "I've done all I can here, Marshall. We should get him to the office so I can get him cleaned up proper."

14

We searched around outside of the Cot-tonwood Springs, looking for any sign, evidence that might provide us with some details as to Strode mysteriously showing up on the whorehouse porch, but found nothing.

Before sundown we loaded up Strode and helped Doc Mayfair get him back to town and into the doctor's office.

After we got Strode settled, Hawkins left Davy and Danny to watch guard.

"Make damn sure no one comes in here," Hawkins said to his deputies, "and if Strode comes to, make damn sure he don't get out of here, either. Remember, this man is a prisoner."

Brisbane was at the reins of the two-seater, Holly was by his side, and Comstock and Ellsworth were still seated in the back when Webb, Virgil, and I exited Mayfair's office.

"Let me buy you boys supper," Comstock said. "Got a fancy lit-tle place that feeds a Sunday-night favorite to the do-wellers of San Cristóbal. Might be the last supper I'll be buying for a while."

Virgil looked at me.

"Sure," I said.

We mounted up and followed Brisbane in the buggy as it made its way through town. The road curved and traveled up a steep incline a few blocks. We stopped in front of a showy-looking eatery called the Claremont. Brisbane unloaded Comstock and Ellsworth, bid us good night, and moved on in the buggy. When we got inside the place, André, a short French fella wearing a bow tie, walked us to a table in the back of the busy restaurant, and Virgil, Webb, Holly, Ellsworth, Comstock, and I settled around a big oval table covered with a white tablecloth.

"Bring us some snails, André, and some of that good wine, steaks, and those crispy potatoes," Comstock said.

"*Oui,*" André said with a smile as he snapped his heels together.

André pushed through a swinging door and disappeared into the kitchen, spouting orders in French that sounded as if he were calling readying details to a firing squad.

"Well," Comstock said as he removed his Panama hat and laid it on the table. "What now?"

Virgil leaned back in his chair. He smoothed the tablecloth in front of him that didn't need smoothing and leveled a look at the bankers.

"You said Strode was an exceptional banker," Virgil said.

"Yes," Ellsworth said. "He was."

"Highly intelligent," Virgil said. "Made customers feel good, was more suited for the job than you were?"

Ellsworth nodded.

"You ever know him to get sideways with anyone," Virgil said. "Have a fight with anyone, that sort of thing?"

"No," Comstock said, looking at Ellsworth.

"My gosh, no, he was not a fighter," Ellsworth said. "Strode, by all accounts, was a gentleman."

"Tell me about him," Virgil said.

"What would you like to know?" Comstock said.

"He was," Ellsworth said, "in every sense of the word a banker, and a damn fine one, with exceptional acumen."

"How long has he been with you at the bank?" Virgil said.

Comstock looked to Ellsworth for the answer.

"A little over five years," Ellsworth said.

"Where did he come from?" Virgil said.

"He was from Saint Louis," Ellsworth said.

"How do you know that?"

Ellsworth looked to Comstock.

"Well," Ellsworth said. "He showed up here in San Cristóbal, the husband of a woman who hails from a very wealthy family."

"Catherine," Comstock said, looking down with his eyes fixed.

There was lull that settled among the men at the mention of Catherine.

"You care for this woman, Mr. Comstock?" I said.

"Well, of course," Comstock said.

"Didn't seem so before," I said.

"Well," Comstock said with a scoff, "I was, for good reason, feeling she might have been part of this, but now, now with this situation, it seems there is much more to this than I'd previously believed."

"That it?" I said.

Comstock looked to Ellsworth.

"Look," Comstock said. "Catherine comes with a pedigree and, well, she uses that to get what she wants."

"Like what?" Virgil said.

"Let me put it this way," Comstock said. "It's rumored Catherine Wainwright gets around town."

André returned from the kitchen with a tray of glasses, followed by a man about half his size holding a tray with bottles of wine. André set glasses in front of each of us, then took the wine from the small fella's tray and poured us each a glass. When he got done, he stepped back, snapped his heels together again, and followed the little fella back into the kitchen.

"Catherine Wainwright," I said. "Any relation to Jantz E. Wainwright from Saint Louis?"

"Why, yes," Comstock said, "she is. Catherine is Jantz's daughter. Her and Strode were married in Saint Louis. They moved out here together, and Strode operated a securities office for Wainwright."

Virgil looked at me.

"Jantz Wainwright," I said. "Big-shot tycoon. Owns a good portion of Saint Louis."

Comstock nodded.

"He goddamn does," Comstock said. "He was responsible for the railway showing up here in San Cristóbal."

"Wainwright," Ellsworth said, "is the most prominent business owner in San Cristóbal. He resides in Saint Louis but owns a lot of businesses here. Two hotels, a number of goods and service businesses, as well as a big cow-calf operation here that supplies beef back east."

"Wainwright responsible for Strode working at your bank?" Virgil said.

"Yes, he was, so to speak," Comstock said. "As Wainwright's businesses here grew, he felt it better to have our bank handle his assets. He felt our bank was more secure, so we absorbed the Wainwright office and Strode came to work at the bank."

Ellsworth nodded.

"But, like I mentioned," Ellsworth said, "Henry Strode was an excellent banker and was extremely valuable to our organization."

Virgil nodded some, looking at the glass of wine sitting on the table in front of him.

"How much of the money in the vault belonged to Wainwright," Virgil said.

Comstock and Ellsworth looked at each other.

"The majority of the money in the vault belonged to Wainwright," Comstock said.

"He know about the robbery?" I said.

"No," Comstock said, shaking his head. "Least I hope he don't."

15

AFTER FINISHING OFF THE DINNER WITH A
creamy layered dessert named after the French general Napoleon,
we left the bankers, and Constable Holly and Sheriff Hawkins rode
with Virgil and me slowly back to our hotel.

"What do you call those snails we ate?" Virgil said.

"Escargot," I said, spelling it out. "*T* is silent."

Virgil nodded a little.

"Good," Virgil said.

"They were," I said.

Nobody said anything else as we clopped along, listening to our
horses' hooves echoing on the brick street.

When we got to the hotel I got my horse and Virgil's into the
corral, then met Virgil and Hawkins on the front porch. They were
sitting in chairs, smoking cigars and drinking whiskey near a
sconce lantern that was getting attacked by bugs when I walked up.
I pulled up a chair to the small table between them.

"Webb and me were talking about the time I shot him," Virgil
said as he poured me a whiskey.

Hawkins nodded slowly, looking at his whiskey glass resting on the small table. He turned the glass and turned it again before he looked up at me.

"I was a dumbass kid," Hawkins said.

"You were," Virgil said with a smile.

"I was lucky, too."

"Luck didn't have nothing to do with it," Virgil said.

Hawkins threw back his whiskey and looked at Virgil.

"I know," Hawkins said.

"If I wanted to kill you, Webb, I'd 'a done it."

"I know," Hawkins said.

"I didn't want to," Virgil said.

"I'm glad," Hawkins said.

Virgil nodded and poured us all a splash of whiskey.

"I remember what you said to me when you came to see me in jail," Hawkins said.

We looked at Hawkins. He stared at his glass again. He turned it again and turned it yet another time.

"You said . . . make memories you can live with, son," Hawkins said as he looked to Virgil.

Virgil nodded some.

"Now look at you," Virgil said. "A bona fide lawman."

"By God," Hawkins said with firm conviction. "That I am."

Virgil dropped his chin, offering a sharp nod, then took a long, deliberate pull on his cigar.

"So what are your thoughts on the Strode business," Hawkins said to both Virgil and me.

"You know him?" Virgil said.

"Nope," Hawkins said. "I mean, I said hello a few times, but I didn't know him."

"His wife?" Virgil said.

"No," Hawkins said. "Pretty as a picture, though."

"Comstock said she got around town," Virgil said. "Know anything about that?"

Hawkins shook his head.

"Don't," Hawkins said.

Virgil blew out a roll of smoke that drifted up and mixed with the bugs swarming the sconce.

"Tell me about Slingshot," Virgil said.

"I've not had my way with her," Hawkins said, "if that's what you mean."

Virgil shook his head.

"Don't think she's showed her cards," Virgil said.

"What are you thinking?" Hawkins said.

"Don't know for certain," Virgil said. "Everett?"

"Well," I said, "it does seem kind of suspect Strode just showing up on her porch like that."

"Does," Virgil said.

"Makes better sense," I said, "that someone must have left him there."

Virgil nodded a bit.

"That'd be my thinking, too," Virgil said.

"Why would she be holding cards?" Hawkins said.

"Don't know," Virgil said, "but whoever whipped the hell outta Strode is gonna have a few wounds himself."

"What makes you think that?" Hawkins said.

"Both of Strode's hands were buggered up," Virgil said.

"Maybe you and me ought to ride out there, just ask her if she knows more than she's let on," I said.

"Maybe just," Virgil said. "Webb, why don't you see what you can find out about Strode?"

"Like what?"

"Send a wire," Virgil said. "See if you can dig up anything on him that might help us know something we don't know."

16

⌇

IN THE MORNING VIRGIL AND I RODE OUT TO THE
Cottonwood Springs to have a talk with Slingshot Clark. She
greeted us wearing a long gown that was kind of flimsy and open.
One side of it slipped off her shoulder, and it was clear she wore
nothing underneath.

"Well, goodness, what a pleasant surprise. If it's not Marshal
Cole, Deputy Hitch," Slingshot said as she held open the door. "So
nice to see you again."

"Nice to see you again, too," Virgil said.

"I like early customers," she said. "Nothing like starting the day
off with a proper bang."

"Like to ask you a few questions," Virgil said.

"Shucks," Slingshot said. "Is that all you'd like?"

"For the time being," Virgil said.

"That's a crying shame," Slingshot said.

"Need to get at something," Virgil said.

"Most men do," Slingshot said.

"Just a few questions," I said.

"Don't know if I have any answers," Slingshot said. "But come on in, and I'll see what I can conjure up."

I looked down the hall as Slingshot led us into the parlor and saw three gals sitting at the kitchen table. They turned and looked at us.

"Make yourselves comfortable," Slingshot said.

Virgil and I took a seat in the parlor. Slingshot sat across from us and crossed her thin legs. Her gown opened up, revealing her smooth thighs nearly to the folds where they disappeared. She pulled a cigarette from a small wooden box sitting on the table next to her and lit it with a cut-glass flint lighter.

"What can I do you for?" Slingshot said.

"Need to know about Henry Strode," Virgil said.

"What do you need to know?" Slingshot said.

"Need to know how he got on your porch," Virgil said.

"I told you."

"What else?" Virgil said.

"What do you mean?" Slingshot said.

"What else ain't you telling me?" Virgil said.

She shook her head.

"Why," Slingshot said with a smile, "I've told you everything, Marshal Cole."

"You don't seem like the kind of person that would ever need to lie about nothing," Virgil said.

"What kind of person do I seem like?" Slingshot said, with her eyes leveled seductively at Virgil.

"How'd he end up here?" Virgil said.

Slingshot smoked on the cigarette, looking all the time at Virgil. She did not even glance in my direction. She just looked at Virgil.

"Like I told you," Slingshot said. "I opened up the door and there he was."

"Don't seem likely," Virgil said.

"Marshal, I appreciate your straightforward disposition, your tempered, hard resolve," Slingshot said. "But I'm afraid you're barking up the wrong tree."

"Don't fuck with me," Virgil said.

"It would be a far better use of our time," Slingshot said.

Virgil didn't say anything.

Slingshot stared at him.

"This is not just a brothel," Slingshot said. "This is a home away from home for many men. I run this establishment outside of the city limits for one reason: discretion. Discretion is my business."

"Everett?" Virgil said.

"Yep."

"In the interest of discretion," Virgil said, "do me the good turn of letting me and Slingshot here have ourselves a discretion-like chat."

Virgil looked at her. He didn't say anything.

"I'll be right outside," I said.

I left Virgil and Slingshot sitting in the parlor and walked outside onto the porch to the Cottonwood Springs. I glanced back through the window, and I could see the profile of Slingshot through the lace curtains. She took a pull off her cigarette and blew smoke back over her shoulder.

I walked down the steps and out through the weeded scrub to where our horses were tied under the cottonwood. I sat in one of the folding chairs and waited for Virgil.

After about ten minutes I looked back when I heard Virgil exit. I stayed seated as he crossed the yard, walking in my direction.

"How was the discretion?" I said.

"She opened up," Virgil said.

"Nothing like starting the day with a bang," I said.

Virgil shook his head some as he reached for his reins.

"She opened up in a way," Virgil said, "that had more to do with what I was interested in knowing than what she's no doubt good at, and what at another time I'd be more than interested in partaking in."

I got out of the chair and undraped my horse's reins from the low-hanging branch of the cottonwood.

"So she was less discreet than previous?"

"She was," Virgil said. "It seems one of her customers had a hand in helping get Strode in the house, but she said he didn't have a hand in Strode getting beat."

"How's she know that?" I said.

"'Cause he was with her," Virgil said. "He left her in the morning and found Strode on the road."

"You believe her?" I said.

Virgil nodded some, looking at the house, then swung up into the saddle.

"I do," Virgil said. "But we'll have a better idea after we talk to him."

I put my foot in the stirrup, got up, got seated, and we moved on some.

"Who is it?" I said.

"Jantz Wainwright," Virgil said. "Strode's daddy-in-law."

17

ᔰ

WHEN VIRGIL AND I RETURNED TO SAN CRIS-
tóbal, Constable Holly was with Hawkins in front of the sheriff's
office. Hawkins was tightening the cinch on his saddle that was
resting on a tall, dark bay.

"Hell," Hawkins said. "I was on my way out to meet y'all."

"For?" Virgil said.

"For one thing. Strode stirred."

"He talk?" I said.

"No," Hawkins said. "Davy came and got me. I went over there
early this morning before daylight. He mumbled a bit. Doc was
able to get him drinking water, but that was it."

Holly nodded.

"Dr. Mayfair," Holly said. "Told us he'd let us know when he
was cognizant."

"But that's not all," Hawkins said. "We found something important. Something we need to show you."

Hawkins pulled a telegram from his vest.

"Did like you asked," Hawkins said. "Went to the Western
Union office this morning and checked up on Strode. Ellsworth

told me Strode was college-educated. Graduated from a school in New York. A place called Saint John's. I wired them and I got this telegram back right away."

Hawkins handed the telegram to Virgil.

Virgil read the telegram, then handed it to me, and I read it.

"Looks like Strode's a smart fella," Virgil said.

"Top of his class," I said. "Must be."

"That isn't the totality of it," Holly said.

Hawkins's bay was gnawing nonstop on the hitch. He slapped the bay's nose with the tip of his reins as he pulled out another telegram and waved it in the air.

"After that first wire, this came in," Hawkins said as he handed the second telegram to Virgil.

Hawkins and Holly looked to me.

"It's from the Saint John's College, too," Holly said. "Someone there who knew Strode personally."

Virgil read it. His eyes narrowed, and then he handed me the telegram.

"You sure this is right?" Virgil said.

Hawkins and Holly nodded.

"That telegram came less than an hour after the first," Hawkins said.

Virgil looked at me as I read the telegram.

"What do you make of that?" Hawkins said, looking back and forth between Virgil and me.

"Did you follow up with a responding telegram to this person?" I said, handing the telegram back to Hawkins.

"No," Hawkins said. "When I got the wire I figured I needed to find y'all, let y'all know right away."

65

Virgil looked at me a bit, then looked up the street, thinking.

"This is by God something," Hawkins said.

Holly looked at his watch.

"We can wire back, but better get to it 'fore it's too late in the day. Might be too late already, being back east and all."

Virgil nodded slightly.

"Do," Virgil said. "Wire 'em back, find out when, what year, how, and what else they know."

Hawkins and Holly both nodded.

"Any news from Slingshot?" Hawkins said as he mounted up.

"Don't know," Virgil said. "Need to find Jantz Wainwright."

Holly looked at Hawkins.

"Wainwright?" Holly said with a curious rise in his voice. "What does Mr. Wainwright got to do with this, other than losing a pot full of money?"

"Don't know," Virgil said, and offered nothing more.

"Well," Holly said, looking at Hawkins, "I don't know if he's in town."

Hawkins shook his head.

"He comes and goes," Hawkins said. "He's never here very long."

"Got any idea where he might be?" I said.

Hawkins shook his head.

"No," Holly said. "I was at the bank this morning. Place was crowded with folks clamoring. Damn upset. Wanting to know about their money. Didn't see Mr. Wainwright, though."

"Where does he stay when he's here?" I said. "Where's he hang his hat?"

"The Harvey House Hotel on the tracks," Hawkins said, pointing in the direction of the hotel. "He stays there some, or at his ranch near the river."

Holly nodded.

"Good," Virgil said. "Find out what you can about Strode, about who knew him and what. Everett and me will have ourselves a look-see elsewhere."

Hawkins nodded. He turned his bay but stopped short of riding off. He looked at the telegram he was still holding in his hand and shook his head some.

"So," Hawkins said. "If like this telegram says is true and Henry Strode is really dead, then who is the man beat to hell and near death in Doc Mayfair's office?"

"Don't know," Virgil said. "But we aim to find out."

18

⁓

VIRGIL AND I LOCATED THE HARVEY HOUSE Hotel. It was a three-story building made of brick and cornered with limestone.

The Harvey House Hotel was part of a popular franchise of hotels that were located in major cities across the west, from Topeka to Frisco. The hotels were fancily appointed and elegant, with indoor facilities. They were renowned for their quality restaurants famous for their Harvey Girls—a staff of educated and overly polite young women dressed in starched black-and-white maids' uniforms.

When we entered the hotel, we were greeted by two of the Harvey Girls behind the front desk. There was a set of stairs to the left and a set of stairs to the right of the desk.

The women were young. One was small, with sandy-colored hair. The other was taller and brunette. Each was attractive, with her hair tied up tightly under a small hat.

"May we help you," the young women said in tandem, with bright smiles.

"Ladies," Virgil said with a returning smile. "We're looking for a fella that might be staying here. Jantz Wainwright?"

The young women looked at each other, and the taller of the two spoke up.

"We are not allowed to give out information about our guests," the brunette said.

"So," Virgil said. "He is here?"

"Sorry, sir," the brunette said. "We are not allowed."

"No reason to be sorry," Virgil said.

Virgil showed his badge.

"What room?"

The young ladies looked at each other.

"We have very strict orders," the taller woman said with a swallow. "We could lose our jobs."

"Well," I said. "Nobody wants that to happen. Why don't you fetch your manager for us?"

"Indeed, certainly," the brunette said. "Splendid. Please have a seat."

Virgil looked at me, and we walked over to a sitting area in the center of the lobby and took a seat in a pair of stuffed chairs. We watched as the brunette walked up the stairs leading up behind the front desk.

"Splendid," Virgil said under his breath, as if he needed to taste the word.

We waited, and after a moment a smart-looking woman walked down the stairs followed by the brunette. She held her shoulders back and her chin high as she descended. She didn't wear the common starched black-and-white outfit the other Harvey Girls wore.

69

She was dressed in a tight-fitting dress that enhanced the curves of her body, and her wavy blond hair was loosely secured up high, with curls falling around her cheekbones. When she got to the bottom of the stairs I recognized her right away. She was the blond woman with the bright blue eyes Virgil and I saw on the street the day before.

"Gentlemen," she said as Virgil and I got to our feet. "I'm Mary May Chase. I understand you're lawmen?"

"We are," Virgil said, showing his badge. "I'm Marshal Cole, and this is my deputy, Everett Hitch."

"What can I do for you, Marshal?"

"We're looking for Jantz Wainwright," Virgil said.

"Well," Mary May said, "Mr. Wainwright is not in, nor is he staying with us at the moment."

"When was the last time you saw him?" Virgil said.

"Well, I'm not certain," she said.

"You're sure about that?" Virgil said.

The front door of the hotel opened, and a tall man with a full head of graying hair entered, followed by Hawkins.

"Gentlemen," the man said loudly, out of breath. "I'm Jantz Wainwright."

19

---- ᔓᔓ ----

WAINWRIGHT WAS OVER SIX FEET. HE WORE A
tweed suit with his pants tucked into tall spit-polished Rutland
buckle boots. He seemed nervous and anxious. He held out his
hand. He was shaking. I stepped in and shook hands with him.

"Deputy Marshal Everett Hitch," I said. "This is Marshal Virgil
Cole."

Wainwright looked to Mary May.

"Mary May, bring us a bottle of whiskey to the porch. Please,
gentlemen, come, follow me."

Wainwright did not say anything as we walked through the
empty dining area and made our way to the rear door of the hotel.
We took a seat at a small table on the porch overlooking the river.

"I just talked to Sheriff Hawkins here at the depot," Wainwright
said, looking to Hawkins. "I was there to meet my daughter."

Virgil didn't say anything.

"I have a big problem, Marshal," Wainwright said.

"What kind?" Virgil said.

"I'm quite concerned, very concerned."

"'Bout?" Virgil said.

Wainwright watched as Mary May came out with a bottle of whiskey and glasses. She set them on the table in front of Wainwright.

"Anything else?" Mary May said.

"No," Wainwright said. "Thank you."

She smiled, backed away, servant-like, and moved off through the dining room.

Wainwright twisted his hands together in front of him.

"I believe my daughter to be in serious danger . . . or," Wainwright said, "perhaps worse."

Wainwright poured himself a whiskey and slid the bottle to the center of the table. He took a gulp like a drunk needing to calm dry shakes.

"What makes you think that?" Virgil said.

"She was supposed to be on the noon train today," Wainwright said. "But she wasn't."

Wainwright coughed, stood up, moved to the porch rail, and spit. He pulled a handkerchief from his pocket and wiped his mouth. He remained looking off toward the river.

"She was in San Francisco visiting my sister. She was meant to return today, but according to the stationmaster, she came back here to San Cristóbal two days ago."

"Why do you fear for her?" I said.

Wainwright turned to face us. He looked at Hawkins.

"I'm not going to mince my words with you men about anything," Wainwright said. "What I am going to do is provide you with the necessary everything I can provide to get to the bottom of this Henry Strode business. I was the one who found Henry near dead. He was unconscious, lying on the road outside of town. I had no idea about the robbery when I found him. Sheriff Hawkins here just told me about what took place. After I found out she had not arrived, I went to their home. She was not there . . . I was prepared to apprise my daughter of Henry's condition, but now, now that she was apparently already home when this ordeal took place and the fact no one knows of her whereabouts, I fear, as I said, she may be in serious danger."

Wainwright poured himself another drink before he continued.

He took a sip of his drink. It seemed to settle him some.

"I have a ranch outside of town. I have been out there for a few days with my wife and our young son. I came into town yesterday on business and was meant to meet my daughter, today, at the depot before returning to the ranch."

Virgil nodded some.

"What were you doing on the road south of town when you found Strode?" Virgil said.

"I was visiting a whoring establishment," Wainwright said.

Wainwright looked off in the distance across the river.

"You got any idea how he got the living hell beat outta him?" Virgil said.

"No," Wainwright said.

"Any idea who might have done it?" I said. "Somebody that was an enemy of Strode's?"

Wainwright shook his head.

"No," Wainwright said. "Frankly, I don't give a fuck, either."

"You don't give a fuck about Strode?" Virgil said.

"What I give a fuck about is the whereabouts and safety of my daughter."

"Tell me about Strode."

"What would you like to know?"

"How did you get to know him?"

"My daughter married him."

"Where did you meet?"

Wainwright shook his head a little. He looked down with a frown fixed on his face, as if he were trying to remember.

"Well, he first came to the club."

"Club?"

"Polo club. I sponsor a club. He was a fantastic player."

"That where he met your daughter."

"Yes."

"What did you know about him, before they were married?"

"Not much, really. He was a gentleman. Apparently from money, old money back east."

"How do you know that?"

"Well, he wasn't broke. He was well spoken, well educated."

"What was your impression of him?" I said.

Wainwright sat for a moment in thought.

"A good man. Hardworking. I hired him, and he proved to be valuable to my businesses. I will say there was something about him that always seemed, I don't know, peculiar."

"Like?" Virgil said.

"I can't say. He was just different. Aloof. But my daughter, Catherine, was in love with him."

Virgil nodded a bit, then got to his feet.

"We will go about what we got to do here to locate your daughter, Mr. Wainwright," Virgil said. "Might need to find you as we go about that very task."

"I will cooperate with you in every way," Wainwright said.

"In the event we do need to find you," Virgil said, "where might we do so?"

"I was meant to return to Saint Louis in a few days," Wainwright said, "but I will remain here until I know what has happened to my daughter. I will either be here or at my ranch across the river. Sheriff Hawkins knows the road."

We moved off and left Wainwright sitting at the table, looking out across the river.

20

I FOLLOWED VIRGIL AND HAWKINS OUT OF THE dining room and across the lobby toward the door. Virgil and Hawkins crossed the threshold out in front of me as Mary May entered from the hall leading to the downstairs rooms.

"May I have a word with you, Deputy?"

I stopped and turned back to her.

"Sure."

"What on earth is happening?"

"What do you mean?"

She looked back through the restaurant to the porch where Wainwright was sitting.

"Well, about this business with Mr. Wainwright," she said. "Of course."

"Business?"

"Has something happened?"

"I'm sorry, Miz Chase. I'm not at liberty to discuss our business. No offense."

"Oh, well, okay, no offense taken. I'm just concerned. That's all."

"About?"

"Well, I've never seen him like this. He seems, I don't know, upset."

"Let me ask *you* a question," I said.

"Certainly."

"Why did you say you were uncertain the last time you saw Mr. Wainwright?"

"I wasn't uncertain about anything," she said, with her blue eyes leveled at me steadily.

"You said he was not in and he wasn't staying here."

"I did."

"Why?"

"I'm new here to San Cristóbal, Deputy Hitch, but I've been an employee of Mr. Wainwright's for five years. I started working for him in Saint Louis, at his hotel there, and worked my way up, and he helped me get this position. He saved me from, well, a life less appealing, and, well, I'm protective."

"Even if you're interfering with the law?"

"Yes," she said flatly.

I looked at her for a moment, and she raised her chin up just a bit to confirm her position.

"Perfectly understandable," I said.

"It is," she said.

"Might get you in trouble."

"You think?"

"I do."

"You'll just have to arrest me, then, lock me up."

She just looked at me for a lingering moment.

"I'm just concerned, Deputy Hitch," she said as she reached out and touched my arm. "Perhaps you have some idea how I feel."

77

I remained looking at her as she looked at me.

"I do."

"Good," she said.

"I have a good idea how you feel."

"I'm glad," Mary May said. "I'm comforted to know."

"Don't change the fact you could get yourself in trouble by not cooperating."

"I know I have a tendency to make things hard for myself," Mary May said. "To a fault, I know, but when things get too difficult, too hard, you can count on me to cooperate fully. It's just I won't roll over easy. It's not in my nature."

"Good to know," I said.

The whole time I'd been talking with Mary May it seemed her eyes were carrying on a different conversation with me than the nature of the conversation itself, and now I was certain of it. I could feel it in my bones. She was concerned for Wainwright, but she was for certain straight-out dallying with me.

"Do you know Catherine?" I said.

"Mr. Wainwright's daughter?" Mary May said with a slight change of expression.

"Yes."

"Is that what this is about?"

"I'm just asking you."

She shook her head.

"No . . . Well, we've met, on a few occasions."

"So you do know her?"

"Only slightly. Like I said, I'm new to town. I'm sorry I'm not more useful."

I tipped my hat.

"You have a good day, Miz Chase."

"You, too," Mary May said with a smile.

I turned to the door.

"Deputy Hitch?"

"Yes."

"Please know I'm not entirely un-useful," she said.

21

VIRGIL AND HAWKINS SAT THEIR HORSES IN front of the hotel and were waiting on me when I walked out the door. Virgil was lighting a cigar as I stepped off the boardwalk and into the street next to the hitch. After he got the cigar going good he flicked the match into the street.

"Something else?" Virgil said.

I shook my head as I slipped the reins from the hitch and stepped up into the saddle.

"She was curious," I said.

Virgil nodded a bit.

"They're a curious lot," Virgil said.

"They are."

"What was she curious about?" Virgil said.

"She fears for him, it seems," I said.

"That's understandable, ain't it? Money's gone, daughter's gone?" Hawkins said as he jerked back the reins to keep his bay from gnawing the hitch.

"Knows he's sideways 'bout something?" Virgil said.

"Yep," I said. "Seems so."

"Maybe she knows more?" Hawkins said.

"No," I said. "Don't think so."

"How 'bout her?" Virgil said.

"What about her?"

"She buggered up about anything?" Virgil said.

"Like what?"

"Like what women get buggered up about."

I looked to Virgil. He did not smile, but I could tell he was smiling the way Virgil smiled without showing he smiled, and he was enjoying it.

"Marshal Cole!" a voice called out.

We looked to see Constable Holly hurrying toward us on the boardwalk.

"I've got something for you," Holly said.

"What's that?" Virgil said.

Holly stepped off the boardwalk and handed Virgil another telegram.

"Got this telegram back from the wire you asked us to send," Holly said, breathing heavily.

Virgil read the note.

"Took me a while to track this down, but Henry Strode died there in New York, apparently," Holly said. "He died a natural death. Coroner's report said consumption. That's what I received back from my inquiry. Can you believe this? Lands. I just cannot fathom why or how something like this could have happened. Oh, and the other thing it says, you, of course, can read there, Strode was a wealthy man from a well-to-do family, yet with no apparent heir."

Virgil passed the telegram to me and I read it.

"Heir or not. Natural cause or not," I said. "Taking over the role of a wealthy man requires some skill to wrangle money from the estate account."

"Unless you're the, what do you call it, for the family," Hawkins said.

"The executor," Holly said.

"That's right," Hawkins said.

"Or a banker," Virgil said.

Holly nodded.

"A will would provide a directive," Holly said. "And without it, the money, of course, goes to next of kin."

"And in this here case there was no next of kin," Hawkins said.

"So it seems," Holly said.

"Good work, Constable," Virgil said. "If you would, keep pounding the key and see what else you might be able to find out. Just keep at it."

"Certainly," Holly said. "There's also another matter, Marshal."

"Matter being?" Virgil said.

"Alejandro has requested he have a chat with you," Holly said.

"Chat?" Virgil said. "'Bout what?"

"Apparently, he has some information for you," Holly said.

"What kind of information?" I said.

"I don't know," Holly said. "Ira Cross told me, I'm just relaying the message."

"Likely wants to let you know he don't much like his jailer," I said.

"I don't much care for him myself," Virgil said, looking at Hawkins.

Hawkins jerked the bay's reins again to keep him from gnawing.

"Truth be told," Hawkins said. "I don't care for him much, neither."

"Well," Holly said, "he is good at his job."

Hawkins nodded and shrugged a bit, then popped his reins and snapped at his bay, "Blisters! Stop with the goddamn gnawing!"

22

VIRGIL AND I LEFT HOLLY AND HAWKINS TO
check in on Strode's condition, and we made our way back to the
sheriff's office to see what it was Alejandro was interested in chat-
ting about.

Ira Cross led us through the metal door into the hall to the cells.
Alejandro had his boots off and was sitting Indian-style on his
bunk. A short, round fella with rosy cheeks wearing a checkered-
patterned suit with a silk fold tie and high flattop hat was in the
cell next to him. He was passed out snoring with his hands folded
across his big round belly.

"*Hola, mis amigos,*" Alejandro said when we entered.

"Stand up," Ira said.

"Fuck you, old man," Alejandro said.

Cross whacked the bars with his club.

"Why, you brown—"

"Let us sort this out with him, Mr. Cross," I said.

Alejandro just smiled and the drunk in the flattop hat kept on
snoring.

Ira steamed an irritable look to Alejandro, then returned back to the office.

"You wanted to see us," Virgil said.

"*Sí,*" Alejandro said with a smile.

"You got something you'd like to share?" Virgil said.

"Yes," Alejandro said. "But Alejandro's *información* comes at a price."

"Alejandro, you're in no position to put a price on nothing," Virgil said.

"But you do not know what *información* Alejandro has got to share."

Virgil didn't say anything.

"What if I were to tell you Alejandro knows much about the robbery."

"Robbery," I said. "What robbery?"

"Why, the bank robbery, of course."

Alejandro nodded to the drunk in the cell next to him.

"My little amigo here, Proctor Pugh. He writes for the newspaper. He told me."

"What do you got to say, Alejandro?" I said.

"Maybe I know where you could find them."

"Find who?" Virgil said.

"The robbers, of course. To be honest, though, Alejandro should say, I know where they most likely may be."

"Honest?" Virgil said. "That's a notion way outside of your ability, Alejandro."

"Get on with it," I said.

Alejandro shook his head.

"I will share what I know, but only when you want to make Alejandro a deal."

Virgil looked at me, grinning a little.

"You'd tell any lie you could," I said, "to get out of this jail."

Alejandro nodded.

"True, Everett," he said. "But do you think I would have you come here to see me and not have something of importance to share with you?"

"Hell, Alejandro," I said. "It's hard to know what you'd think."

"You will be impressed!" Alejandro said.

Virgil shook his head.

"There is nothing about you that is impressive, and nothing you've got to say, Captain," Virgil said. "When you broke out of jail up in Butch's Bend you shot a friend of ours in the back. Before that you killed two men in this town. Men you'll most likely get strung up for, so wade into what you got to say and say it."

"I did not kill your friend. But let Alejandro start with the two men you say I killed here in San Cristóbal."

"Start," I said.

"Those men. They tried to kill me."

"You'll have an opportunity to tell your side of it to the judge," Virgil said. "Let's go, Everett."

"Wait!"

Alejandro got to his feet and moved closer to the bars.

"There were three men that night that tried to kill me. One of them got away."

"What does this have to do with the robbery?" I said.

"It was his plan."

86

"Whose plan?" I said.

"The one who got away."

Alejandro opened one side of his naval jacket and put his finger through an in-and-out hole in the jacket's side, showing us an apparent bullet hole.

"He shot at Alejandro one last time. Two men coming out of the church saw us in the street. They say I killed the men, but they do not know the whole story. I jumped on my horse running north, and the man who shot at me jumped on his horse running south. I have not seen him since, but he is the man responsible for robbing the bank. This much I know."

Virgil looked at me.

"You expect us to believe you?" I said.

"*Sí*," Alejandro said with a broad smile. "He was planning to rob the bank then. I found out about it and tried to stop them."

"That was months ago," I said.

"*Sí*."

Virgil shook his head.

"Tell the judge."

Virgil and I turned for the door.

"Okay," Alejandro said. "They tried to cut me out of the deal, Everett . . . They tried to kill Alejandro."

"Who you talking about here?" I said.

Alejandro shook his head.

"There is one thing I can tell you," Alejandro said. "He is perhaps the Diablo himself."

"Who?" I said.

"I have to hold a few cards, Everett," Alejandro said, "you know that . . . I am a very good card player, but you have to help Alejandro."

"We don't have to do nothing," Virgil said, and walked out.

I gave one last look to Alejandro and followed Virgil into the office. Then we heard Alejandro call.

"What if I told you I know Henry Strode is not Henry Strode?"

23

"**WAKE UP,**" **CROSS SAID.**

Cross poked the newspaperman, Proctor Pugh, in his round belly with the police club.

"What?" Pugh said with a fright. "Good God!"

Pugh talked out of the corner of his mouth, as if one side of it was stitched together. He rambled as he spoke and stretched his words longer than they needed stretching.

"Lord have mercy!" Pugh said with a disoriented look on his face. "What? What is it? What time is the print?"

Pugh pulled out his pocket watch and held it at arm's length, trying to focus on the time.

"Time to wake up, Pugh," Cross said.

Pugh looked around. He looked at Virgil and me, then pocketed his watch, leaned back, and closed his eyes.

Cross poked him again.

"Up," Cross said. "Wake up."

"Oh, good God," Pugh said. "Can't a lady get any rest? I'll get up when I'm exceptionally good and ready."

"You'll get up right now," Cross said, and pulled Pugh to his feet.

Pugh's hat tumbled off his head. Cross picked it up and put it back on Pugh's round head.

"All right," Pugh said, swatting Cross away like he was a pesky fly. "All right! I can manage. I can get around quite well on my own volition, thank you very much."

Pugh turned, looking for his hat, and then turned again until he realized it was on his head. He took the hat off, looked at it, and placed it back atop his head. He started out of the cell and looked Virgil and me up and down.

"Proctor Pugh," he said with a tip of his hat. "And whom do I have the pleasure of meeting on such a postulate occasion?"

"Get!" Cross said.

"Mr. Cross," Pugh said. "Never have I had the displeasure of knowing a character of such unimaginable insolence as I have with the likes of you."

Cross jerked Pugh from the cell and walked him out, leaving us alone with Alejandro.

Alejandro was on his feet behind the bars. Virgil faced him.

"What do you have to say, Captain," Virgil said, "about Henry Strode?"

"I know him since I was a boy," Alejandro said.

"Who is he?" I said.

"Will you help me?" Alejandro said.

"You are a prisoner," Virgil said. "Start answering. Depending on what you got to say will determine what I might and might not do."

"That does not sound too good for Alejandro."

"Alejandro don't got much choice."

"He is," Alejandro said, "a *huérfano,* from my country."

"Orphan?" I said.

"*Sí.* His brother, too, and me."

"What's his name?" I said. "His real name?"

"Joe."

I looked at Virgil. His arms were crossed in front of him, and he leaned with his shoulder to a post. He was looking at Alejandro with a fixed expression of distrust.

"We came to America together. Me, Joe, and his brother, Jack."

"Keep going," I said. "Last name?"

Alejandro shook his head.

"I did not kill your friend, and I did not kill those men. I kill only to protect myself, same as you, Virgil Cole."

"Don't go comparing yourself to me," Virgil said.

"Don't ask me to help you for nothing," Alejandro said.

Virgil walked out, and I followed.

"You let me out," Alejandro called out. "I will take you to where you need to go! Otherwise you will never, ever find him! Ever!"

Ira Cross was sweeping the floor. He stopped and looked to us.

"That Mezkin brown bean is full of shit," Cross said as he continued to sweep.

"You hear him talking to the newspaperman?" I said.

"Newspaperman my ass," Cross said. "Proctor Pugh gets paid some to write for the newspaper, but he ain't nothing but a damn drunk."

"Did you?" Virgil said.

"Nope, I did not hear them talking," Cross said, and went back to sweeping the already swept-clean floor.

"Where is Proctor Pugh?" Virgil said.

"I don't know. I sent the rat on his way. Why?"

"Where would we most likely find him?" I said.

"That's easy," Cross said as he swept. "He's bellied up at the closest place for him to get liquored up, no doubt."

Virgil looked at me as Cross continued to sweep.

"Where would that be, Mr. Cross?" I said.

Cross stopped sweeping. He pointed.

"Up the street here, there is a joint called the Gold River Saloon."

"Appreciate it, Mr. Cross," I said.

Cross nodded and resumed sweeping as I followed Virgil to the door.

"Most likely, though," Cross said without looking at us as he dragged the broom in small whisking moves across the floor, "he's at Benedict Arnold's Saloon, down the street, on the right."

24

BENEDICT ARNOLD'S WAS A DARK, DANK PLACE,
and it was near empty except for a couple of teamsters sitting in the
corner playing a contemplative game of checkers, and, like crotchety
Cross had thought, the newspaperman Proctor Pugh was there, too.
He was sitting at the bar, finishing off a mug of beer.

"Pugh," Virgil said.

He turned, looked at us, and removed the mug from his lips.

"A rose by any other name," Pugh said with a crooked smile.

His upper lip retained the froth from the mug.

"I'm Deputy Marshal Everett Hitch, and this is Marshal Virgil
Cole," I said. "Like to have a word with you."

"Well, you've come to the right place," Pugh said. "Words are
my forte. I'm never without them."

"Good," Virgil said.

"They, the words, however, are sometimes without me, which
provides embarrassing discomfort for a man such as myself con-
fined to the vocation of journalism."

Virgil looked at me. He smiled some.

"And," Pugh said, "as of late, they, the words, have just been leaving me by the wayside, I tell you, the absolute wayside. It's troubling, aggravating for that sort of—"

"Three beers," I said to the bartender.

"And an aperitif of some sort, my good man," Pugh said with urgency to the bartender. "The good stuff."

The bartender looked and me and I nodded.

"I've seen you fellows before," Pugh said, tapping his temple with his stubby first finger. "I never forget a face."

"That's good," I said. "You just saw us, when we saw you at the jail a short time ago."

"So I did," Pugh said. "So I did. I stop in there now and again to see what might be newsworthy. I'm always on the job, you see. They are my friends there—well, with the exception of that specimen of leather they refer to as the jailer. He's not going to heaven, I tell you, I'm sure of it, but the jailhouse is a good place to gather information."

"That's what we want to talk about with you," I said.

Pugh looked at the whiskey and the beer the barkeep set in front of him.

"Outstanding," Pugh said, and downed the whiskey. "My vocabulary is becoming more bountiful by the minute."

"Good," Virgil said. "Talk to us about the fella that was in the cell next to you."

"The Mexican?" Pugh said.

"Yes," I said. "What was the nature of your conversation you had with him?"

"His English is very good," Pugh said.

"Do you remember?" I said.

"Well, of course," Pugh said. "I remember everything, Deputy. I have a mind like a steel trap."

"The conversation?" Virgil said.

"Yes, well, we discussed his incarceration, naturally," Pugh said. "Always a common topic of discussion for a man behind bars."

Pugh drank a big gulp of beer.

"What did you tell him about the bank?" I said.

"The bank, the bank," Pugh said, as if he was trying to remember.

"Let's not fuck around here," Virgil said.

Pugh cocked his head and backed it up into the grimy collar of his shirt and looked at Virgil with a sideways glance.

"Well, since you put it that way," Pugh said. "A proclivity I've managed to avoid in my fifty-plus years, mind you, I will say I told the Mexican—Alejandro, that is—about the robbery, that I did."

Pugh took another gulp of beer.

"How did you know about the robbery?" I said.

"Well," Pugh said with a belch, "I was engaged in a winning game of rummy the previous evening with a few colleagues. Our game ended about the time the bank opened, and there was some god-awful bellyaching spindrift swirling about in front of the bank. Naturally, I caught wind of what was happening and I cornered one of the tellers. That's what I do, you know? I investigate. Anyway, he divulged to me what had happened."

"What did the teller tell you?" I said.

"He told me the bank's president, Henry Strode, had robbed the bank. Ha! I rushed to the office with the breaking news but only made it to the corner of Fifth before I got into an altercation with

Gertrud Bavenger, a bitch wolf in heat, I tell you. Anyway, as a result, I was escorted to the jail for a little respite."

"Did the Mexican share anything with you about Strode?" I said.

"As a matter of fact he did," Pugh said. "He told me he knew the man—he told me they were old friends."

"Anything else?" I said.

"Like what?"

"He tell you where they were from?" I said.

Pugh shook his head.

"Nope," Pugh said.

Pugh looked back and forth between Virgil and me.

"This is a corroborative effort on your part, is it not?" Pugh said.

Virgil looked at me.

"That's right," I said to Pugh. "We are trying to verify a few things."

Hawkins came through the door followed by Holly. He spotted us at the end of the bar and stumbled over a chair in the dark room as he hurried over to us with Holly on his heels.

"We have a problem," Hawkins said. "A big goddamn problem!"

25

HAWKINS'S ANNOUNCEMENT AWAKENED PUGH'S journalistic curiosity like a wasp's nest getting hit by a swiftly thrown rock. Pugh tumbled his round body off the bar stool with the intention of following us out of Benedict Arnold's, but Virgil turned on him and talked to him like a house dog.

"Stay put," Virgil said.

Pugh looked back and forth between Virgil and me and nodded.

"Don't mind if I do," Pugh said.

He removed his hat, bowed, and crawled back up on the bar stool and repeated himself, "Don't mind if I do."

We walked out of the darkness of Benedict Arnold's and into the blazing bright sunlight of the afternoon. Virgil and I kept stride with Hawkins as he moved up the street. Holly was behind us, doing his best to keep up.

"Dr. Mayfair, Davy, and Danny were all tied up," Hawkins said.

"Just awful," Holly said, "awful. We found them locked in a closet in Mayfair's office."

"They hurt?" Virgil said.

Hawkins shook his head.

"Pride's all," Hawkins said.

"They've not been harmed," Holly said. "Thank God!"

"They're good and angry," Hawkins said.

"How'd it happen?" I said.

"Early this morning," Hawkins said. "Strode woke up, whispered 'water.'"

"His first words!" Holly said.

"Davy got close to Strode," Hawkins said. "Strode snatched Davy's Colt."

"Strode did that!" Holly said. "Can you believe it?"

"Anybody else have a hand in this?" I said.

"No," Hawkins said. "Don't seem like it."

"He told Davy to rip up bedding, of all things," Holly said. "And tie up Dr. Mayfair and Danny."

Hawkins nodded.

"Told Davy to tie up his own feet," Hawkins said. "Goddamn man. And lay facedown with his hands behind his back. Strode snugged Davy's hands."

"Gagged them, too," Holly said. "And left the three of them in the closet. Can you believe it?"

"We found them when we got there," Hawkins said.

"Any idea where he is?" Virgil said. "Anybody see him?"

"Don't know nothing yet," Hawkins said.

"With one exception," Holly said. "We know he's gone—that much we do know."

"He stole the Rangfield brothers' horses," Hawkins said.

"Indeed he did," Holly said. "His crimes are mounting—first the bank, now this hostage saga, horse thievery. Lord knows what's next."

"Anybody see him?" I said.

"Don't know," Hawkins said. "Not found that out yet, anyway."

"No telling where he is," Holly said.

"We already got Davy and Danny on other mounts," Hawkins said. "I gathered some of the deputy boys, and they're asking around, looking for Strode or anybody that's seen him."

When we got to Doc Mayfair's, the doctor was sitting out front on the steps, smoking a cigarette.

"Gents," Mayfair said, looking up at us.

For the moment that was it; that was the total of what the doctor had to say.

"I gave them the whole of it, Doc," Hawkins said.

Mayfair nodded, slowly smoking the cigarette.

"Strode say anything?" I said.

Mayfair shook his head.

"No," he said.

Virgil nodded a little, then looked around as if he were looking for something.

"How long?" Virgil said.

Mayfair clinched his cigarette between his teeth, leaned back slightly, pulled his watch from his vest, and opened it.

"He's been gone for about six hours," Mayfair said.

Mayfair closed the lid on the watch and slid it back into his pocket, then flicked his cigarette into the street.

"He's weak," Mayfair said. "There's one thing for certain. He's not moving too fast."

Virgil looked to Hawkins.

"He take anything," Virgil said.

"He did," Mayfair said. "He took some supplies, morphine, bandages, a shaded pair of syphilis spectacles."

"Like to get over to Strode's place," Virgil said. "Have us a look around."

"Sure thing," Hawkins said.

"Anything else you can tell us?" I said to Mayfair.

"No," Mayfair said quietly as he rolled a cigarette.

26

⤳

VIRGIL, HAWKINS, AND I RODE OUT TO HENRY
and Catherine Strode's place on the edge of town. As we neared,
Hawkins pointed.

"That's it there," he said.

"Let's pull up," Virgil said.

We stopped maybe a hundred yards from the house.

"Let's be on the smart side of doin'," Virgil said.

"You don't think he's dumb enough to have come back here, do
you, Cole," Hawkins said.

"Don't," Virgil said. "But let's just take 'er easy anyway."

We tied our horses to a solid hackberry tree in front of a small
home and walked on up the road to Strode's place.

Virgil did not want to take any chances, and not knowing what
to expect, we readied ourselves with our pistols when we got close
to the house.

Strode's place was a quality-built home with a white picket fence
surrounding the property and a well-kept garden.

"Go on around back, Everett," Virgil said quietly.

I nodded and continued on.

Virgil and Hawkins entered through the front gate and stopped as I walked around the outside of the fence to the rear of the house. I looked back to Virgil. He nodded, and they started toward the front door.

The back door was unlocked, and I entered the house just as Virgil and Hawkins entered from the front.

The front door was visible from the back door. Virgil and Hawkins stopped and listened. I did the same.

"Strode?" I called out as I looked to Virgil and Hawkins.

The three of us stood silently for a moment, but there was no reply, no sounds. I walked the narrow hall to Virgil and Hawkins.

The house was a two-story structure with fine furniture. The downstairs area was a loop of connecting rooms surrounding a staircase to the second floor. We walked around the first floor through the living area and into the kitchen. Virgil was looking at nothing and everything. In the kitchen there was a polished step-back hutch with glass-covered doors, and behind the doors there were stacks of glazed plates and saucers. There was an open can of peaches sitting on the counter with a spoon resting in it. The can was empty. We walked through the dining room. The doors of a liquor cabinet were open, and with the exception of a single bottle of plum brandy, the cabinet was empty. There was a vase with wilted flowers sitting on the dinner table. Two glass candleholders sat on opposite sides of the vase. They were covered with hardened wax that had dripped and pooled in folds spreading out on the tabletop. Virgil continued on up the stairs and Hawkins and I followed. Upstairs consisted of two bedrooms and a small powder room with a fancy vanity. Both of the beds were made up. In the larger bedroom, Virgil opened the doors of a carved-wood armoire that was divided by narrow shelves. On one side of the shelves hung Strode's suits, and on the other side there was a good number of frilly dresses.

Virgil stood there looking at the clothes. He looked through the drawers, and they were full of dressing pieces, scarves, ties, and ribbons.

Virgil turned, walked to a window, and pushed back the lace curtain to have a look out.

"There been anybody else here?" Virgil said. "Since the robbery?"

"No," Hawkins said.

"Nobody touch nothing?" Virgil said.

"No," Hawkins said. "Everything seems pretty much like it was when I came here before. This was, of course, the first place I looked."

"What about the peaches?" Virgil said.

"Peaches?" Hawkins said.

"You eat those peaches," Virgil said. "The open can on the counter?"

"No," Hawkins said. "Why?"

Virgil looked out the window for a moment before he looked back to Hawkins and me.

"Strode didn't have everything to do with this robbery," Virgil said. "Fact, he might not have had a hand in it at all."

Hawkins looked to Virgil, then looked to me.

"What makes you think that?" Hawkins said.

Virgil turned from the window.

"Somebody made him do it," Virgil said.

"What?" Hawkins said.

"Somebody was here," Virgil said.

"Who?" Hawkins said.

Virgil shrugged and shook his head some.

"Don't know."

"That table downstairs is a nice table," Virgil said.

Hawkins looked at me, then back to Virgil.

"It is a nice hardwood," Virgil said. "Cherry, I believe."

Hawkins squinted like he was trying to see Virgil clearly.

"Cherrywood? What are you getting at, Cole?"

"It's never had wax on it," Virgil said. "Ever."

Hawkins looked back and forth between Virgil and me.

"The can of peaches," Virgil said, shaking his head.

"The peaches?" Hawkins said. "What about them?"

"Someone else ate those peaches," Virgil said.

Hawkins removed his hat and scratched his head.

"Someone let the candles burn to the quick," Virgil said.

Virgil looked at me.

I nodded.

"Sounds right," I said.

"Does," Virgil said. "This home is full of proper, proper for everything. Those clothes are all well tailored and taken care of—everything in this house is. Got bottoms for glasses to protect the tables and fancy dishes to eat peaches from."

Virgil looked back out the window, thinking.

"Don't think Catherine," Virgil said, "*or* Henry Strode would eat peaches from a can."

27

IT WAS NOW LATE IN THE AFTERNOON. THE NEWS
of the bank robbery and the subsequent disappearance of Strode
had spread across the city of San Cristóbal. We joined Hawkins and
his team of deputies and searched the town for any sign of Strode or
anyone that might have seen him but came up with nothing. Hawkins instructed the Rangfield brothers and four other deputies to
continue the hunt as Virgil, Hawkins, and I gathered in front of the
sheriff's office, where Constable Holly stood on the porch.

"He's not out there?" Holly said.

"Goddamn ghost," Hawkins said.

"Hard to believe he's gone," Holly said. "And not a single person
has seen him?"

"No. Goddamn ghost," Hawkins said again. "What the hell
now, Cole?"

Virgil sat his horse, looking down the street toward the lower-
ing sun.

"Everett?"

"Be dark soon," I said.

"Too late to get started with a posse," Hawkins said.

Virgil nodded a bit.

"Nobody seeing him," Hawkins said, "be goddamn hard to know where, or even which way to go."

"Someone," Holly said, "somewhere, surely has seen him."

"You'd think," Hawkins said.

"Hurt like he is," Holly said, "it would certainly seem so."

"At some point," Hawkins said, "he'll die, right?"

"My Lord," Holly said. "My Lord."

Virgil continued looking west.

"We got four roads in and out," Hawkins said.

Hawkins pointed west.

"He goes that way, he's got those mountains to contend with," Hawkins said.

Hawkins looked back over his shoulder to the east.

"Hell," Hawkins said. "He's got mountains that way, too."

"No matter," Virgil said. "He's going the direction he needs to go."

"The direction he *needs* to go?" Holly said.

"Yep," Virgil said.

Hawkins bit on the edge of his mustache, thinking, as he looked at Virgil.

"What's the closest town south?" Virgil said.

"Elk City," Hawkins said. "Fifteen miles."

"North?" Virgil said.

"Rushing Springs," Holly said. "That's twenty-five miles. There is, of course, various homes, farms, ranches, and a few businesses on the way to both Elk City and Rushing Springs."

Hawkins nodded.

"So," Hawkins said. "If he didn't do this, why is he running?"

"He ain't running," Virgil said.

Hawkins looked at Virgil for a moment.

"He's not, is he?" Hawkins said.

"No," Virgil said.

"He's on the hunt," Hawkins said.

"He is," Virgil said.

"The hunt?" Holly said. "I'm confused."

Hawkins looked in the direction Virgil was looking, toward the setting sun, then looked to Holly.

"He's going after whoever whipped the hell out of him," Hawkins said flatly to Holly.

"Yep," I said. "And whoever let the candles burn down to the quick on the cherrywood table."

"And whoever ate the goddamn peaches," Hawkins said.

"Peaches?" Holly said.

Virgil nodded.

"That's right," Virgil said. "Whoever ate the peaches, and whoever run off with his wife."

28

AS SOON AS WE GOT CONSTABLE HOLLY APPRISED of what we believed to be the circumstances regarding the disappearance of Henry Strode and the robbery, Davy and Danny Rangfield rounded the corner on their mounts and pulled up to a stop where Virgil, Hawkins, and I sat our horses.

"Hey, Marshal," Danny said. "Deputy."

"Boys," Virgil said.

Davy stayed back behind Danny some. I don't think he liked the idea that Strode had snatched his Colt away, tied him up, and left him in a broom closet.

"Find anything?" Hawkins said.

"No," Danny said. "Not really."

"What do you mean, 'not really'?"

"Old man Letts said he heard some horses this morning before dark," Danny said.

"But you know old man Letts," Davy grumbled.

"Yeah," Danny agreed. "He'd say anything just so to hear himself talk."

"We stopped at Wolfgang's store and all the houses that way," Davy said. "Nothing."

Hawkins circled his bay in the street.

"Let me go talk to Letts," Hawkins said.

"Fair enough," Danny said.

Danny and Davy turned to follow. Hawkins looked to Virgil.

"We'll keep looking, Cole, checking out what we can. Least till we're dark-bit."

Hawkins clucked Blisters and moved on up the street, followed by the Rangfield brothers.

"Constable Holly?" Virgil said.

"Yes, Marshal?" Holly said.

"What kind of telegraph records do you keep here in Cristóbal?" Virgil said.

"Well," Holly said. "We run an efficient office. Why?"

"How far back would you have records of telegrams sent?" Virgil said.

"A few years, I think," Holly said. "But I'm not certain. They get rid of them after a while. I'm uncertain as to the last removal. What do you need?"

"I want you to check the months before the shootout Alejandro had with those fellas just before Christmas," Virgil said. "Check and see if there is any record of Alejandro sending a telegram to anyone."

"Alejandro?" Holly said with a befuddled look on his face.

Virgil looked at me and shrugged some.

I nodded.

"Yes," Virgil said to Holly. "Alejandro."

"Telegraph sent to who?" Holly said.

"Don't know," Virgil said. "That's what I aim to find out."

Holly looked back and forth between the two of us.

"Does this have to do with Alejandro wanting to talk to you?" Holly said.

"You'll check for me?" Virgil said, politely ignoring Holly's question.

"Well, well, certainly," Holly said. "Might take some time sorting through, but I suppose it can be done."

"Good," Virgil said.

"Let us know what you find, Constable," I said.

"I assume this is imminent?"

Virgil looked at me.

"You bet," I said to Holly. "It's pronto."

Holly nodded.

"Indeed," Holly said with a little grin. "Like it were yesterday."

"Or the day before," Virgil said without a smile.

"Or the day before," Holly said with a nervous chuckle. "Yes, well, okay, then."

With that, Holly smiled slightly, turned, and moved on up the boardwalk. We watched him walk a ways.

"Worth a try," I said.

"Is."

"You're thinking if what Alejandro said is correct, he'd have to have contacted the brother somehow."

"That'd be my thinking."

"Unless Alejandro and the brother were together."

"Yep," Virgil said.

"Or if the brother was close to here."

"Providing there even is a brother," Virgil said.

"True," I said. "Alejandro might be, and most likely is, just bullshitting us about the brother?"

"Don't know," Virgil said. "But he seems convicted to convince us he does."

"A way outta jail."

"Is."

"Let's say he does know and Holly don't find a telegram," I said. "What then?"

"Don't know."

29

AFTER SUNDOWN, HAWKINS FOUND VIRGIL AND me on the porch of the Holly Hotel. We sat at the same table underneath the sconce swarming with moths, mosquitos, and bugs of June. Virgil had an after-dinner cigar going, and the smoke lingered over the table in the hot and muggy evening air. Virgil pushed out a chair with his boot as Hawkins trudged slowly up the steps to the porch.

"Get yourself a seat, Webb."

"Don't mind if I do."

Hawkins dropped in the chair like he was done for the day.

"Nothing?" I said.

"Nope," Hawkins said, shaking his head gradually.

I stepped inside and got a glass for Hawkins and poured him a whiskey.

"Fucking tired," Hawkins said as he pulled his shoulders back, trying to get something inside his big body to crack.

Virgil blew out a roll of smoke that twisted and swirled in the light.

"That all?" Virgil said.

"No. My ass is sore, too."

Virgil grinned a little.

"Blisters give you some blisters?" Virgil said.

"He damn sure did," Hawkins said.

Hawkins took his hat off, set it on the table, and took a sip of whiskey.

"I did talk to old man Letts, though. He's the one who said he'd heard horses in the morning."

"What'd he allow?" I said.

"Said he heard 'em, but it's hard to make out whether Letts is just carrying on or not. He's got a gift to gab."

"Which way is his place?" Virgil said.

"He's south, about halfway to Elk City."

"And nobody else has seen or heard anything?"

"Nope. I told the boys to get some sleep and start looking again at first light. Got to be somebody somewhere that's seen Strode, least so we know a direction to look."

"You'd think," I said.

The three of us rested with our thoughts for a moment and sipped some whiskey.

"Saw you got Holly looking for a wire?"

"Do," Virgil said.

"That's a good idea," Hawkins said.

"That's what we thought," Virgil said.

"So far he's found nothing," Hawkins said. "I put two of my boys there to help sift through."

Virgil nodded.

"Good."

"Cross told me that Alejandro's been going on about something he knows."

"He has at that," Virgil said.

"You believe him?"

Virgil shrugged a little.

"Judge Bing's got Alejandro's hearing set for the day after tomorrow," Hawkins said.

"Soon," I said.

"He figures since Alejandro escaped the first time," Hawkins said, "he's not wanting to take any chances."

"Evidently," Virgil said.

"Bing don't tolerate gunplay," Hawkins said.

"No," Virgil said. "He don't."

"We know that."

"We do."

"Known Judge Bing for a good while," I said.

Hawkins nodded.

"He was a territorial circuit judge for a while 'fore settling down here, wasn't he?" Hawkins said.

"Was," Virgil said.

"We've not seen him since," I said.

"Well, I'm sure he's even tougher than when y'all last saw him. Not tolerating gunplay is only one of his displeasures. He damn sure don't tolerate escaping prisoners—he's even less appreciating of that. Put the two of them together and you got his attention."

"Bing is tough," I said. "I'll give you that."

"Goddamn right he is," Hawkins said. "He's got a big trial going on right now. A dispute between two large mining outfits, and from what I hear he's not making it easy on nobody. Shitloads of people, landowners, and mining officials will be here this week, but he's gonna get Alejandro out of the way."

"Who's the prosecutor?" I said.

"Baxter Beazley. He's a mean sonofabitch, out to make a name for himself here in San Cristóbal. The court-appointed attorney is Charlie Chubb—he's more of a drunk than the newspaperman Proctor Pugh, so, needless to say, Alejandro's days are numbered."

"He's been saying he's innocent," I said.

"He damn sure ain't the first man to try and slip out of the high knot," Hawkins said.

"Nope," Virgil said. "He damn sure ain't."

"Marshal!" Holly called.

We looked to see Holly coming up the boardwalk.

"You were right. I found the correspondence. My gosh. How could you have known?"

30

⤳⤳

THE CORRESPONDENCE CONSTABLE HOLLY DIS-
covered at the Western Union office was a telegram sent from Alejandro to a man named Dalton McCord. Holly read it aloud. It was
a short telegram that simply stated: *San Cristóbal—Found your
brother, Jedediah.* The note back from Dalton McCord was even
shorter. It read: *On my way.*

"Where from?" Virgil said.

"Why, La Mesilla," Holly said.

"La Mesilla's a half day's ride south," Hawkins said.

"Vernon Talmadge still the sheriff there?" I said.

"Yes, he is," Hawkins said.

"Rowdy goddamn place," I said.

"Indeed it is," Holly agreed. "Vernon is respected, though. He
keeps a strong hand on the place."

"He has got his hands full," Hawkins said. "That's for sure."

"Would you like for us to try and contact Vernon, Marshal?"
Holly said. "See if he knows this Dalton McCord or see if he can
find out anything about him?"

Virgil thought about that for a moment.

"Do," Virgil said. "But I don't want him doing nothing. Just find out what he knows, if Dalton is there. In the meantime, Everett, let's you and me have a visit with Captain Alejandro."

༄

When Virgil and I got in the office, Cross opened up the big door leading into the cells. Alejandro was lying on his side facing the wall with his back turned toward us.

"Up!" Cross said too loudly.

Alejandro didn't budge.

Cross whacked the bars with his club.

"Up!"

"Go to hell," Alejandro said quietly, without turning.

"Need to talk with you, Alejandro," I said.

Alejandro rolled over some and looked at Virgil and me.

"Everett. *Mi amigo.*"

"You got no goddamn friends here," Cross growled. "Get your ass up!"

"Go on, Cross," Virgil said.

"Get up!" Cross said as he walked out the door, returning to the office.

Alejandro sat up slowly and pushed his long hair back with both of his hands.

"I was dreaming . . . about my mother," Alejandro said with a smile.

"Thought you didn't have no mother," Cross interjected loudly from the other room. "Thought you was a Mezkin orphan?"

I closed the door, blocking out Cross, so we could have a

conversation with Alejandro without the interference of a man no one in the city of San Cristóbal much liked, including Virgil and me.

"Everybody has a mother. Even Alejandro," he said with a weak smile as he got to his feet.

Alejandro scooped a ladle of water from a small bucket that was provided for him in his cell.

"My mother, she was killed during the Guerra de Reforma. I was three. My father, he died, too, in battle, but my mother, she died in my home, in front of me. She was raped and murdered."

We didn't say anything.

"Then I was sent to the orphanage."

"McCord," Virgil said.

A slow smile came to Alejandro's face.

"Everett," Alejandro said. "Virgil Cole. He is a smart man."

"He is."

Alejandro walked to the bars to face us.

"Dalton McCord," Virgil continued.

Alejandro grinned fully, showing his white teeth.

"Jedediah McCord," Virgil said.

"*Sí.*"

"You sent a wire to Dalton," Virgil said. "About Jedediah."

"*Sí.*"

"What were you doing here?" Virgil said. "In San Cristóbal?"

"Trying to find work."

Virgil shook his head.

"You never tried to find work a day in your life."

"Well, you know, work is hard to find," Alejandro said with a smile. "Especially when you are trying to find it."

"What was Dalton doing in La Mesilla?"

"Like everybody in La Mesilla, gambling and whoring."

"You and him partners?"

"No. I know him forever."

"You lied before. You said his name was Joe, his brother was Jack."

"*Sí.*"

"You want my help. Start talking, don't lie."

"What do you want to know from Alejandro?"

"You told him you found his brother."

"*Sí.*"

"Why? Why did you send the telegram to Dalton saying you found Jedediah?"

"It's *complicado.*"

"What's *complicado* about it?" I said.

"When we came to America together, many years ago. We, Jedediah, Dalton, and me, Alejandro, we got into some trouble."

"What kind of trouble?"

"We were just *niños.* We robbed a bank and a man was killed. Dalton and Alejandro were caught, and we go to jail. Jedediah, he did not, he went free."

"Go on."

"Jedediah told the *autoridades* it was Dalton who killed the man. Jedediah, he went free. I was not in jail too long, but Dalton stay behind bars for many years. When he got out, he looked for his brother. He wanted to kill him but never found him, until Alejandro find him."

"Where?"

"Here."

119

"In San Cristóbal?"

"*Sí.* I was in town. I was walking the street and I saw a man, older now, but I knew it was Jedediah. He was walking down the street, too, with fat men. They were all wearing fancy clothes. I stop him. I said, Jedediah, but he said I had the wrong person, but Alejandro is like Virgil Cole. Alejandro is smart and I knew this man was for certain Jedediah."

"After you sent a telegram to Dalton, telling him you found his brother," I said. "He came here?"

"*Sí,* Everett. Two days later, Dalton, he come to San Cristóbal. He come with two amigos. Two amigos Alejandro not like."

31

⁓

"**WHERE ARE THESE TWO AMIGOS NOW?**"

"Dead. I told you they wanted to cut Alejandro out of the deal. They tried to kill me. I shot them to save Alejandro's life."

"And Dalton took off, left town?"

"*Sí.*"

"Where did he go?"

"I do not know. I told you, he jump on his horse and I jump on mine and we go opposite direction."

"You seen him since?" Virgil said.

Alejandro shook his head.

"No. But when I hear bank get robbed, Alejandro knows who did it and how."

"And you know where to find him?"

"I have idea."

"Idea?"

Alejandro nodded.

"I could only show you," he said.

"The telegram you sent before was to La Mesilla," I said.

"*Sí.*"

Virgil looked at me.

"That where he is?" I said.

"Could be," Alejandro said with a smile. "But Alejandro does not think so."

"So where?"

"Many places to look but an *especial* place is where."

"What *especial* place, Alejandro?"

Alejandro shook his head. He turned away from the bars for a moment, then started talking without looking at us.

"I can help you," Alejandro said. "I can show you."

He stopped talking for a moment, then turned back to face us.

"Virgil Cole, I swear to you on my mother's grave I only shot those men in self-defense. Your friend, in Butch's Bend, I did not kill, either. The other *hombre* in the jail did that. You do not have to believe me, but if you want Alejandro's help, I can help you, but Alejandro will have to show you where to go."

Virgil did not say anything.

"You said you know about the how?" I said. "The how about the plan you said you were cut out of months ago?"

"*Sí.*"

"Tell us?" I said.

"One day, Dalton and Alejandro visit bank. Dalton was very smart, like Alejandro, like Virgil Cole. He asked the teller if he could talk to Mr. Henry Strode. Henry come out. He stopped and looked at Dalton."

Alejandro grinned, thinking about the moment.

"Mr. Henry Strode was . . . how do you say, without voice?"

"Speechless."

"*Sí,*" Alejandro said. "Speechless. He was in shock to see Dalton."

"They did not talk?"

"Not at first, but they got around to talking."

"What did they talk about?" I said.

"It was a friendly visit. Friendly from Dalton's position anyway," Alejandro said with a smile. "You can imagine, Jedediah was not so happy to see his brother. Dalton tell him he was *muy* impressed with Mr. Henry Strode's position. Such a big, important man."

"What about the how," Virgil said. "The plan?"

"*Sí.* It took some time to complete. Dalton, um . . . play with them."

"Play?" I said. "With who?"

"Jedediah and his wife."

I looked at Virgil.

"One evening, when Jedediah come home from work, Dalton, he was drinking tea with Jedediah's wife," Alejandro said with a grin. "She is *muy bonita.* Like Jedediah, Dalton is a very handsome man. The *mujeres,* they like him. They like Alejandro, too, but they like Dalton more. The *mujeres,* they always like Dalton."

"What happened that evening?" I said.

"He tell her he is Henry Strode's brother. She say, 'Really!' She did not know Henry had a brother. Jedediah, he come home from bank, and his wife say, 'Look, look who is here.'"

"How do you know this?" I said.

"Dalton, he tell Alejandro. Dalton make friends with Jedediah's wife."

"Friends."

"*Sí.* Maybe more than friends."

"What are you saying?" I said.

"Dalton make nice with her."

"What kind of nice?"

"He stopped by house more than once."

"Are you saying he had relations with her?" I said.

"Relations?"

"Fucking."

"I do not know, Everett," Alejandro said with a laugh. "But he wanted her. Dalton told Jedediah, not in front of his wife, that he would make Jedediah's life hell."

"So what about the robbery plan?" I said.

Alejandro shook his head.

"Dalton wanted to take Jedediah's wife," Alejandro said.

"Take her?" I said. "Where?"

"Take her to be his."

Virgil looked at me.

"That was the plan?"

"No."

"So what was it, Alejandro?"

"Dalton would go to Jedediah's home and tell Jedediah if he did not get all the money from the bank, he would kill his wife."

"I thought you said he wanted to take her."

"*Sí.*"

"But he told Jedediah he would kill her?"

"*Sí.*"

"What you are saying does not make sense, Alejandro."

"He was to keep her, tell Jedediah he would kill her if he did not get the money from the bank. But Dalton made things bad for Jedediah. He hold her, how do you say . . . ?"

"Hostage?"

"*Sí*, hostage. He hold her hostage while Jedediah get the money. After, instead of kill her, he was going to just take her. Dalton gets the money and he also gets Jedediah's wife. *Venganza!*"

I looked at Virgil.

"Revenge."

"*Sí*," Alejandro said. "Revenge."

32

WE LEFT THE SHERIFF'S OFFICE AND STARTED walking back toward our hotel. Virgil and I didn't talk for a while. We just walked, thinking about the conversation with Alejandro. In the distance we heard the evening train approaching, and as it got closer it let out one long blast of the whistle.

"Hell of a deal," I said.

"Is."

"This Jedediah fella," I said. "Buffalos Jantz Wainwright, his daughter Catherine, the bankers, and everyone in between into believing he was someone else."

"Yep."

"Think he knows where Dalton is?"

"Hard to say."

"Maybe Dalton went back to La Mesilla."

"Could have," Virgil said. "Nobody knows him as the bank robber."

"La Mesilla's a big place."

"Is."

"What about the woman?" I said. "Catherine?"

"Don't know," Virgil said.

"She damn well may have run off with him."

"Or he took her."

"If Vernon Talmadge in La Mesilla don't know him or know of him, or know where to look for him, then what?"

"Only got one option that might offer an upside."

"Gamble on Alejandro as a pathfinder."

"Yep."

"Not the most favorable of circumstances."

"Nope."

"Judge Bing's not gonna be too interested in us bargaining with Alejandro."

"No, don't think he will."

"That prosecutor, neither."

"No," Virgil said. "Him, neither."

"If Alejandro is not arraigned, he's just in custody," I said. "He gets arraigned and a trial is set, then Judge Bing can't help us."

"I thought about that, too," Virgil said. "If we are gonna wrangle him, it's got to be before the arraignment."

"There's also a good chance Alejandro doesn't have a goddamn clue where to go, or look."

"There's that, too."

"One thing's for certain," I said. "We don't find Dalton in La Mesilla, we'll most assuredly be on our own."

"Yep."

"Without someone providing us with some necessary information, be hard to know where to begin to look for him."

"Like trying to find a goose in a gaggle."

"Is."

Four horsemen rounded the corner ahead of us and came in our direction. As they got closer we could tell it was Danny and Davy and two younger posse boys.

"Hey, boys," Virgil said as they pulled up. "Anything?"

"No, sir," Danny said. "We've been all over hell."

"We're headed to the house," Davy said. "Get after the sonofabitch tomorrow."

We watched them ride off. Then walked on a ways.

"Don't think Dalton ate the peaches," Virgil said.

"You think he had help with the robbery?"

"Do."

"You think like before, he had hands working with him?"

"That'd be my thinking."

"Dalton came to town before with two gun hands, they got crossways, shot it out with Alejandro. That much we know happened."

Virgil nodded.

"Yep," Virgil said. "Dalton leaves town after that, lets everything settle down, then comes back, does it again."

"Same scheme."

"Yep."

We continued on for a bit and turned the corner, walking down the street toward the Harvey House Hotel.

"Maybe he had the hands go to the house and hold Catherine hostage while his brother cleaned out the vault?"

"Maybe so."

"So he'd save face."

"You think this Dalton McCord was fucking Strode's wife?" I said.

"Jedediah McCord's wife, you mean?"

"That's right, Jedediah."

"Hard to know."

"Sort of sounds like it."

"Does."

We passed by the Harvey House. I stopped and looked up to the hotel. Virgil stopped.

"Think I just might mosey in here, have a visit with Mary May," I said. "See what she's got to allow."

Virgil looked up to the doors of the hotel. He nodded a bit.

"Mosey right on."

33

VIRGIL WALKED ON BACK TO OUR HOTEL, AND I stepped into the doors of the Harvey House. There was a grandfather clock that echoed in the wood-paneled lobby, letting me know it was nine o'clock when I walked to the front desk. The place was empty of any guest, and there were not any Harvey Girls behind the counter, just the night man with his head stuck in a thick book. He was a scrawny fella with a pleasant, almost sweet disposition. He smiled.

"May I help you?" he said.

"Sure. Like to see Mary May."

He looked to the clock.

"Miss Chase, I believe, has turned in for the evening."

"You believe?"

"I do."

I showed the fella my badge.

"I'm here on official business."

"What sort of official business?"

"No affront, but it's no business of yours."

He looked at me for an extended moment. Then he put a book-marker in his fat book and slipped off the stool he was sitting on.

"Let me see."

"Please do."

"May I tell her who's calling?"

"My name is Hitch. Deputy Marshal Everett Hitch."

"One moment, Deputy."

I watched as the scrawny fella scampered effortlessly up the steps, then I walked toward the doors leading into the restaurant. They were open, but the place was empty, closed for business, and there wasn't anyone in sight.

I drifted around the lobby, looking at the paintings on the walls as I waited, and after some time the scrawny fella floated, dancer-like, back down the steps.

"Deputy Hitch. Miz Chase told me to tell you she would be down subsequently."

"Appreciate it."

"She said if you'd like to wait for her on the back porch, to please feel free."

I looked through the restaurant toward the back porch, where we had previously sat with Wainwright.

"Believe I will feel free."

He dipped his head politely, turned, scurried back behind the desk, and hopped back on his stool.

I walked among the tables and chairs of the empty dining room and out to the back porch. The evening was still warm, but the swift waters off the river cooled the humid night air.

I strolled the length of the porch, looking at the river. There were no lamps burning, but the high moon was bright and I could see its near-full reflection in the swift-moving waters. I sat on the rail and waited.

It took some time for Mary May to appear.

"Deputy Hitch," she said.

I turned to see her. I took a step toward her.

She was standing in the doorway, and the light behind her gave me a good look at the outline of her curvaceous figure.

"Miz Chase. Hello. Sorry for the hour."

"Not at all. No sheep counted."

"Good to know."

"It's warm this evening."

"Is."

"What a pleasant surprise."

"Better to know."

"My knitting puts me in knots and not to sleep, I'm afraid."

She moved a bit closer. Her blond hair was long and fell nearly to her waist. She was wearing a summer sleeping gown. A thin robe hung loosely from her sharp shoulders, and she was barefoot.

"What can I offer?"

"Just had a few questions."

"Oh, well, only a few and not a few too many?"

"Maybe more than a few."

"I hope I have an answer or two."

"Me, too."

"Providing they're not too difficult. I fluster with difficulty."

"I have some questions about Catherine Strode."

"Oh . . . What would you like to know?"

"You know Catherine."

A silent moment hung in the space between us, then she said, "As I said. Not well."

"Well enough."

Mary May looked down as she moved to the porch edge. She lifted up on her toes and slid her bottom on top of the rail with her back to a post. She gazed toward the river.

"Any reason you didn't want to tell me that you know her?"

"What is it you want from me?"

I moved a little closer and leaned my hip on the rail facing her.

"You know she is gone? She's missing."

"I do know, yes."

"You know anything that could help me find her?"

"No, I'm afraid I don't."

"Sure?"

"Yes, I'm sure. If I did, I'd tell you."

"Know Henry, too?"

"No. I'd only met him, said hello."

"How'd you know Catherine was missing?"

"The girls informed me."

"How'd they know?"

She laughed a little.

"They know everything."

A breeze kicked up off the river and pushed some of Mary May's blond hair across her face. She hooked her little finger under the long strands, pulling her hair back out of her eyes, and smiled at me.

"Everyone knows everything. About the bank, how badly hurt Mr. Strode was, and now he is gone. The girls tell me everything. They, of course, know from the posse boys. The girls and the boys, they talk."

"Did you know Henry Strode's brother?"

34

MARY MAY LOOKED AT ME BLANKLY FOR A moment.

"No."

"But you know he had a brother?"

"Yes."

"And how do you know that?"

Mary May looked out toward the river for a moment, then gazed back to me.

"I've not lied to you, Deputy."

"Everett."

"Everett," she said with a smile. "I do not know Catherine well, but ever since I started working here, she looked up to me, like a big sister. She confided in me that she met someone she cared for."

"Henry's brother?"

Mary May nodded.

"You know him?"

"No, I never met him."

"You ever see him?"

She shook her head.

"No. I didn't. She just told me about him and that he was very handsome and he made her laugh."

"Did she talk of leaving Henry?"

"She mentioned she would like to."

"Where is she?"

"I honestly do not know."

"What do you know?"

"She told me she met Henry's brother and she had feelings for him, but that was months ago, and then one day she came to me crying like a baby. She was devastated. She told me he just left town. That is all I know."

"Was this last year?"

Mary May thought for a moment.

"Why, yes. Winter. December, I believe. Listen, I don't think it was her first infatuation. I believe she might . . . most likely had others, I don't know. I told her to forget about him and to remember she has a fine husband with a fine job. A husband that loves her."

Mary May slid off the rail.

"That's all I know."

"Okay."

"I'm not sorry for her."

"Meaning?"

"She has everything when so many have nothing."

She took a step closer to me.

"I've had to fight every step of the way," she said. "I do not suffer fools lightly."

She smiled.

I smiled.

"I appreciate it."

"You're entirely welcome. Now, if you don't mind, I'm going to return to my room and drink some wine."

"You do that," I said with a tip of my hat.

"This way," she said.

She walked the length of the porch to a rear stairwell, then turned back to me.

"Coming?"

"You'd like me to come?"

"Mr. Hitch."

"Everett."

"Yes, Everett," she said. "You've been further around than most have ventured in a gunnysack or a bushel basket. I would not think I'd need to put out bread crumbs or draw you a map."

35

By the close of the evening there had been no word back from La Mesilla's sheriff, Vernon Talmadge. In the early morning, Virgil and I sat drinking coffee on the porch of our hotel. We were watching a bunch of crows across the street moving back and forth between a big boardwalk sycamore and the telegraph lines. They were making more noise than they should be making for such a pleasant morning as I filled Virgil in about the talking part of my evening visit with Mary May.

"So Catherine's a woman with inclinations?" Virgil said.

"Might be."

"And she had a hankering for the brother?"

"Seems," I said.

"He have a real hankering for her?"

"Don't know."

"Got no idea?" Virgil said.

"Don't."

"Mary May?"

"She don't know."

"Maybe it was like Alejandro said," Virgil said.

"He played with her?"

"Yep."

"Could be."

We thought about that for a moment as we watched a team of Roman-headed horses pulling a small load of freshly cut saplings.

"We do know she ain't here," I said.

"That we do."

"Odds are better than good she left with him?"

"They are," Virgil said.

"Willingly, maybe," I said.

"Or might have took her?"

"One way or the other," I said.

Virgil nodded and drank some coffee.

"Mary May?" Virgil said.

"She don't know."

"What more does she know?"

"Thinks Catherine's spoiled."

"'Spect she is."

"Thinks Catherine's a fool."

"Got Catherine's cards counted?" Virgil said.

I nodded.

"Told Catherine she had a good husband," I said.

"She didn't listen?"

"Hard to know."

"Maybe Catherine got to thinking she had herself a geld," Virgil said.

"Maybe."

"And a stud comes along."

"Might have happened."

"Wouldn't be the first mare to drift."

"Or the first stud to move in."

"Wouldn't," Virgil said.

"Not uncommon."

"No, by God, it goddamn isn't."

"Fact, Mary May thought this might not be Catherine's first trip out of the barn."

"So," Virgil said, "she does have herself inclinations?"

"That's what Mary May said."

"Maybe that's what Comstock was saying but not saying directly. Maybe he knew something."

"Don't think he was fucking her?"

"Naw," Virgil said, shaking his head.

"It's a big town," I said, "but it's also a small town, so no telling about what's said about the rich man's daughter."

"Or the banker's wife."

"People talk."

"They do."

"But inclinations are inclinations."

"They are," Virgil said.

We drank our coffee, thinking about inclinations.

I was certain Virgil was thinking about his Allie back in Appaloosa and her inclinations, because I know I was thinking about her and her inclinations.

It was never an uneasy proposition, Virgil leaving Allison French behind when we were away with a job to do. His leaving was not so much an uneasy proposition for Virgil as it was for Allie. More times than not, when we were away Allie would wander into some kind of compromising circumstance with some other fella interested in her wayfaring inclinations. In a few of those compromising circumstances the fellas didn't fare too well in terms of still being upright and alive.

A half block away Hawkins rounded the corner on his bay, Blisters. Walking next to him on the boardwalk was Holly. They were talking with each other as they neared.

We could not hear what was being said, but Holly was shaking his head back and forth like he had a foul taste in his mouth.

Hawkins spotted us and kicked Blisters ahead of Holly some. He reined up in front of Virgil and me. Blisters shook his head hard with an obvious disfavor for the hard bit in his mouth.

"Got some real goddamn bad news," Hawkins said.

"What?" Virgil said.

36

"**La Mesilla's sheriff, Vernon Talmadge,**
was shot and killed last night," Hawkins said.

Virgil looked at me and grimaced a bit.

"Is bad news," I said.

"Is," Virgil said.

"Vernon was a good lawman," Hawkins said.

"Who done it?" Virgil said.

"Got some other bad news," Hawkins said.

"Dalton do it?" Virgil said.

"No," Hawkins said. "But it was some of Dalton's men."

Virgil shook his head.

"How'd it happen?"

Holly arrived in front of the hotel. He sat quickly on the steps.
He was sweating and breathing hard from his brisk walk.

"Vernon was killed," Hawkins said, "when him and one of his
deputies were involved in a skirmish with a handful of Dalton's
men at a La Mesilla billiard joint."

"You tell him I didn't want him to do nothing?"

"We did," Holly said. "Most certainly."

Hawkins shook his head.

"But he must've done something anyway," Hawkins said.

"Something that got him killed," I said.

Holly nodded and took a deep breath.

"Seems Dalton McCord has been a fixture in La Mesilla for a while," Holly said.

"Dalton part of it?" Virgil said. "He there?"

"Don't know," Hawkins said.

"Apparently," Holly said, "Dalton McCord has a gang of men he runs with that have been giving the authorities fits."

"Dead ain't fits," Virgil said.

"No," Holly said. "Indeed, of course not."

"Where are these men now?" I said.

"Don't know," Hawkins said.

"Well, what should we do?" Holly said.

Virgil looked at me and I looked at him.

"Goose waddled out of the gaggle," Virgil said.

"Did."

Virgil looked at Holly.

"Get a message back," Virgil said. "Tell them not to do nothing till we get there."

Holly nodded.

❧

At half past nine in the morning Virgil, Hawkins, and I rode to La Mesilla to find out what we could about Dalton McCord and his gang.

The two-rut road from San Cristóbal to La Mesilla was a fairly easy ride. The sun was hot, the land was dry, and the wheat-colored dirt blew easy as we rode. We traveled through six small towns and settlements on our way to La Mesilla. In each we passed through, we made inquiries with various folks, asking if they'd seen Henry Strode.

La Mesilla was a crossroads town, the intersection of the Butter-field and the Santa Fe stage lines, and was the destination of many, but mostly young men seeking festivities. It was a happy, lively place, with more drinking, gambling, and whoring than most towns its size. In fact, you could even say the major commerce in La Mesilla was drinking, gambling, and whoring. The town was spread out and the place was open for business twenty-four hours a day.

We arrived in La Mesilla one hour past sundown, and the streets were already a bustle of activity. We passed an open-air saloon where a Mexican brass band was playing some fandango. Dancing girls in colorful dresses were kicking up their feet to the music. The girls resembled a lively flock of starlings swerving around one another as they snapped castanets and banged on tambourines.

"Not changed much," I said.

"Just bigger," Hawkins said. "More people."

"Same lot," Virgil said.

We rode past a few working girls sitting on the porch of a green-painted brothel called Lucky's. We passed, paying them little atten-tion as they whistled and lifted their dresses.

We rode down Main Street and found the sheriff's office at the edge of town. A young deputy was waiting for us. He came out the door and onto the office porch when we dismounted.

He was a slim, clean-cut fella with tidy clothes. His sandy hair was cut short, tight to his scalp, and he looked to be no more than twenty. His belt buckle was a leftover emblem of his days in the service, and judging by his youth, it was obvious he'd spent a limited time in uniform.

"Come in," the young deputy said with a Southern twang. "Been waiting on y'all."

We followed the deputy into the office.

"Got y'all some fresh coffee."

Once we were inside the light of the office, I could tell the young man was upset about the death of Vernon, and it was obvious to us he'd been doing some crying. He introduced himself as Lesley Bright and after we made our introductions and Bright got us a cup, Virgil wasted no time with the pressing question that had been on our minds since leaving San Cristóbal.

"Where's Dalton McCord?"

37

"I DON'T KNOW," BRIGHT SAID, SHAKING HIS
head.

"When was the last time you saw Dalton?" Virgil said.

"I saw him the day before yesterday, in the morning," Bright
said.

"Where?"

"The sonofabitch was eating breakfast at a café on Second."

"With who?"

"The bunch of 'em."

"How many he run with?" I said.

"Off and on, there's about ten of 'em. They've been getting more
and more swagger. Think they own the place."

"Dalton have a woman with him?" I said.

"He always has women with him," Bright said.

"At the café?" Virgil said.

"We're looking for one woman," I said. "A pretty, young
woman?"

"Don't know," Bright said. "Maybe, can't say for sure. Fact is I
wasn't in the café, I just walked by, but I saw Dalton for sure."

"Where does he stay?" Virgil said. "Dalton?"

"Them boys stay at hotels and with whores," Bright said.

"Dalton?" Virgil said.

"Him, too, I reckon. Don't think one place. Least I know."

"How many hotels are here?" I said.

"La Mesilla is a big place. There's a lot of people and a bunch of places to shack. There's a bunch of hotels. A few are fairly decent, none of them are too nice. Don't know if Dalton stays in 'em or not. Got two of the nicest on Third and one here on Main. There's other, smaller hotels all over, a bunch of flophouses, though, too, and whoring establishments that shack fellas up regularly. There are also outlaying little houses all through the brakes."

"How did Vernon get shot?" Virgil said.

"Late last night there was a ruckus at Lily's, a pool hall down the street here," Bright said. "That ain't unusual—there's a ruckus damn near ever' hour 'round here, generally harmless, and nobody ever gets into the spit with Vernon and Shep, least not until last night."

"Shep Walker," Hawkins said, looking at Virgil and me, "been with Vernon for years."

Bright nodded.

"That's right," Bright said. "He might be little, but nobody messes with Shep Walker."

"So what happened?" I said.

"Vernon and Shep went down there," Bright said. "There was seven Dalton McCord hands in there, and they was drunk and slapping a couple of coolies around, said they was going to hang them. The bartender cut 'em off and told them to leave the coolies alone and to get out. They got mad, said they'd hang the bartender instead. They got a rope, threw it over a beam, and was gonna hang the bartender, but Vernon and Shep stepped in and stopped 'em. Nobody had the cojones to stand up to Vernon and Shep, and them boys left. Vernon and Shep was walking back up the street, and one of them shits shot Vernon in the back. Shep chased 'em. Cornered two of 'em behind the feed store, but they took some shots at Shep and got away. They all scattered."

"Where are they now."

"Don't know," Bright said. "We got word y'all was coming and for us not to stir up the pot."

"Was Dalton one of them at the pool hall?" Virgil said.

"I don't know for sure," Bright said. "Don't think so. So much has happened. You'd have to ask Shep."

"So you've not seen any of the hands since?" I said.

"No, sir, I ain't, no. Shep told us deputies to just keep our eyes and ears open."

"Where are the other deputies?" I said.

"They're around," Bright said sadly. "I sure hope y'all get these fellas that done this. We're all sure tore up 'bout this, 'specially Shep."

"Where is Shep?" Hawkins said.

"He's been with Vernon's wife," Bright said. "They're at Vernon's place. There's a bunch of folks there with Vernon's wife and all. She's taking it awful hard."

Bright looked down, not wanting to cry, but the young man couldn't keep from it. A few tears rolled down his cheek, and he wiped them away with the back of his hand.

"Like to kill all them," Bright said. "Vernon was like a dad to me. Like a dad to a bunch of us."

Bright got to his feet. He pulled a Winchester from a gun rack and snugged his hat down tightly on his head.

"Shep told me to wait on y'all and to fetch him when y'all got here, so I'll do that. He'll be able to give y'all more details," Bright said. "Be back directly."

38

SHEP WALKER WALKED INTO THE SHERIFF'S
office with the young deputy, Lesley Bright, just past seven-thirty
in the evening. Shep was for sure a short fella, but tough-looking.
He was fit and carried himself like he was the largest man in the
room. He reminded me of a jockey. After we made our introductions, Shep poured a coffee and took a seat.

"Good of you to come here," Shep said, looking at each of us.

"Damn sorry about Vernon," Hawkins said.

Shep nodded a little, then tipped his head to Deputy Bright.

"Lesley here told me he filled you in on what went down last
night," Shep said.

"He did," I said.

"Was Dalton with them?" Virgil said.

"No," Shep said. "He wasn't there, but it was his boys."

"You know where he is?" Virgil said.

"I don't," Shep said.

"Had you and Vernon been looking for Dalton?" Virgil said.

"No," Shep said. "We was waiting word. We knew he must have
stepped into some shit, but we didn't try and roust him or nothing."

"How was it you got in a to-do with his men?" Virgil said.

"Those fellas have been causing trouble almost nightly," Shep said.

"You cornered two of them and they shot at you?" I said.

"They did," Shep said. "I chased them into the alley. They took a few dark shots and ran. Tried to find them and the others up until late last night, but they scattered."

"Any idea where they are?"

Shep shook his head.

"They know they fucked up by shooting Vernon," Shep said. "Vernon was a friend to almost everybody in this town. He'd give the worst drunk his last penny to get something to eat."

Bright held back his emotions and nodded in agreement.

"They are a brazen bunch, though," Shep said. "They're likely not to stray too far. Plus, the shot that killed Vernon was a rifle shot to the back. They weren't close. They will rant on, saying they didn't do nothing."

"These boys are certain compadres of Dalton's?" Virgil said.

"They are," Shep said. "This town has got a lot of troublemakers, but we know who is who. Most are of no account. Seen these boys coming and going enough to know who they are and what they're about."

"When did you last see Dalton McCord?" Virgil said.

"I saw him day before yesterday," Shep said. "But he was not around last night when all this happened."

"When you saw him yesterday," Virgil said. "Who was he with?"

"Nobody," Shep said. "Saw him on his own. He was on a stocky gray, trotting out south on Main Street."

"You see him with a woman at all?" I said. "Anytime before?"

Shep shook his head.

"Dalton McCord is most often with a woman," Shep said. "They like him."

"You look for any of them today?" Virgil said.

"Some, this morning," Shep said. "But I had to deal with Vernon and the undertaker and whatnot and Vernon's wife . . . so I got no idea."

"Either of you seen a man come to town on a skewbald," Virgil said. "He might have had another horse, too."

Virgil looked to Hawkins.

"Light bay," Hawkins said.

Virgil nodded.

"Riding one or the other."

"He's also not looking so good," I said. "Been beat up bad. Face is swollen and cut up."

Shep shook his head.

"No," Shep said, then looked to Deputy Bright. "You?"

Bright shook his head.

"No, sir. I have not."

Virgil nodded a little, looking at the two of them.

"I know I do not have to tell you how mad I am," Shep said.

"No," Virgil said. "You don't."

"I've heard a lot about you, Marshal Cole," Shep said. "You, too, Hitch. I know you boys been riding together for a good go of it."

"We have," I said.

"Vernon and me were a lot like you and Hitch, Marshal Cole," Shep said. "Maybe not known for our steady resolve as good gun hands or for being as far in the stretch as you two have been, but we'd been together for long enough. I'm gonna miss the sonofabitch, I can tell you that."

"You know where Dalton is staying?"

"No," Shep said, "but we can get to looking."

39

SHEP PUT TOGETHER A SEARCH LIST, AND WE SET out from the jail and began looking for Dalton McCord. We divided up the town. Virgil, Hawkins, and Deputy Bright had a list of hotels, brothels, and flophouses on the east side of town. Shep and I had places on the western half of town to look.

Shep and I made our first stop at a big hotel called the Champion, but Dalton had not been there, nor had he ever stayed there. We continued on, making our way from one establishment to the next.

We checked a few boardinghouses and a few boarding brothels but had yet to find anyone who'd seen Dalton of recent.

We met some of the working ladies along the way, and for the most part they had nothing but bad things to say about Dalton. We left a place called Lucy's, and like a few of the other ladies we'd talked to, Lucy offered disparaging remarks on the way out.

"Tell him when you find him," Lucy said, "he's not welcome back."

Shep and I walked across the street and through an alley to the next block.

"Thought you said the ladies liked him," I said.

"They do," Shep said. "Can't you tell? That's why they got nothing nice to say."

When we stepped out of the alley onto the next street, there was a big hotel catty-corner across the way.

"This is the Winchester Inn," Shep said. "Might be the nicest hotel we got in this town."

The hotel was a big place. On one side of the lobby there was a fireplace with sofas surrounding it, and on the other there was a set of doors leading to the Winchester Saloon.

The man behind the desk looked up, seeing us, and offered a sad smile to Shep when we approached.

"Hello, Dave," Shep said.

"Shep," Dave said. "Me and Ginny were real sorry to hear about Vernon."

"Thank you, Dave," Shep said. "Dave, this is Deputy Marshal Everett Hitch. He's here to help us solve this crime."

Dave nodded.

"What can I offer?" Dave said.

"Dalton McCord," I said. "He staying here?"

"No," Dave said.

"He ever stayed here?" Shep said.

"He has some in the past a few times, but he's not here now. Why?" Dave said. "Did he do this? Did he kill Vernon?"

"We don't know, Dave," Shep said. "We need to talk with him, got a few questions for him."

"Sorry, Deputy, Shep," Dave said. "He's not here."

"You seen him?" I said. "Or have any idea where he might be?"

Dave shook his head.

"Ask Roger," Dave said.

Dave pointed to the saloon across the lobby.

"He knows way more than he should," Dave said. "Maybe he knows something."

"Much obliged," I said.

Shep and I walked across the lobby and into the saloon. For all of La Mesilla's breach and banner, the Winchester Saloon was quiet and low-key. Right away I could tell this was a place for serious gamblers with money. There were a number of card games happening in the room, and the players paid us no mind as they focused on their respective games.

Roger, the bartender, was a big man with a mustache that went from side to side nearly ear to ear. Like Dave, Roger offered his sympathies to Shep, and without too much talk of condolence we got to our business.

"Looking for Dalton McCord?" I said.

"Not seen him," Roger said. "Not tonight, anyway."

"But you have seen him?" I said.

"He doesn't come in here much," Roger said. "Unless he's got money to gamble."

An old gambler behind me playing stud turned in his chair and looked up to me.

"I saw him," the old gambler said.

"That right?" I said.

"That's right," the gambler said. "He won a bunch of money off me."

"Where?" I said.

"Mitch's Room," the gambler said.

"Mitch's is a high-stakes gambling room," Shep said. "On the edge of town."

"When?" I said.

"Night before last."

"You have any idea where he is?" I said. "Where he's staying?"

"I don't," the old gambler said. "He took me for a big pot, though. Said it was his lady luck."

"Lady luck?" I said.

"Yep," the old man said. "He had a young blond lady with him, said she was his lady luck."

40

SHEP AND I WENT TO THE EAST SIDE, LOOKING
for Virgil, Hawkins, and Deputy Bright. We stopped at a few places
they had visited before we found them walking out of a boarding-
house on the edge of town.

"Virgil?" I said.

He turned, seeing us walking up the boardwalk toward him.

"Find him?" Virgil said.

"No," I said. "But a gambler saw him night before last. He said
there was a woman with him."

"Catherine?" Virgil said.

"Sounds like it."

"He said she was young and pretty," I said. "His description
sounded like it was her."

"He talk to her?" Virgil said.

"He said he didn't," Shep said.

I shook my head.

"The gambler said she just sat there," Shep said.

"Said Dalton told her to watch and not talk," I said.

"You think she's his hostage?" Hawkins said.

"I asked the gambler," I said. "He said he couldn't say for certain."

"Said she just sat there," Shep said, "with her hands in her lap and did not say a word."

Virgil nodded a bit.

"Least we know she ain't dead," Virgil said.

Two riders came fast into town at a hard gallop. They rode past us, but when they saw Shep they pulled up and circled back. They stopped in front of us in a cloud of street dirt. We could see right off they wore deputy badges.

Both of the riders were on dark bay horses, and the horses were winded. They'd been ridden hard for a while. One of the deputies was a lanky kid with long hair. The other was a young Mexican. The Mexican was carrying a Springfield .55 trapdoor carbine in one hand and the reins of the bay in the other.

The bay horses kicked some street dirt around a bit, trying to get settled. The deputies looked to us. They looked to Shep, then back to us, then back to Shep.

"What's afoot, Cliff?" Shep said to the tall fella with the long hair.

Cliff's horse was moving, wanting something other than standing still. Cliff reined the horse in a quick semicircle as he spoke.

"Guess what, Shep?" Cliff said.

"Goddamn, Cliff," Shep said. "I'm here with territorial marshals. We're dealing with some very important business here and I got no fucking interest to guess nothing! What?"

"We run into Mosley and Mike McGrew," the Mexican deputy said.

"*What, José?*" Shep said impatiently.

"The McGrews," Cliff said. "Told us they was coming back from moving cattle for Bryson and stopped in at the Last Chance for a beer."

"Get to it!" Shep said.

"They said Dalton McCord's hands were in there. They were bragging to a couple of the gals, saying they done away with Sheriff Vernon for good."

"Where are Dalton's hands now?" Shep said.

"Still there, I reckon," José said.

"Dalton one of 'em?" Virgil said.

"Don't know," Cliff said.

"Where are the McGrew brothers?" Shep said.

"They gone on," José said.

"But they told us there was six of them in there," Cliff said. "Dalton McCord's hands."

José nodded.

"Said they were carrying on something fierce," José said.

"Where is the Last Chance, Shep?" I said.

Shep pointed.

"'Bout thirty or so minutes that way," Shep said.

"Amos rode on out to there, to the Last Chance," José said.

"What?" Shep said excitedly.

"He said he'd keep a lookout in case they left," Cliff said. "That's all."

"Hellfire," Shep said. "He better not by God try and go about showing his scrawny worth."

"He's not, Shep," Cliff said.

"Said he'd stay off the road," José said. "Shy of the place, till you come."

"Who's Amos?" I said to Shep.

"One of our deputies," Shep said. "My son."

41

WE LEFT THE YOUNG DEPUTIES TO CARRY ON
with their city deputy duties, and Virgil, Shep, Hawkins, and I rode
south out of La Mesilla at a half past nine in the evening.

The night was bright. It was almost a full moon, and we could
see clearly as we rode. After about a thirty-minute ride we neared
the Last Chance. We rounded a curve and came to a section of the
road that looked to once be some kind of community, with broken-
down buildings on each side of the road. Behind the last dilapidated building on the left we saw some movement, a horse and
rider. We stopped and waited for a moment, then we heard Shep's
son speak up.

"Daddy?"

"Amos?"

Amos moved out onto the road and edged his way toward us.

"Hey, Daddy," Amos said. "I ain't done nothing but just sit here
and wait."

"They still in there?" Shep said.

"They are," Amos said. "Likely drunker than waltzing pissants
by now."

"Good, Amos," Shep said.

"What do you want me to do?" Amos said.

"You go on back, Amos," Shep said.

"Aw, really?" Amos said.

"Aw, really," Shep said.

"Okay," Amos said dejectedly.

"Go on, son," Shep said. "We got these marshals here. They got me covered."

"Okay," Amos said. "Be careful, Daddy."

"I will, son," Shep said. "Go on."

Amos turned his horse and took off for town.

We rode on up the road, and in a few minutes we arrived at the Last Chance.

The place was a converted barn, and for being away from town, it was obviously a popular destination. There were twenty horses tied to trees and hitches. Inside, we could hear a piano clanking and people laughing and singing.

Virgil took the lead. We followed him and rode around the backside of the Last Chance toward the remnants of an old corral. We dismounted. I pulled my eight-gauge from the scabbard, and we left our horses tied to a section of sturdy rail thirty feet behind the barn. We walked up a ways to the back side of the place. The rear door was open, and we could hear the people inside talking and laughing. The piano started up a new tune, "Jeanie with the Light Brown Hair," and a few people began to sing along.

Virgil stopped in the shadows, avoiding the light that was spilling out of the rear door. From where we stood, we could see clearly the front entrance through the open rear door. Virgil turned back to the rest of us following him.

"Shep," Virgil said. "You will know these hands when you see them?"

Shep nodded.

"I will."

"And they will know you?"

"Oh," he said. "They will."

"You and Hawkins go around and enter from the front door. Everett and me will be able to see you, and we will come through the back, at the same time."

"Then what?" Hawkins said.

"Walk in," Virgil said.

Hawkins looked to Shep.

"We go in normal-like," Virgil said.

"No telling what they will do," Shep said.

"No telling," Virgil said.

"We'll see firsthand what they are made of," I said.

"Will," Virgil said.

"All right, then," Hawkins said.

"Providing their balls are not too tight and they're not jumpy, I'll make the necessary introductions," Virgil said. "Then, Shep, you can help me to know who is who. Call 'em out and cull 'em. See where we go from there."

"If they pull," Hawkins said.

"Shoot straight," Virgil said.

Shep and Hawkins nodded and started to move to the front.

"One thing," Virgil said, stopping Shep and Hawkins. "Make no mistake, this here is a see-to situation we'll be stepping into. Though if the situation provides us the possibility, it be good if we could keep at least one of them alive."

Shep and Hawkins moved on around the building, and Virgil and I stepped closer toward the rear door.

"I'll come up this side," Virgil said. "Out of the light. You come up the other."

Virgil crossed the path of the spilling light coming from the door. He remained in shadow as he moved up one side of the light and I moved up the other.

When we got to the back of the barn we stayed out of the light of the open door. I had the better angle, looking at the front door, and could see when Hawkins and Shep entered. We waited, and after a short time I nodded to Virgil and we stepped into the rear door of the Last Chance.

42

VIRGIL AND I SLIPPED INTO THE BACK DOOR AS
Shep and Hawkins entered from the front. The interior of the barn
had been constructed into a regular saloon. A wood floor had been
installed and the barn loft was converted into a second-floor open
mezzanine.

To the left there was a long bar, and to the right was a set of
stairs. Under the stairs sat the piano, and a small round woman with
bright red hair was pounding on it like she was trying to hurt it.

A few drunken fellas and another chubby gal wearing a dark
pink saloon dress were doing the singing.

Shep entered, followed by Hawkins. Shep's appearance quieted
the room some, but the pianist and the singers continued to dis-
grace what otherwise was a beautiful tune.

At a table in the center of the room sat four men playing poker.
One of them, a wiry fella wearing a flattop derby, had a small
woman sitting on his lap. She fell to the floor when he stood up,
seeing Shep. The other three men at the table followed suit.

They were all up fast with their hands on their handles.

"Don't!" Virgil said.

I cocked my eight-gauge. It had an effect on the room, and everyone turned, looking at Virgil and me, including the piano player and her chorus.

The man with the flattop derby looked at Virgil, then back to Shep. His hand was still resting on the grip of his pistol.

"Easy," Virgil said. "Don't do nothing stupid."

Virgil was relaxed, with his arms to his sides.

"Who the hell are you?" the fella in the flattop said with a drunken smirk.

"I'm Territorial Marshal Virgil Cole. This fella here next to me with the eight-gauge is Deputy Marshal Everett Hitch. Across the way there is La Mesilla deputy Shep Walker. Most of you likely know who he is. The big man next to him is Webb Hawkins, sheriff of San Cristóbal."

One of the men was a big bearded man with his hand on a Colt. He had a second Colt with a pearl handle tucked in his belt.

"So what," the bearded man said.

"No reason for you boys to get riled up," Virgil said. "Just here to conduct some business."

Two other men stepped away from the bar. They pulled back their jackets, showing us they were heeled. One of them, a mean-looking man with shifty dark eyes, spoke.

"Yeah?" he said. "What kind of business?"

"Official business," Virgil said.

The mean-looking fella with the dark eyes took a meaningful step toward Virgil.

"What sort of official business?" he said.

"I suspect by now you know the sheriff of La Mesilla, Vernon Talmadge, was murdered," Virgil said.

"What of it?" the dark-eyed man said.

"Shep?" Virgil said, without taking his eyes off the dark-eyed man. "Any of these boys here with their hands on their handles at the pool hall the night Sheriff Talmadge was shot?"

"They were," Shep said. "The six of them."

"How about Dalton McCord?" Virgil said.

"Don't see him," Shep said.

"Any of you boys know where he is?" Virgil said.

The big bearded man laughed, and the other men joined him.

"What's funny?" Virgil said.

"You coming in here acting like you think we'd be scared of you. That's what."

"We're not acting," Virgil said. "You being scared is another matter altogether."

"We ain't scared," he said defensively.

The other men nodded.

"Well, all right, then," Virgil said. "Then I reckon it's not going to be hard for you to tell me which one of you shot Sheriff Talmadge in the back?"

The man with the shifty dark eyes took another step toward Virgil.

"You got to be fucking kidding," the dark-eyed man said.

"Not," Virgil said.

"You know who I am?" the dark-eyed man said.

"Don't," Virgil said.

"I'm somebody you do not want to fuck with."

"Good," Virgil said. "It was one shot. So there is only one of you who did the murdering. That means one of you that's not scared can let me know which one of you did it, then you'll be in good favor with the court."

"I'm Ozark Atkins," the dark-eyed man said impatiently. "This is my brother Kale."

Kale squared himself some.

Ozark looked at each of the other men in turn. It was the brazen look Virgil and I had seen many times. That telltale look when a man was about to plant his foot on the rail and go for it.

"You don't want to pull on me," Virgil said.

"Why?" Ozark said. "You think you're faster than me?"

"No," Virgil said. "I know I am."

Ozark and Kale went for their pistols.

43

 ﹏

VIRGIL SHOT BOTH OZARK AND HIS BROTHER Kale before they could clear leather and was aiming his Colt at the head of the bearded man who stood frozen with his hand on the grip of his Colt as gun smoke churned and drifted leisurely near the bar.

Shep, Hawkins, and I had not pulled the trigger. The other men around the table held their hands away from their pistols, stunned.

Virgil spoke softly, almost like he was talking to a child, as he coaxed the bearded man.

"Just take your hand off that .44 and I won't put lead in your head," Virgil said. "Not tonight."

"Goddamn," the bearded man said as he removed his hand from the grip of his Colt. "Goddamn."

"Shep, Webb," Virgil said. "Let's relieve these boys of some of their unnecessary equipment."

Shep and Hawkins moved to the men and took their pistols.

Virgil walked over and looked down at Ozark and Kale. They'd both been shot in the head.

Virgil opened the loading gate of his revolver and removed the two spent casings as he looked at Ozark and Kale.

"You ever heard of this man, Everett?" Virgil said. "Ozark?"

"Nope."

Virgil put two new rounds in the revolver's chamber and snapped the loading gate closed.

"Me, neither," Virgil said.

"He said his name like it was a name you should, or would, recognize," I said.

"He did."

"Ozark," I said. "Seems like a name you'd remember."

"Does," Virgil said.

"Don't ring a bell?" I said.

"Don't," Virgil said.

"Maybe he was thinking in the future?" I said.

Virgil nodded.

"Maybe."

Virgil looked over to the men at the poker table.

"Boys," Virgil said.

He walked toward them.

"Everett and me are gonna ask you a few questions."

"You ain't getting shit outta me!" the fella with the flattop said with a steely-eyed slur.

"Only two questions," Virgil said, friendly-like.

"You just shot Ozark and Kale," Flattop said.

"They had a chance," Virgil said.

"They was my friends," Flattop said.

"Everett, take those two boys there," Virgil said with a point.

He was pointing to the one with the flattop derby that was doing the talking and the big man with the beard.

"You and Hawkins take them out back and ask them two questions," Virgil said.

"Who shot Sheriff Vernon Talmadge being one of the questions?" I said.

"Yep," Virgil said. "That be one question."

"The other being, where is Dalton McCord?"

"That'd be the other," Virgil said.

Virgil looked to the other two men sitting at the table.

"Shep, you and me will ask these two fellas here the same questions," Virgil said.

"Then," I said, "we'll compare their answers."

"We will," Virgil said. "If they are not the same answers, then we'll have a big problem."

"What kind of problem?" Flattop said with a frown.

"If any of you lie to Everett or me," Virgil said. "If your answers to the questions do not match the answers of your amigos here, you will be arrested for the murder of Sheriff Vernon Talmadge. You'll get convicted, and you will hang for it."

"Don't listen to this crap!" Flattop said to his buddies. "This is bullshit!"

"No bullshit," Virgil said.

Virgil looked at all four men.

"You tell me and Everett the truth, then you will only be an accessory to murder."

"A much lesser charge," I said.

"Providing you find yourself an attorney with some hooks," Virgil said. "There's a good chance you'd go free."

"Shit," Flattop said.

"Unless one of you pulled the trigger," I said.

The four men looked at one another. Flattop shook his head.

Virgil looked to Shep.

"That sound like the right call, Shep?"

"It does," Shep said.

"Those will be the main questions," Virgil said. "We'll be asking some other questions while we are at it."

"What?" Flattop said.

"Might be easier questions for you," Virgil said. "See how you boys fare."

"Goddamn it!" Flattop said. "I don't understand this shit."

"Think of it like a game of truth," Virgil said. "Whoever don't tell the truth is seriously fucked."

44

HAWKINS AND I STEPPED OUTSIDE WITH THE
fella wearing the flattop derby and the bearded man.

"Have a seat," I said.

They sat side by side on a hay bale near the back door.

"What's your names," I said.

The two men looked at each other.

"This is not a trick question," I said.

"Be the easiest one you'll have to answer," Hawkins said.

"I'm Chuck," the bearded man said. "Chuck Page."

"You?" Hawkins said to the fella in the flattop derby.

"Delbert Chastain," he said.

"Good," I said.

"That wasn't too hard, was it?" Hawkins said.

They shook their heads in tandem.

"Where is Dalton McCord?" I said.

"I don't know," Chuck said.

"Why," I said. "What do you mean you don't know?"

"He took off," Chuck said. "Left us. He didn't say where he was going."

"When?"

Chuck looked to Delbert.

"Yesterday," Chuck said.

"You know where he is, Delbert?"

"No," he said, shaking his head.

"Who did he leave with?"

"Drummer and EG," Chuck said.

"Who is Drummer and EG?"

"His close friends," Delbert said. "They're two big guys from Yuma Prison days."

"They been with Dalton awhile," Chuck said.

"Just the three of them?" Hawkins said.

"Yep," Chuck said.

"What about a woman?" I said.

"A woman?" Chuck said.

"Yep. Was there a woman with Dalton?" I said. "A pretty young blond woman?"

Chuck and Delbert looked at each other, then nodded.

"There was a woman," Chuck said.

"So Dalton took off with Drummer, EG, and a woman?"

They nodded.

"So it was the four of them?" I said. "Not three that took off?"

"Yes," Chuck said.

Hawkins looked at me.

"What's her name?" Hawkins said.

Delbert looked to Chuck.

"I don't know," Chuck said.

"Me, neither," Delbert said.

"He showed up with her," Chuck said. "Then moved on with her."

"What do you mean he showed up with her?" I said.

"He took off for a while, and when he came back, she was with him."

"Where'd he take off to for a while, before he came back?" Hawkins said.

"We don't know," Chuck said. "Him, Drummer, and EG was gone for like a month. When they come back, she was with Dalton."

"And they didn't say where they'd been?" Hawkins said.

"Nope," Chuck said. "Drummer and EG don't talk much."

"Tell me about the woman," I said.

"Damn pretty," Delbert said.

"Was she happy?" Hawkins said.

"What?" Delbert said.

"Answer the question," I said.

"Hell, I don't know if she was happy or not," Delbert said.

"We never met her," Chuck said. "Or talked to her, even. She came to the café and ate, but I didn't talk to her."

"Well," Delbert said. "No shit. Why would she talk to you?"

"Fuck you, Delbert," Chuck said.

"Drummer and EG didn't say nothing to you about her," I said.

"No," Chuck said. "Fact, they never say nothing about much of nothing."

"No shit," Delbert said.

"What did Dalton say to you when he took off?" I said.

"Said good-bye," Chuck said. "Said he wouldn't be coming back to La Mesilla."

"He didn't say nothing to me," Delbert said.

"He didn't like you," Chuck said.

"Fuck you!"

"He didn't."

"That ain't true," Delbert said. "He gave me as much money as he gave you."

"Money," I said. "What money?"

"He gave each of us a new fifty-dollar bill when he left," Chuck said.

"And you got no idea where they went?"

"I don't," Delbert said.

Chuck shook his head.

"Me, neither," he said.

"Anybody show up in La Mesilla looking for Dalton?"

"You," Delbert said with a sneer.

"You see a man," I said, "or know about a man, hear about a man looking for Dalton?"

"In the last day or so?" Hawkins said.

"Nope," Chuck said.

Delbert shook his head.

"Where was Dalton staying the days before he left?"

"The Oracle Hotel," Chuck said. "On Fourth."

"Who killed the La Mesilla sheriff, Vernon Talmadge?" I said.

45

Debased and as drunk as they were, we learned a good deal from our question-and-answer session with Dalton McCord's men. They provided us with some important details but left us with nothing to go on in respect to where Dalton, Catherine, and his two men were headed. We also learned that the man who killed Sheriff Vernon Talmadge was dead. It was Ozark Atkins's younger brother Kale who shot Vernon in the back.

We left the Last Chance and rode back to La Mesilla with the six men from Dalton McCord's gang. Four of them were upright in their saddles. Two of them, Ozark and Kale, were draped over their saddles, their hands and feet secured and snugged with a half hitch.

When we got back to La Mesilla we dropped off the dead men with the undertaker, locked up the other four in the jail, and made our way over to the Oracle Hotel on the east side of town.

It was close to eleven-thirty in the evening when Virgil, Hawkins, Shep, and I entered the hotel.

The Oracle Hotel was a small establishment, but it was clean. The small lobby had hanging lanterns covered with tin canisters. The canisters had holes punched in them, and the light shining through the holes made the narrow room look like it was covered with stars.

A burly man was asleep in a chair by the front window with his trousers unbuckled, giving his big belly a breather. He awoke when Shep called his name.

"Buster," Shep said.

Buster opened his eyes. He looked at Shep as if he didn't recognize him at first, then offered a big smile.

"Hey, Shep," Buster said.

Buster gazed up at the rest of us looking at him.

"What's going on?" Buster said.

"Got some questions for you, Buster," Shep said.

"Well, sure, Shep."

Buster lifted himself out of the chair and buckled his trousers. Shep made our introductions.

"What can I do for you?" Buster said.

"Want to ask you some questions about Dalton McCord," Virgil said.

"Dalton McCord," Buster said. "Well, sure. What would you like to know, Marshal?"

"He been staying here?" Virgil said.

"Until yesterday, he was," Buster said.

"How long had he been here?"

"Oh. Let's see, he'd only been staying here for a few days," Buster said. "But then he up and left."

"You have any idea where he left to?"

"No, sir," Buster said. "I don't."

"He have a young lady with him?" Virgil said.

"As a matter of fact, he did," Buster said. "Pretty young thing.

He had two rooms. There was four of them altogether, but they all took off."

"You got any idea where the other two took off to?" Virgil said. "Where they went?"

"I don't know," Buster said.

"You speak with the woman?"

Buster shook his head, looking back and forth between all of us.

"No, Marshal," Buster said. "I only saw her once, and that was when they checked in."

"You see anything or have reason to believe she may have been with Dalton unwillingly," I said.

"Unwillingly?" Buster said.

"Yes," Virgil said.

"From what you witnessed," I said. "You have any reason to believe that might have been the case?"

"Oh, Lord," Buster said. "No, I don't believe so."

"You said there were four altogether," I said. "Did you speak to the other two?"

"EG and Drummer," Buster said. "No, didn't talk with them. They all left before daylight while I was asleep. I didn't see them leave."

"EG and Drummer," I said. "You know them?"

"Know of them," Buster said.

"They been around La Mesilla awhile," Shep said.

"They were both quiet, didn't talk," Buster said.

Shep nodded.

"Those two got rattlesnake in 'em," Shep said.

"Anything else you might be able to tell us," I said. "Anything helpful?"

Buster shook his head.

"All I can say is you're not the only ones asking about Dalton McCord," Buster said.

I looked at Virgil.

"Who else," Virgil said.

"Don't know. A man came in here yesterday asking about Dalton and if I knew where he was."

"What'd he look like?" Virgil said.

"Well," Buster said. "He was wearing dark spectacles, and he looked like he'd been in on the losing end of a damn tussle with a badger."

"He ask you anything else?" I said.

Buster thought for a moment, then nodded.

46

"**HE ASKED ME WHERE THE CLOSEST TRAIN STA-** tion was located," Buster said.

"What'd you tell him?" Virgil said.

"Well, Navarro," Buster said. "That's the closest."

Virgil looked to Shep.

"Navarro's a day's ride," Shep said. "Small place, small depot."

Virgil, Hawkins, Shep, and I stepped out of the Oracle Hotel and started back to the jail. La Mesilla didn't do much in the way of mourning Vernon Talmadge. The streets were crowded with hon-yocks and rabble-rousers making their way from one joint to the next.

"How do you think Strode," Hawkins said, "or Jedediah, or whatever his name is, knew to look for Dalton here in La Mesilla?"

"Hard to know," Virgil said.

"But he knew," Hawkins said.

"Damn sure did," I said.

"But how did he know?" Hawkins said. "And of all places, he locates the sonofabitch in this hotel?"

"They *are* brothers," I said.

"They are," Virgil said.

"Together as orphans," I said. "Close, or were close."

"They got history."

"They do," I said.

"Like wolves," Virgil said.

"They are."

"You can only separate them so much," Virgil said.

"They find each other," I said.

"Like now," Virgil said.

"Yep."

"More like a couple of coyotes, if you ask me," Hawkins said.

We stopped on the boardwalk and waited as a dirty white Percheron pulling a heavy wagonload full of barrels of beer maneuvered around the corner.

"No matter," Virgil said. "One thing is for certain. Orphans, wolves, coyotes, whatever, we got brother dogging brother."

"And they got a day's jump on us," I said.

"That they do," Virgil said.

After the beer wagon cleared, we crossed the street and made our way up the boardwalk, heading for the jail.

"Day's jump or not," Hawkins said. "Now what?"

"I can put together a posse in the morning," Shep said. "See what we might be able to find."

"Good luck with that," Hawkins said.

"Worth a look," Shep said.

"'Spose it is, Shep," Hawkins said. "But these two brothers have proved hard to find. Probably have better luck looking for renegade Mescalero."

ROBERT KNOTT

"Least I can get down to Navarro Station," Shep said. "See what we can find out in that direction. See if anybody knows anything or has seen them."

"Where do you think they're headed, Cole?" Hawkins said.

"Everett?" Virgil said.

We walked for a moment before I answered.

"Mexico," I said.

We continued to walk. Virgil didn't say anything until Hawkins posed him with the question.

"You think that, too?" Hawkins said.

"Do," Virgil said.

"Where they came from," I said.

"It is," Virgil said.

"It's what they know," I said.

"It is."

"Big damn country, Mexico," Hawkins said. "Might not ever find them."

Nobody said anything for a bit while we walked. We passed a tiny gambling shack with two gals out front offering their goods, but we paid them no mind.

"Good Lord," Hawkins said. "You ain't thinking you'd angle to get Alejandro to show you where he was talking, are you?"

"Maybe," Virgil said.

"Goddamn," Hawkins said.

"Mexico is my hunch," Virgil said. "Everett's, too. And a good hunch, considering. But I want to make sure and check the train records at Navarro Station. See who went north and who went south before we do anything."

"And if they went south?" Hawkins said.

182

"We follow," Virgil said. "North or south."

"But your hunch is south?" Hawkins said.

"Is," Virgil said.

"To that *especial* place Alejandro was talking about," I said.

"Which means asking Judge Bing for Alejandro's help?" Hawkins said.

"Does," Virgil said.

"Judge Bing won't like it," Hawkins said.

"No," Virgil said. "Don't expect he will."

"If so," Hawkins said. "Best get back to San Cristóbal and see the judge before Alejandro is arraigned."

"That's what we're gonna do," Virgil said. "Shep, you do your posse tomorrow, but before you do, wire Navarro Station first thing in the morning and find out who boarded headed north and who headed south."

"Will do," Shep said.

We walked back through the busy streets, making our way to our horses at the jail.

We drank some coffee with Shep. Then Shep packed us with some hardtack and jerky, and we mounted up just after midnight.

Virgil, Hawkins, and I sat our horses in front of the jail and bid good-bye to Shep.

"I don't have to tell you, Shep, but I will," Virgil said. "If for some reason these fellas we are after did not get on that train. If they're still milling about for some reason. You be sure and tell that troop of deputies of yours to not act like heroes if by chance somebody does find Dalton and/ or his brother."

"We'll keep a tight circle, Virgil," Shep said. "Been enough killing here for a while."

"Don't you go getting into it with 'em yourself, either, Shep," Virgil said.

Shep nodded.

"Don't worry 'bout me," Shep said. "I ain't interested in dying, either."

We left Shep standing in front of the jail, and we rode out of La Mesilla.

~

It was a bright evening. The moon was a glint fuller than the night I'd previously spent with Mary May Chase.

It was also a hell of a lot better evening than tonight. I stopped thinking about Dalton and Strode, or Jedediah and where in the hell they may or may not be, and thought about being with Mary May as we rode.

I'd never met anyone quite like her before. She was a freethinker, and though she managed herself very well and with genuine craft while we were under the covers, she was no church-house mouse when it came to upright issues concerning women and women's rights.

We had had ourselves a spirited debate about the thirteenth amendment, and we both agreed all people, no matter their race, religion, or gender, should have the right to vote. She was as appreciative as I was sympathetic with her and her views. And she showed her appreciation in ways that made me do what I was doing now as we rode along the road back to San Cristóbal . . . *yawn*.

47

VIRGIL, HAWKINS, AND I MADE IT BACK TO SAN
Cristóbal by morning. The night ride returning to San Cristóbal
was considerably easier than our heat-of-the-day ride to La Mesilla,
and we made much better time.

We were sleepy as we rode into town, but we knew we had to
keep moving. The streets were starting to come alive with folks
going about their day when we made our first stop at the Western
Union office to see if there was any word from Shep concerning
passengers boarding in Navarro.

Virgil and I sat our horses, waiting on Hawkins as he checked
with the operator in the office. After a moment Hawkins looked
out through the window at Virgil and me and nodded. Hawkins
waited on the operator to give him the telegram and walked out.

"You were right," Hawkins said.

"They get on board in Navarro?" Virgil said.

"They did," Hawkins said.

"South?"

Hawkins nodded.

"Got to be them," Hawkins said.

Virgil looked to me.

"Here we go," I said.

Virgil nodded.

"No passenger names on the manifest, but Shep's wire says five people booked south passage out of Navarro and nobody north."

"All on the same train?" Virgil said.

"No," Hawkins said. "Four on Tuesday at four-thirty and one the following day at six-thirty."

"Book stock?" Virgil said.

"Shit, don't know," Hawkins said. "Shep's wire didn't say. You want me to wire and see?"

Virgil nodded.

"Will do," Hawkins said.

I looked at Virgil.

"Stock or no stock," I said. "We need to get right behind them?"

"We do."

"Goddamn lot of country south into Mexico," Hawkins said.

"There is," Virgil said.

"Looks like it's that *especial* place Alejandro was talking about," I said.

"Does," Virgil said.

"Don't think he's just bullshitting you?" Hawkins said.

"Oh, he's get freedom on his mind," Virgil said. "No doubt about that. All men behind bars do."

"They do," I said. "All they can think about."

Virgil nodded.

"There is a history with these three men, though," Virgil said.

Virgil had both of his hands draped across the horn of his saddle, looking off. He thought for a minute.

186

"Everett," Virgil said. "Let's you and me go have us a final conversation with Captain Alejandro. Maybe we can get us some answers, some direction."

I nodded.

"And Webb," Virgil said. "Why don't you see if you could let Judge Bing know we'd like to have a visit with him before the arraignment of Alejandro."

"You got it," Hawkins said. "I'll let him know right away, then get back here and send a wire, see what I can find out about stock or no stock."

"Good," Virgil said.

Hawkins climbed onto Blisters and trotted off up the street, and Virgil and I rode back to the sheriff's office.

48

∾

CROSS WAS SLEEPING WHEN WE STEPPED INTO the room but nearly jumped out of his chair when he heard us.

"Easy, Mr. Cross," I said. "We're just here to pay the captain a little visit."

Cross was still half asleep and much more pleasant because of it. He didn't have much to say as he unlocked the door leading to the cells. We stepped in and closed the door behind us.

Alejandro was shirtless, standing over the cell bucket, splashing his face with water. He turned, looking at us, and smiled wide.

"Everett," Alejandro said. *"Mi amigo!* I'm very honored you come to see Alejandro this morning."

"You ever mention to Henry Strode," Virgil said, "that Dalton had been staying in La Mesilla?"

Alejandro looked back and forth between Virgil and me as if he did not understand the question.

"When you were here before," I said, "did you ever have a discussion with Jedediah?"

"You mean Mr. Strode?" Alejandro said with a big smile.

"I do."

"No," Alejandro said.

"When you were with Dalton," Virgil said, "you said you two paid Jedediah a visit at the bank."

"*Sí.*"

"Dalton tell Jedediah he was, had been, in La Mesilla?" I said.

Alejandro looked curiously back and forth between Virgil and me.

"You find Dalton in La Mesilla?" Alejandro said with a surprised expression on his face.

"Don't get sidetracked," Virgil said.

"I had no talk with Jedediah," Alejandro said. "Jedediah looked right through Alejandro as if he did not know me . . . So you find Dalton?"

"No," I said. "Jedediah was found. He was beaten badly."

Alejandro frowned and shook his head some.

"Alejandro tell you before and Alejandro not lie, his brother is the Diablo himself."

"Jedediah is also gone," I said.

"Looking for his brother Dalton," Virgil said.

"And maybe his wife," I said.

Alejandro again shifted his eyes back and forth between Virgil and me.

He pointed to his temple.

"Alejandro is smart," he said. "And you are telling this to Alejandro for a reason?"

"*Sí,*" I said.

"The reason is you want to know *how* Alejandro would know where to find them?"

"We know which direction they are headed," I said.

"*Sí,* because you are smart like Alejandro and you know they are not traveling *el norte.*"

"Where?" I said. "Where is this *especial* place?"

Alejandro smiled, shaking his head.

"I told you," Alejandro said, "you would never find this place. Like Alejandro told you before, ever. Even if I were to tell you, and I will not tell you, you would not find this *especial* place."

Virgil looked at me.

"*Especial* place you can't even find," Virgil said.

Alejandro shook his head and pointed to his temple again.

"Alejandro knows," he said. "He knows Dalton, too, knows how Dalton thinks and where Dalton will go and even what Jedediah would do."

"You can find this place?" I said.

"*Sí.*"

I looked at Virgil. He was leaning on a post with the thumbs of both his hands hooked in his belt. He was staring at Alejandro like he was studying auction stock at a crooked sale barn.

"You know," I said. "If you were to lead us astray it would make what's left of your life a whole lot worse."

"Everetttttt," Alejandro said. "You would not be disappointed in Alejandro."

"If, and I say if, that were to happen, Alejandro," I said, "we'd need to know where we are going. We'd need to know how far."

Alejandro looked at me out of the corner of his eye. He thought for a moment, then paced. He walked to one wall, then back to the other. He looked at Virgil. Virgil had not moved from leaning on the post.

"Got to get close," I said, "so we can get to this place sooner than later."

Alejandro stopped and moved close to the bars, as if he had a secret to tell.

"Mexico City," Alejandro said.

I looked to Virgil.

Virgil shook his head like something had a disappointing flavor.

"Long damn way," I said.

"*Sí*," Alejandro said.

"Captain?" Virgil said.

Alejandro looked to Virgil.

"You are our prisoner."

"*Sí*," Alejandro said as he looked back and forth between Virgil and me as if he didn't completely understand Virgil's statement.

"You, by God, will remain our prisoner," Virgil said. "We don't find them, you will continue to be our prisoner."

Alejandro smiled.

"And if Alejandro finds them?"

"You will still be our prisoner."

Alejandro narrowed his eyes and shook his head.

"So what is good for Alejandro?"

"I will tell you what is good for Alejandro," Virgil said. "Dalton has proved himself to be a no-good. You prove yourself not to be a no-good, then we will let the judge know. But you have to prove yourself and not fuck up."

49

⌒

VIRGIL AND I THOUGHT IT'D BE RESPECTFUL TO be somewhat presentable before the judge, so we went about the business of freeing ourselves of some of the road dirt we collected on our ride. We washed up in a bathhouse behind the hotel, changed into some clean clothes, and took a seat on the hotel porch and drank some coffee.

I was pouring us some more coffee when I saw Hawkins coming down the street on Blisters. He pulled up and stopped in front of us.

"I waited around for Judge Bing, but he wouldn't talk to me," Hawkins said. "He was busy—man's always busy, fishing or working. Best get over there and see if you can roust him yourself."

"Appreciate it," Virgil said.

We made our way up the street to the courthouse a half hour before the scheduled arraignment of Alejandro. We let the bailiff know right away we needed to see Judge Bing before the arraignment business of Alejandro got under way.

"Sheriff Hawkins already told me that!" the bailiff said.

"Good, then," Virgil said. "You'll let him know."

The bailiff was a stern, unpleasant old fella.

"The judge has been busy in his chamber since sunup," the bailiff said. "I will let him know."

"Let him know it's Virgil and Everett," I said.

"Just take a seat. Everybody wants to talk to the judge! But I will tell you like I told Sheriff Hawkins and everybody else—you have to wait your turn!"

The bailiff turned and left us standing in the courtroom lobby.

Virgil shook his head.

"Might be out of the same litter as the jailer, Cross," I said.

"Might."

"Or drinking from the same well."

Virgil and I stood around for a while, watching the people file into the court for the miners' trial. After some time we moved into the courtroom with them, took a seat, and waited. Then waited some more.

It was now past ten, the courtroom was full of people, there was no sign of Judge Bing, and the early day was already hot.

Virgil and I sat at the back of the room. After a while I leaned my head back on the bench and tilted my hat over my eyes.

Sitting in courtrooms was my least enjoyable part of law work, and it seemed to me no matter how big or how small the court, waiting was a big piece of the talking part of the justice system.

After about twenty minutes, Alejandro was escorted in from the back room by Cross and Constable Holly; they were followed by the prosecutor, dapper Baxter Beazley, and the court-appointed attorney for Alejandro, Charlie Chubb. Chubb was a slack-faced thin man with hunched shoulders, stringy thin gray hair, and large ears.

Cross pushed Alejandro down into a chair.

"Don't think the bailiff heeded our request," Virgil said.

I lifted my head from the back of the bench and tilted the brim of my hat back.

"Don't look like it."

"Must be on the side of the prosecutor."

"Must," I said. "Now what?"

"Make a fuss, I reckon."

"Do some objection of sorts?"

Virgil nodded.

"Yep."

I looked around the crowded and stuffy room, and it seemed to be fuller than when I'd previously shaded my eyes. There were people whispering in the crammed-full room, but for the most part it was quiet. I could hear the whine of the steam turbine on the courthouse roof laboring away under the hot morning sun.

As early as it was, it was damn hot out, and the turbine-powered belt system snaking through the many pulleys driving the six ceiling fans whirling overhead provided very little relief from the full room and summer heat. Everyone had a good shine going from the sweat; most were trying to get rid of it by waving some kind of makeshift fan in their faces.

Judge Bing entered from his chamber. Judge Bing was a big, older man but had a head full of thick brown hair. He had a voice that reminded me of an opera baritone, and he always chewed tobacco. He was country, too. He grew up on an Arkansas dirt farm but was college-educated and well read. He had a vocabulary that kept most attorneys' heads stuck in a dictionary. He was a no-nonsense, can-do man, and his court was his kingdom.

The bailiff called out loudly, "All rise!"

After Judge Bing got settled behind the bench, the bailiff called out, "Be seated."

Everyone except Alejandro took a seat.

Judge Bing looked up over the top of his spectacles at Alejandro and offered a smile that didn't match the words that came up.

"Sit your ass down, Mr. Vasquez."

Alejandro had his black shiny hair combed back. He flashed his ivory-white teeth at the jury before taking his seat.

"Mr. Vasquez," Bing said. "This is not your jury, so do not waste your time, my time, or their time by trying to impress them. They do not give a hoot about you."

Judge Bing explained to the court that he had some arraignment business to attend to before the trial that was scheduled. He banged his gavel, and just as he did there was a loud pop. Everyone in the courtroom watched as the overhead fans slowly came to a stop.

"Not again," Judge Bing said as he shook his head. "Derwood. Do us the obligatory deed of communicating with Jasper and see if he can determine what is happening with this fallacious contraption?"

Derwood, a fat redheaded fellow with short pants, hurried out.

Bing stood up.

"All rise!" the bailiff said.

Judge Bing leaned a little to get a good look at Virgil and me.

"Virgil. Everett?" Bing said.

He motioned for us to follow.

"My chambers," Judge Bing said.

He banged the gavel.

"We'll take a recess," Bing said. "See if we can get these twirling things twirling."

50

WHEN WE ENTERED JUDGE BING'S CHAMBERS HE
stood up and greeted us. His office was full of everything to do
with fishing. There was a shiny stuffed bigmouth bass hanging on
the wall behind his desk, a bunch of fishing poles leaning in one
corner, and a framed tintype of the judge standing on an ocean
dock next to a swordfish.

"Virgil Cole and Everett Hitch, good to see you," Bing said.

"Good to see you, Judge," Virgil said.

"Been awhile," I said.

"It has," Bing said. "It damn sure has."

"You're looking well," I said.

"Fishing keeps me from getting too fat," Bing said. "Not the
fishing itself, but just getting out there and getting back."

"It's good to move," Virgil said.

"It is," Bing said. "Heard you boys were still in town, and I'm
glad to know it."

"We are," Virgil said.

"Please have a seat in these comfortable chairs," Bing said.
"Damn good to see the both of you."

Bing bit off an edge of tobacco from a plug he pulled from his pocket and started to chew on it.

Bing waved Alejandro's warrant in the air.

"My congratulations to you both for bringing in this fugitive," Bing said.

I nodded. Virgil didn't say anything.

"Captain Alejandro Vasquez," Bing said.

"That he is," Virgil said.

"Where did you find him?"

"Border town," I said. "El Encanto."

"I understand some of his desperadoes were not lucky enough to be captured along with Alejandro?"

"That's right," Virgil said. "They weren't."

"They had other ideas," I said.

"Well," Bing said, followed by spitting a stream of tobacco juice into a spittoon. "'Bout time he was apprehended. Not a respectable occurrence to have men gunned down in the town where the judge presides."

"Not," Virgil said.

"I know Captain Alejandro says he did what he did in self-defense," Bing said.

"He does."

"We'll see about that, in the court," Bing said, then spit again.

"After we got him locked up," Virgil said, "we'd meant to come see you before now, Judge. But things have been more expectant here in San Cristóbal than we expected."

"I know that. The damn bank robbery. Lot of damn money."

"Was," Virgil said.

"Good thing I didn't have money in that bank."

"Real good," Virgil said.

"Any news on who beat the hell out of Henry Strode."

"Some," Virgil said.

"Obviously, he didn't rob the bank alone."

"No," Virgil said. "He didn't."

"I suspect whoever whipped up on him was in on it, got greedy?"

"He was."

"What's Strode's condition?"

"You didn't hear?" I said.

"Hear what?"

"His condition is better," I said.

"It is," Virgil said.

"That's good," Bing said.

"It's good enough he took off."

"What?"

"He escaped," I said.

"Escaped?"

"Yep," Virgil said. "Came to and took off."

"Not sure why I was not informed of this," Bing said. "Seems like I'm always the last to know."

"You're a busy man, Judge," I said.

"Any idea where he is?" Bing said.

"We do," Virgil said. "But not exactly."

"We've been looking for him," I said.

"Well, goddamn," Bing said, and spit.

I nodded in agreement.

"Got a proposition for you, Judge," Virgil said.

"What sort of proposition?"

"Like to borrow Alejandro."

51

BING LOOKED AT VIRGIL LIKE HE DIDN'T HEAR
him. He pulled his spittoon a little closer. He kept his eye on Virgil
as he spit.

"Borrow him?"

"Yep."

"You mean like someone might borrow a book or a cup of sugar,
or a fishing pole?"

"Like that," Virgil said.

"What in the hell do you want to borrow him *for*, might I ask?"

"He knows where to find the bank robbers," I said.

Bing looked at Virgil for a long moment, then looked to me.

"What?"

I nodded. Virgil nodded.

"*Alejandro?*" Bing said.

"Yes, sir," I said.

Virgil nodded.

Bing squinted and shook his head like he had a fly in his ear.
Then he sat back in his chair.

"Elaborate, gentlemen."

"Just that," Virgil said.

"That's not elaborating, Virgil," Bing said.

"We believe he knows the whereabouts of the robbers," I said.

"What in the hell has he got to do with Strode and the robbery?"

"He says he knows where they are," I said.

"And you believe him?"

"Given a set of circumstances," I said, "we do."

Bing chewed his plug hard and then spit.

"What set of circumstances?"

Virgil looked at me.

"He provided us with information that proves to us he knows those responsible for the robbery," Virgil said.

"Strode?"

"And others."

"What others?"

"The one that beat Strode," I said.

Bing shook his head.

"Alejandro is to stand trial for murder," Bing said.

I nodded.

"You ever heard of Baxter Beazley?" Bing said.

"Have," Virgil said.

"Know he's a tough prosecutor," I said. "Out to make a name for himself."

Bing nodded.

"That he is," Bing said.

"This is not a request we'd ask for, Judge," Virgil said. "But there is more to this than this robbery."

"What more?"

"We believe Strode's wife was kidnapped when this robbery took place."

"Jantz Wainwright's daughter?" Bing said.

"Yes," Virgil said.

"By who?"

"We believe Strode had a brother behind the robbery," I said.

"Oh, Lord," Bing said, and then spit.

"If it weren't for the fact there's a woman's life at stake here," I said, "we wouldn't be asking this of you, Judge Bing."

Bing looked at us for an extended moment. He moved forward with his elbows resting on his desk, and he put the tips of his fingers together. He gazed at Virgil and me as he thought about our request.

"Well," Bing said. "It's your good fortune that goddamn fan quit."

Virgil did not say anything, and I didn't say anything.

"This goes against my better judgment," Bing said. "You understand that, don't you?"

"We do," Virgil said.

"But seeing how it's the two of you asking and not some of the other, less-qualified lawmen I have to deal with, it goes in your favor."

Virgil nodded. I nodded.

"Right now, Alejandro is in custody," Bing said. "That's all. After his arraignment he will be in the system supported by the law. Currently, however, if he by chance were to be gone, it would be outside of my bailiwick. After the arraignment, the situation would be different."

"Understand," Virgil said.

"Well, I hope you do," Bing said. "I could lose my job over this."

"That's why we wanted to discuss this with you now," Virgil said.

"When do you want to do this?" Bing said.

"We figure to get a fresh start in the morning," Virgil said.

Bing looked at us for a long minute, then spit.

52

HAWKINS WAS SITTING ON THE STEPS WHEN VIR-
gil and I walked out of the courthouse.

"What'd he say?" Hawkins said.

"Wasn't happy about it," I said. "But with Catherine missing, he
somehow convinced himself."

Hawkins nodded a bit.

"Navarro Depot wired back right away," Hawkins said, "and all
five passengers that boarded south had stock."

"Good to know," Virgil said.

"Don't know about the two of you, but I could use some sleep,"
Hawkins said. "Guess that will have to wait, though."

Hawkins got slowly to his feet.

"Holly told me Wainwright sent his wife and son back to Saint
Louis," Hawkins said. "Wainwright told Holly he'd be at his ranch
and for us to let him know when and if we found out anything."

Virgil nodded.

"'Spect we ought to do that," Hawkins said. "Let him know
about his daughter. Don't you think, Cole?"

"I do."

"You want me to just ride out there and tell him?" Hawkins said.

"No," Virgil said. "Wouldn't want you to have to row that boat alone, Webb."

"Appreciate it," Hawkins said. "Damn glad to hear."

"He know about his son-in-law being gone?" I said.

"He does," Hawkins said.

Virgil nodded a little but didn't say anything.

"I'll get us some fresh horses," Hawkins said.

"Good," Virgil said.

"All right, then," Hawkins said. "I'll meet you back at your hotel and ride you out."

"Appreciate it," Virgil said.

※

It was scorching hot out when Hawkins showed up in front of our hotel. He was riding a thick-necked roan and was pulling a tall dun and a dapple gray.

Virgil and I saddled the horses with our tack. Virgil took the dun, and I climbed atop the dapple gray. We took off, traveling east out of San Cristóbal. We crossed the river at a low ford and rode for about forty minutes toward the mountains and arrived at Wainwright's ranch just before noon.

On one side of the road leading to a big house, backed up to a stand of huge sycamores, there were fine-looking Thoroughbred horses behind a fence, watching us as we rode by. Off in the distance on the other side of the road, hundreds of cattle grazed on rolling hills of lush grass.

"'Bout the nicest place I believe I've ever seen," I said.

"Is," Virgil said.

"Ain't it, though?" Hawkins said. "It runs all the way as far as you can see. All the way to the bottom of those mountains there."

When we arrived at the big house, two Mexican barn attendants greeted us. They took our horses and told us Wainwright was on the back porch. They showed us to a path between rows of pepper trees that led to the back of the house.

Wainwright was sitting alone on the tall porch, reading a San Francisco newspaper, when we walked up.

"Mr. Wainwright," Hawkins said.

"Sheriff," Wainwright said, getting to his feet. "Marshal, Deputy. Come up. Please."

Wainwright called into the house.

"Josefa!"

An older Mexican woman stepped out, and Wainwright told her in Spanish to bring lemonade.

"Please sit," Wainwright said nervously. "As you might imagine, I'm, well, damn anxious. What do you know? Have you found Catherine? Is she okay? Have you—"

Virgil held up his hand, and Wainwright stopped talking.

"We know she is alive."

Tears came to Wainwright's eyes.

"Thank God!" he said, and dropped in his chair. "Thank God! Where is she?"

"Mexico," Virgil said.

"*Mexico!*" Wainwright said. "But how? What has happened?"

"She was taken," Virgil said.

Wainwright squinted. He looked as though he might vomit.

"By who?"

"Turns out your son-in-law is not who he says he is," Virgil said.

Wainwright looked at each of us in turn, then rested his eyes on Virgil.

"What?"

"He's a fella originally from Mexico," Virgil said.

"Mexico?" Wainwright said. "I'm sorry. I do not understand. If he's not Henry Strode, then who, who the hell is he?"

Virgil looked at me.

"He assumed the identity of a man who died, Henry Strode," I said. "And by all accounts he was doing a good job of it until his brother found him."

"What? His brother? I didn't know Henry had a brother."

"Well, like Everett said," Virgil said. "He ain't Henry, and he did have a brother."

"Henry's real name is Jedediah McCord," I said.

Wainwright shook his head in disbelief.

"Turns out the brothers didn't get on so well," Virgil said.

"His brother's name is Dalton," I said. "We're not completely sure how it happened, but Dalton and a few of his men were behind Jedediah cleaning out the vault."

"They beat him," Wainwright said, staring at the floor. "They beat him, left him for dead, and took my Catherine?"

Wainwright looked to Virgil.

Virgil nodded.

"But why Catherine?" Wainwright said. "Why Mexico?"

"We don't know all the particulars," Virgil said. "But we are determined to find her."

"Where in Mexico?"

"We believe near Mexico City."

"Mexico City!" Wainwright said, shaking his head. "My Lord . . . Constable Holly told me about Henry, or . . . ?"

"Jedediah," I said.

Wainwright nodded.

"Yes, Jedediah," Wainwright said, pronouncing the real name of his son-in-law for the first time. "Holly told me he escaped."

"He has," I said. "He's dogging his brother. He, too, is determined to find your daughter."

"And his wife," Virgil said.

53

WHEN WE GOT BACK TO TOWN, VIRGIL AND I rode over to the depot to book our travel south to Mexico.

The outbound would depart San Cristóbal the following morning at eleven. The journey would take us through Navarro, then to Ciudad Juárez, Mexico. From Ciudad, we'd take the Mexican Central Railway down to Mexico City.

Virgil and I left the depot at about three and set about our chores, getting ready for the long journey.

After we got outfitted we settled into our hotel café for some early supper. We ate some ham with potatoes and cornbread, then made our way to our rooms for some much-needed shut-eye.

A knock on the door shortly after seven woke me. I got up, opened the door. It was Mary May.

She smiled.

"Am I disturbing you?" she said.

"You're not."

"May I come in?" she said.

"Be disappointed if you didn't."

"Well," she said. "I'm flattered and glad you feel that way and are not disappointed."

She smiled. I smelled her perfume as she walked past me. I closed the door behind her and turned to find her lips on mine. She kissed me. I kissed her back.

She pulled away some, looking at my face. She put her hand to my cheek and stared at me.

"What?" I said.

"Nice face, Mr. Hitch."

I smiled.

"Everett," I said.

"You're not blushing, are you, Everett?" she said.

"Not," I said.

She turned from me and looked around the small room.

"I wanted to have a look at Harvey House's competition."

"That what you wanted?"

She smiled.

"Don't think there's much competition here," she said.

She pushed the bed, checking its firmness.

"Nice bed."

She sat on the bed.

"Comfortable," she said.

She propped herself up at the headboard with a pillow behind her back. She crossed her arms.

"I hear you found Catherine," Mary May said.

"Where'd you hear that?"

"I also know her husband had some sort of getaway," she said. "You didn't mention that before, but I knew."

"Your girls, no doubt?" I said.

"I told you. They know everything."

"They ought to get into police work," I said.

"Yes. They should. It's hard for them not to know everything that's going on in San Cristóbal. I'm relieved to know you found her. What I said before about her being spoiled was true, but I believe she has a good heart."

"We located her," I said. "Haven't found her."

"Is she okay?"

"She's with him," I said.

Mary May just looked at me.

"I'd have to say it might not be the most pleasant of circumstances for her," I said.

Mary May was silent for a moment.

"When you play with fire," Mary May said.

"Hard to know just what has happened," I said. "But whatever did happen, I don't think it's got the makings for a lasting relationship."

"She was taken, Everett," Mary May said. "I told you she maybe wanted to leave with him, but that is the fantasy of many young women with too much time on their hands, and in her case too much money and time. Their husbands work all day and they feel neglected, and then a charmer comes along."

"You know that for certain?"

"Yes," Mary May said. "Certain enough."

I thought about what she said for a moment.

"What happens now?" Mary May said.

"We go get her," I said.

"Have you told Mr. Wainwright?"

"Your girls didn't say?"

She shook her head.

"He's been at his ranch," she said.

"We have," I said. "We went out, talked to him."

"How is he?" Mary May said.

"Happy she's alive," I said.

She shook her head again.

"I wish I could have done something to protect her," Mary May said. "I really do."

"We were not certain how things were with Catherine, and we didn't fill her father in on all the details, and I don't suppose you will, either."

"Of course not," she said. "Poor man."

"Poor he is not."

"Poor choice of words," she said.

"He's upset," I said. "But like I said, he's happy to know she is alive."

"Me, too," Mary May said. "Me, too."

I nodded, looking at Mary May, and smiled a little.

She smiled a little, too.

"When do you leave?" she said.

"Tomorrow."

"What are your plans for tonight?"

"I don't have any plans."

"You don't?"

"No."

"You haven't thought ahead?"

"Nope."

"I have a few thoughts," she said.

"Me, too."

"I wonder if your thoughts are the same as mine?"

"I hope so."

"Me, too," she said.

Mary May reached up and removed a few long pins holding up her hair.

212

54

THE FOLLOWING MORNING, CONSTABLE HOLLY
and the bankers, Walter Comstock and Truitt Ellsworth, stopped
at the hotel when Virgil and I were drinking coffee with Hawkins
on the front porch.

"What an ordeal," Holly said. "What an ordeal."

"What ordeal you talking about, Constable?" Virgil said.

"Constable Holly here told us everything," Comstock said. "And,
well, it is a goddamn ordeal!"

"Yes," Holly said, "quite the ordeal!"

Virgil looked at me.

"What exactly are you getting at?" I said.

"Well," Holly said. "Everything. First, the two men who were in
town to rob the bank last Christmas getting killed in the street,
then you hunt and apprehend Alejandro for their murder, then he
escapes and you find him again and bring him back to finally face
the charges, then the bank robbery, and Mr. Strode being someone else other than who he pretended to be. Then Sheriff Talmadge
getting killed in La Mesilla and you having to face two gunmen
and them being killed, and Strode having a brother on the run with

the money and Jantz Wainwright's daughter in tow. And Strode, or whoever he is, in pursuit, and now you are taking Alejandro to find them."

Virgil looked at me.

"Guess that is quite the ordeal," Virgil said.

"Is," I said.

"It goddamn is!" Comstock said.

Virgil looked at me.

"'Spect there's gonna be more of the ordeal to come," Virgil said.

"You'd think," I said.

"Would," Virgil said.

"Henry Strode," Ellsworth said, "working for us all this time and we had no idea he was an imposter."

"He was a good goddamn imposter, too," Comstock said.

"Yes," Holly said, "and his wife, Catherine, now in trouble. The poor dear."

"Mr. Comstock," I said. "When we were eating at that French restaurant, you said Catherine got around town."

"I said it was rumored she got around town," Comstock said.

"Where'd you hear that rumor?" I said.

"Well," Comstock said, looking to Ellsworth.

"He heard that from me," Ellsworth said.

"What did he hear from you?" I said.

"Shortly before the robbery," Ellsworth said, "I saw her walking down the street with a fellow."

"What fellow?" I said.

"I don't know who he was," Ellsworth said. "He was a handsome man."

"That's it?" I said. "You saw them walking down the street?"

"Well, yes," Ellsworth said. "He was laughing, she was laughing, and it looked like they were having a fine time of it."

"That's all?" I said.

"Yes," Ellsworth said.

"Catherine is a vivacious sort," Holly said.

"Goddamn flirtatious," Comstock said.

Ellsworth nodded.

"Well, you might say so," Ellsworth said. "But I believe she loved Henry, and I know Henry was in love with her. He adored her. He was always showering her with gifts. She would come to the bank and just sit and wait for him to finish work. For hours she'd sit in the lobby reading and, well, rumors are rumors."

"So you have no evidence she was with someone?" I said.

"In the biblical sense," Ellsworth said, "no."

Comstock nodded.

"I'm sorry we was part of the mill," Comstock said.

"Well," Holly said, "let me just say I'm very grateful to you both for your help in solving all this."

"Not solved yet," I said.

"Nope," Virgil said. "Far from it."

"Well," Holly said. "Nonetheless, I want you to know Sheriff Hawkins and I are very appreciative of everything you have done and are continuing to do."

"Agreed," Hawkins said.

Virgil nodded a bit.

"It's what we do," I said. "Constable."

"It is," Virgil said.

"I hope the hell you find them," Comstock said.

"We are gonna do our best to find them," Virgil said, "and straighten the rest of this ordeal out, Constable."

"I hope the hell so," Comstock said.

"You need to know something, though, Mr. Comstock," Virgil said.

"What's that, Marshal?" Comstock said.

"We got criminal elements we're dealing with here," Virgil said. "Everett and me will do what we can, but there ain't no guarantee you'll get your money back. And maybe not Catherine."

55

IT WAS THE BEGINNINGS OF YET ANOTHER HOT
day when we loaded up our horses on the eleven-o'clock train
headed for Mexico. Much to Alejandro's dislike, we had him in
shackles, and in the short walk from the jail to the depot, he'd
already perturbed the hell out of Virgil.

Hawkins stood on the porch of the depot with us as we boarded.

"I'd go with you if I didn't have a town to police," Hawkins said.

"I know, Webb," Virgil said.

"Hell of an ordeal," Hawkins said with a grin.

"Is," Virgil said. "Hell of an ordeal."

Hawkins turned to Alejandro.

"Where is the *especial* place you been talking about, Alejandro?"
Hawkins said, as if he were throwing a dart at Alejandro.

Alejandro laughed.

"Alejandro can't show his face card, Sheriff Hawkins. God knows
Sheriff Hawkins knows Alejandro is smarter than that."

"Well," Hawkins said. "Sheriff Hawkins knows and God knows
you better not get down there to Mexico and lose your sense of
direction."

Alejandro raised his hand, pointing to his temple. His shackles required both his hands to make the trip up to his head.

"Alejandro knows like pigeon."

"Just what makes you sure this *especial* place is the place to find Dalton McCord?" Hawkins said, as if he were throwing a second dart but harder.

Alejandro smiled. He looked to Virgil, then to me and back to Hawkins. Then he stopped smiling.

"I will give you a clue how Alejandro knows."

"Good," Hawkins said. "Why don't you? We're listening to you, Captain Alejandro."

"When we was children in the orphanage," Alejandro said, "we visited this *especial* place. We always said when we were rich and happy, we would return."

"Well, bullshit," Hawkins said. "That ain't no kind of guarantee."

"I never gave Virgil and *mi amigo* Everett no guarantee, but Alejandro knows Dalton, and this place, the *especial* place, has much to do with Dalton, especially for Dalton."

Hawkins looked at Alejandro for a bit, then said, "Don't fuck up."

"Alejandro will not fuck up. You will see, Sheriff Hawkins."

Hawkins shook his head a little and looked back to Virgil.

"Not the most ideal travel companion," Hawkins said.

"He'll have no option but to show his worth," Virgil said.

Hawkins pulled out a handful of cigars that were resting in his shirt pocket and handed them to Virgil.

"Good ones," Hawkins said.

"Appreciate everything you've done," Virgil said.

"I'll be right here. Send word if you need something."

"Will," Virgil said.

"I could use some keys to get these irons off," Alejandro said.

Hawkins didn't pay any attention to Alejandro, and neither did Virgil. Virgil just nodded for me to get Alejandro on the train.

"Good-bye, Sheriff Hawkins," Alejandro said as I pulled him up the steps of the car. "Good-bye, San Cristóbal."

We were in the sixth car back. It was the smoking car, and the only other passengers were men. We sat in the back seats. I put Alejandro next to the window, and I sat next to him.

"We have a long way to go," I said.

"*Sí,*" he said. "It is a far travel."

"Is," I said.

"Mexico is beautiful," Alejandro said. "*Viva la México.*"

"Yep. *Viva la México.*"

Alejandro looked out the window like an excited kid riding the train for the first time.

"Like you to do me a favor, Alejandro," I said.

"Anything for *mi amigo.*"

"Do your best not to talk," I said.

Alejandro looked at me like I hurt his feelings.

"It'd be best for the both of us if you just kept quiet," I said.

"But how will you know the directions, unless Alejandro can talk?"

"Well, like you said, it's far travels to Mexico City," I said. "When we get there, and we need to know how to get to the *especial* place, then it would be a good time for you to talk."

Virgil stepped on board just as the engineer pulled the cord and the whistle let out one short blast. Virgil sat across the aisle from me. He leaned forward and looked over to Alejandro. Alejandro smiled.

Virgil didn't smile back, and he didn't say anything.

56

THE TRIP SOUTH INTO MEXICO CITY WAS NOT without troubles. Alejandro didn't heed my request entirely. He talked more than he needed, and, as expected, Virgil continued to be annoyed by his unnecessary travel commentary about Mexico and its culture.

Virgil and I took turns watching Alejandro while the other slept. The days to Mexico City were long and hot. A few nights on the trip we camped near the depot, exercised the horses, and Virgil and I played gin to pass the time. We were three stations away from Mexico City when Virgil figured it was time to press Alejandro for details.

"Now that we are good and down here," Virgil said, "and closing in on Mexico City, it's time you tell us just where the hell we are headed, Captain."

"Virgil Cole," Alejandro said. "Alejandro told you. Without trying to be tricky, if Alejandro were to say, try to tell you, you would never find where."

"Where about?" Virgil said.

Alejandro looked at us for a long moment.

"East out of Mexico City," he said. "We will have to travel east."

"How far east?" Virgil said.

"A week with horses," Alejandro said.

Virgil looked at me and shook his head some.

"A week?" I said.

"*Sí,*" Alejandro said.

"First Mexico City," I said. "Now you're saying elsewhere east?"

"Alejandro said we travel to Mexico City," he said. "Then Alejandro will provide the instructions."

"Just get to those instructions, Alejandro," I said.

"When we get to Mexico City, there is a train, Ferrocarril Interoceánico, that will travel east a ways. That would be faster."

"A ways?" I said.

"*Sí,*" Alejandro said. "The rail is not complete. At least last time Alejandro was down here it was not complete. We will see, but I don't think so. Mexicans do not work so fast like the Americans."

"When were you last here?" I said.

"A year, a little more," he said.

"Why?" I said.

"Oh, I come back to my people. I have many friends here."

"Where?"

"Alejandro have friends all over Mexico," he said.

"No," Virgil said. "Where, east?"

"Where is very hard to find," he said. "Alejandro is not lying. He will have to show you, Virgil Cole."

Alejandro smiled, then looked out the window.

We arrived in busy Estación Ferrocarril in Mexico City early in the afternoon. Virgil took Alejandro with him to inquire about booking travel east, and I retrieved our horses from the stock car. I walked them around the station and waited on Virgil near the arches of the entrance.

The street in front of the station was crowded with people and vendors selling their goods. Unlike most of the cities in America, the buildings were old, built of stone, and built to last. In the distance I could see a cathedral rising above the buildings that looked to be centuries old and hundreds of feet tall.

After some time, Virgil walked out with Alejandro. He found me near a trough I'd located across from the station for our horses to drink.

"We're booked to a place called Córdoba," Virgil said. "End of the line."

"Córdoba?" I said.

"Yep."

"That's almost to the Gulf."

"Is."

"Veracruz."

Virgil looked to Alejandro.

"It is," Virgil said.

"How far?"

"Two days."

"This is good," Alejandro said. "The rail is longer than when Alejandro was here before. From there, it is not far. We have only a day's ride."

"When?" I said.

"Leaves this evening," Virgil said. "Departs at seven."

"Córdoba is a beautiful place," Alejandro said. "You will see."

Virgil shook his head.

"Beautiful place or not," Virgil said. "First you say Mexico City, now this. You lead us on a rabbit hunt, you will have hell to pay."

"There will be no rabbits," he said, "and Alejandro will not pay hell."

57

THE TRAIN BROKE DOWN TWICE ON THE JOURNEY
to Córdoba. The second time it stopped we were less than halfway to
Córdoba. We unloaded our horses and rode to the next village depot.

There were two Federales sitting on the depot porch when we
rode up. One of the Federales was a big man with a pockmarked
face. He was cleaning his fingernails with a large knife.

"*¿De dónde viene?*" the big Federal said.

"America," I said.

"*¿A dónde va?*"

"Córdoba," I said.

He eyed me with a curious look, then glanced west up the track
in the direction we had come from. I told him the train broke down
five miles back.

"*¿Quiénes son?*"

"*Soy un* Territorial Deputy Marshal, Everett Hitch," I said. "*Este
es* Marshal Virgil Cole."

The Federal stood up and looked to Alejandro in his shackles.
Alejandro smiled.

"*¿Quién es el prisionero?*"

"Alejandro," I said.

"*¿Y su apellido?*"

"Vasquez," I said. "*Su nombre es Alejandro Vasquez.*"

"*¿Qué hizo?*" the Federal said.

"*El es un ladrón de caballos,*" I said.

"*No soy un ladrón!*" Alejandro said.

"He claims he is innocent," I said.

The Federal looked at me and frowned.

"He does not understand you, Everett. The Federales are not very smart like American police, and they don't know English," Alejandro said.

"*Él dice que es inocente,*" I said.

The Federal nodded and laughed.

"*Inocente,*" he said.

He looked to the other Federal. They both laughed.

I explained to him in brief the nature of our mission.

He moved closer to the edge of the porch, looking at Alejandro as if he was a slave trader and Alejandro was for sale. He smiled, but it was not a friendly smile. After a long stare, he nodded sharply.

Virgil clicked and moved Cortez away from the depot, and Alejandro and I followed.

"Why did you tell the Federal that Alejandro was a horse thief?" Alejandro said.

"You prefer he told him what you really are?" Virgil said.

We found some shade, away from the depot under a stand of oaks. We removed our saddles and hobbled the horses to graze as we waited.

We waited under the trees the better part of the day, and just as the sun began to set we heard the train approaching from the west.

After the train took on water and coal at the depot, we got our horses into the stock car and boarded for the final leg to Córdoba.

The Federal with the pockmarked face eyed us as we took our seats in the coach. When the train pulled out of the depot, the Federal got to his feet and watched us as the train built up steam and started thumping away from the depot.

"Don't think that Federal fella much cares for you, Alejandro," Virgil said as the train began to move away down the track.

"*No, mi amigo,*" Alejandro said. "All Mexico love Alejandro."

"Amigo?" Virgil said with a smile. "I am an officer of the law, you are my prisoner."

"You will see, Marshal Cole," Alejandro said as he leaned forward, looking past me to Virgil across the aisle. "I will not let you down."

Virgil looked at Alejandro for a moment.

"Everett," Virgil said. "Providing the train don't quit on us again, what time do you figure we'll get to Córdoba?"

I looked at my watch.

"I'd say nine, ten in the morning."

The coach we were in was fairly empty of passengers now. Virgil looked out the window, watching a man in a big straw sombrero herding sheep, as the train picked up speed.

Virgil pulled a cigar from his pocket. He bit the tip and spat it out the window. He fished a match from his pocket, dragged the head of it on the back of the seat in front of him, and lit the cigar. After he got it going good, he looked over to Alejandro sitting by me. Alejandro was looking out the window next to him. Virgil looked at me and shook his head a little.

"Hope to hell we're not pissing in the wind," Virgil said.

58

WHEN WE ARRIVED IN CÓRDOBA IT WAS ELEVEN
in the morning. The station was a bustle of activity, and to our surprise, a group of Federales were waiting for us when we stepped off
the train.

Their leader was a lean man with a scraggly beard and
friendly dancing eyes. He had a black-handled Colt with a backward Slim Jim holster. He wore a flat canvas police hat with a short
leather brim and a green jacket with medals pinned next to both
lapels.

"Marshal Virgil Cole?" he said.

"I am," Virgil said.

"Everett Hitch?" he said.

I nodded.

"My name is Lieutenant Sebastian Diaz. This is Sergeant Major
Acero. We are with the Córdoba Federales. We have been waiting
for you."

The lieutenant spoke perfect English. His manner was pleasant
and slightly formal. He showed no sign of drunkenness, but it was
obvious by his smell that he was no teetotaler. His sergeant major

stood a half step behind him. He was a burly, mean-looking hombre with dark slits for eyes and void of expression.

"Waiting for us for what?" Virgil said.

Virgil looked to me.

"We are here to assist you," the lieutenant said.

"Assist us with what?"

The lieutenant looked to Alejandro.

"You are Alejandro Miguel Vasquez, are you not?"

"What are you here to assist us with, Lieutenant?" Virgil said.

"The stop west on the rail," the lieutenant said. "You met one of my cousins. I have many. He sent a wire letting me know you were coming. He wrote, stating your prisoner said my cousin was not smart. My cousin is amusing. Contrary to his ugly looks, he is very smart. He knew he remembered the name Alejandro Miguel Vasquez, the man with the naval captain's jacket, the man with the fancy breeches and sombrero. He has a good memory. So my cousin sent a telegram to me inquiring about this Alejandro Vasquez. And sure enough, wouldn't you know, Alejandro Miguel Vasquez is wanted here, too, in Córdoba. My *jefe* learns from me two Americano law officials, Virgil Cole and Everett Hitch, have one of our wanted men, Alejandro Vasquez, and it was his orders, my *jefe*'s orders, we assist you . . ."

He pulled a piece of paper from his pocket.

"I have an arrest warrant for Alejandro Vasquez right here," the lieutenant said. "We appreciate you bringing him to us."

Alejandro shook his head and started to speak, but I jerked the back of his belt. He shut up.

"Didn't bring him to you," Virgil said. "This man is my prisoner."

"Yes," the lieutenant said. "But you are in Córdoba now, and he is a wanted man here in Córdoba. So he is now *our* prisoner."

"Wanted for what?" Virgil said.

"Robbery," the lieutenant said. "Alejandro robbed one of our statesmen's haciendas. A rather high-profile robbery, too, so you might imagine how fortunate it is for you that you apprehended him for us and brought him back here to face trial."

Alejandro shook his head, and I jerked him again by his belt.

"You can't have him, Lieutenant," Virgil said.

The lieutenant smiled.

"We have brought this man here to Córdoba to help us locate some hombres who abducted a woman," Virgil said. "And we ain't leaving until he helps us do what we brought him down here to do."

"How much is she worth?" the lieutenant said.

"There is no price."

"Aw, but surely there is a price on a woman from America?"

"There is none."

"You have come to Mexico to find a woman and there is no ransom involved?"

"That's right."

The lieutenant crossed his arms high across his chest, looking at Virgil. He was no longer smiling.

"How can this man help you? He is a thief, a common criminal."

"He knows the whereabouts of the woman," Virgil said.

The lieutenant looked Alejandro up and down.

"You believe him?" the lieutenant said.

"Do. Until he proves himself otherwise, I got no choice."

"You do have a choice," he said. "An obvious choice it is."

"That choice being?" Virgil said.

The lieutenant looked back to his sergeant major.

"You just have to persuade him to tell you where to go," the lieutenant said. "Did you think of that?"

"Didn't," Virgil said.

"Well," the lieutenant said. "You are in luck, because my sergeant major can persuade him easily."

The slit-eyed sergeant major showed no visible emotion.

Alejandro wanted to run, but I held him by the back of his belt.

The lieutenant folded the warrant carefully and handed it to one of his seconds, then put his hands behind his back.

"It should not take long," the lieutenant said.

"No," Virgil said.

"No?" the lieutenant said.

"No."

"It's no trouble," he said with a stern face. "No trouble at all."

"We are here now," Virgil said. "Come a long way, took us a while to get here. I will complete what I set out to do with him."

"Seriously?" the lieutenant said.

"More than seriously," Virgil said.

The lieutenant looked at Virgil for a steady moment.

"We will assist you," the lieutenant said.

"With what?"

"We will assist you and help you find the woman."

Virgil shook his head.

"Won't be necessary," Virgil said.

"I insist," the lieutenant said. "And when we are done, we will arrest this man."

59

VIRGIL AND I GOT OUR HORSES OUT OF THE STOCK car and made our way to a hotel across Córdoba's busy plaza. After we booked a room, I walked the horses around the plaza a few times, then boarded them in a livery near the hotel. The lieutenant moved on but left the surly sergeant major and one of his other Federales in the hotel lobby, making sure we didn't have plans to carry on without them. Virgil and I walked Alejandro up the stairs of the old hotel.

"After I find Dalton and Jedediah's wife," he said, "you will, of course, be taking Alejandro back to America, won't you, Virgil Cole? You won't be leaving me with the fucking Federales in Córdoba, will you?"

Virgil didn't say anything as we walked the hall to the room.

"Will you?" Alejandro said.

Virgil didn't respond as we entered the hotel room. It was a big, open room with two beds. It had high ceilings and a balcony facing the plaza. There was a small room that had no windows connecting to the main room, and in the corner of the small room there was a bunk for Alejandro. We shackled Alejandro to the heavy iron frame of the bunk.

"Aw Everett," Alejandro said. "You do not need to keep cuffing me. You must know I have no interest whatever in not being with you, Everett, and you, too, Virgil Cole. You must believe Alejandro."

"We got a ways to go, Captain," Virgil said. "How this plays out is unforeseen."

"Well, I want to thank you, Virgil Cole. I have very much gratitude for what you did back there at the station. Those Federales have a different way of dealing with situations than the Americanos do. They would harm Alejandro. Probably, most likely, kill Alejandro."

"Thought all Mexico loved Captain Alejandro," Virgil said.

"Most Mexico, yes, not everywhere. Córdoba, they are a little different. That is why America is now my home."

"Your navy jacket," I said. "It carries a mark for you, Alejandro. Might consider losing that."

"Aw. No. Never. This was my father's jacket."

Alejandro looked at the jacket admiringly, as if he were looking at it for the first time.

"He was in the navy?" I said.

"*Sí.*"

Virgil was leaning on the doorjamb, looking at Alejandro, with his arms folded across his ribs.

"I do not remember my father. My mother tell me all about him. He was a very great man. This jacket is my shield. He was my hero. Alejandro, too, will one day be a hero like my father."

"Heroes don't go around killing and robbing people," Virgil said.

"Alejandro is not a killer," he said.

"You told us when you, Dalton, and Jedediah were *niños* you robbed a bank and got caught?" I said.

"*Sí,*" Alejandro said.

"How old were you?"

"Sixteen."

"Jedediah and Dalton?"

"Jedediah was seventeen, Dalton eighteen."

"Not hardly *niños,*" Virgil said.

"*Niños* enough."

"Where was the bank?"

"Nogales."

"You said an hombre was killed."

"*Sí.*"

"Who got killed?"

"The hombre who owned the bank."

"You kill him?"

"No, Dalton. The hombre chased us out of the bank. He shot at us, and Dalton chased him down and shot him."

"Dalton chased the banker down?" Virgil said.

"*Sí,*" Alejandro said, nodding. "That is Dalton."

"You and Dalton got caught?"

"*Sí.* We were convicted and went to prison in Yuma. It was not a good place. I got out in one year. Dalton stayed for twelve years."

"Jedediah got away and you've not seen him since?" I said.

"No."

"You said Jedediah told the authorities on Dalton."

Alejandro nodded.

"He did. He wanted to leave, get away from his brother Dalton."

"Why?"

Alejandro shook his head.

"They had been together too long, too close for too long . . . Too many fucking bad things had happened."

60

"**Dalton and Jedediah were tough hombres.**
Like no hombres I've known. They were rough with each other."

"What way rough?" I said.

"Fight, bad fights. Most always started by Dalton. A few times, very bloody fights, like animals. Once I thought they would kill each other."

Virgil looked to me.

"They would play games on each other, not friendly games."

"What kind of games?"

Alejandro narrowed his eyes as if he needed to make a point.

"Dalton mostly, he was always causing trouble for Jedediah."

"What kind of trouble?"

"They would steal things from each other, hide things. They would make each other suffer. Food, horses . . . *niñas.*"

"*Niñas?*"

"*Sí,* like now. This is what is happening."

"This has happened before?" I said.

"*Sí.* Dalton had a sweetheart in Silver City. One week we had jobs. We move some sheep for a rancher. We were on our way back to Silver City. We stopped and washed in a creek. Dalton took Jedediah's clothes while Jedediah was in the water. He also took his horse. He left the bridle of Jedediah's horse tied to a tree, but we left with Jedediah's horse. Dalton and me rode back to Silver City and left Jedediah with no clothes and no horse. I told Dalton we must go back and get Jedediah, but Dalton would not. We played seven-up in a cantina that *noche*. Later, when we left the cantina, Dalton's horse is not there and Jedediah's horse is gone also. Dalton's bridle is still tied to the hitch. Dalton was mad, but he became really angry when he was to find out his sweetheart, Otilia, was also not to be found."

"Jedediah took her?"

"*Sí.* They were always trouble for each other."

"Where did he take her?"

"No place," Alejandro said. "He rode around with her. Then, next day, come riding his horse and pulling Dalton's horse with a lead. Otilia was on Dalton's horse. Jedediah dropped the lead and rode on."

"Jedediah have his way with her?" I said.

"Do you mean did he fuck her?"

"Yes," I said.

"No," Alejandro said.

"They share women?" I said.

"No."

"And you think this is what happened, now?"

"Now is different," Alejandro said.

"In what way?" I said.

"They were bad, but they were brothers. After they would do something bad, fight, steal, they would love each other for some time, everything would be no problem. But Alejandro would know, always be ready, this would happen at any moment, like cocks, studs, they would bite . . . Dalton most of the time would win the fights. Finally, Jedediah had a chance to get away. But now, too much has happened, life changed. Dalton spent so much time in Yuma Prison. Jedediah become someone else, acted as though he did not know me. Dalton tried to kill me. This is no game no more, no more boys."

"How did Jedediah get away?"

"After the three of us got caught, the authorities questioned each of us separate. Dalton and me were arrested and Jedediah was not."

"And you never saw Jedediah again," I said.

"No."

"Until you saw him on the street in San Cristóbal just before you killed those two hombres," Virgil said.

"The sonofabitch tried to kill me."

"Well, you have killed, so you can't make a claim you're no killer," Virgil said.

"I never killed a man that did not deserve it."

"Think the thieving business is another situation altogether," Virgil said. "Seems everyone, including the Federales, and Captain Alejandro himself, knows Alejandro is a thief."

"Before the orphanage, I was on the street after my mother was killed. I was just a boy. I had to learn to live the best way I could."

"What about the other two," I said. "Dalton and Jedediah? How did two American boys end up in a Mexico City orphanage?"

"The orphanage is here," Alejandro said.

"In Córdoba?" I said.

237

"*Sí.* They lost their mother and father to sickness," Alejandro said. "Their mother and father were missionaries from America. They had traveled south to heathen country, but they got sick, they died of the terrible plague. Many people died."

"How long were you with them in the orphanage?" I said.

"I was there for two years," he said. "But it was no orphanage! It was a very bad time for us. The orphanage was not a good place. It was dirty hell. We were slaves there, Everett, that is all."

"How'd you get out?" I said.

"We escaped. We were just *niños.* I was only *nueve,* Jedediah was just a year older, and Dalton was two years older than me. We just chose to no longer be slaves. The three of us, we climbed over a very high wall and left."

"Where to?" I said. "Where'd you go?"

"To look for my father."

"I thought your father died in the Guerra de Reforma?" I said.

"He did. Alejandro did not know he was dead when we looked for him. He died in the Reforma at the battle of Antón Lizardo."

"Where?" I said. "Where did you look for your father?"

Alejandro looked to Virgil and then to me.

"Where we will be traveling to tomorrow," he said with a smile.

I pulled a map out of my saddlebag.

"Picked this up in the plaza," I said.

I unfolded the map and spread it out across a small table. I pulled the table close to the bed where Alejandro was shackled so he could have a look.

"Where?" I said.

61

ALEJANDRO LOOKED BACK AND FORTH BETWEEN
Virgil and me.

"Where we are going is not on any map," he said. "*Exactamente* can only be found by Alejandro."

"Don't concern yourself about *exactamente*," I said. "We got you down here and you're taking us where we need to go and there is no going back on that."

Virgil looked at me and nodded a little.

"Where're we going, Alejandro?" I said. "What area on this map?"

Alejandro looked at Virgil and me for a moment, then leaned over, looking at the map. He studied it, and then he placed his free hand flat on the map. Then he made a circle with his finger around where he placed his hand, indicating an area.

"In this area here," Alejandro said.

Virgil and I looked at the map. The area Alejandro circled was the coastal city of Veracruz.

"That's where you went?" I said. "When you were kids and you escaped from the orphanage? You went there to look for your father?"

"*Sí.*"

Virgil looked at me.

"How'd you get from here to there?" I said. "Long travel for kids."

"We stole a horse," he said. "I told Dalton and Jedediah my father would take care of us. He would make soldiers, sailors of us."

Alejandro sat back on the bed and stared at the map for a moment.

"It did not work out like I had planned," he said.

"What happened?" I said.

Alejandro got quiet.

"Alejandro?" I said.

"Took us many days. We went to the ships looking for my father. They were *magnífico*. We find a captain. A very good man, Captain José Chapa. Captain Chapa is not like me, he is a real sea captain. No navy man, but he was fisherman. He was good to us boys. He fed us, and we stayed overnight on his fishing boat. Captain Chapa took me to a naval office. There we learn about my father. Alejandro's father was dead."

Alejandro sat quiet for another moment.

"The navy could not help you boys?" I said.

Alejandro shook his head.

"No, I received my father's jacket and a few mementos, that is all."

"And Captain Chapa," I said. "What of him?"

"He was a busy captain," Alejandro said. "His ship was leaving. Captain Chapa, he left."

Alejandro looked up to Virgil. Virgil remained leaning on the doorjamb. He didn't say anything.

"That is what happened. The three of us were there, Captain Chapa was gone, my father was gone."

Alejandro grinned.

"The jacket, it was left. It was very big, but I wore my father's jacket, no matter. Jedediah and Dalton, they thought it funny Alejandro wearing big navy man's jacket. They started calling me Captain Alejandro, this is how I got the name."

"Where did you boys go?" I said.

"We had no place to go. It was night, we followed a road. The weather was very bad. We found a big hacienda. We hid for many days in a barn, then many weeks. A villa looking over the ocean. We were safe until an hombre found Jedediah stealing food and beat him, bad."

"What hombre?"

"The *propietario* of the villa."

"You were there for weeks and no one knew?" I said.

"*Sí.* The *propietario* was never at the hacienda. Just workers—one very old herder knew but did not care. He brought us fruit."

Alejandro stared at the map as if the past were present.

"This is where everything change for us . . . Dalton and me were hidden in the loft above, watching. Jedediah was hurt, then the hombre tried to take Jedediah—he wanted to, you know, fuck him."

Alejandro looked at us with a serious expression on his face.

"Dalton jumped down from the loft with pitchfork and killed the *propietario.* He stabbed him many times like he was chopping a tree. He continued to stab him until Dalton himself collapsed."

"Then what?" I said.

"Then we left there. We did what we could do to survive after. We were together for many years. We made our way to America."

"Why would Dalton come back here?" I said.

"He told me he would do so."

Virgil looked at me and shook his head.

"He told the hombre when he killed him, too. One day the villa would be his, but the hombre, he was dead."

"Dalton been back here since then?" I said.

"No," Alejandro said.

"Tall lie," Virgil said.

"No lie, Virgil Cole. We loved it there on the ocean."

Virgil looked at me, shaking his head some.

"So what makes you so sure," I said, "Dalton would come here?"

"That Christmas night. When things went bad and Dalton's hombres turned against me and Dalton, too, he turned against me. In San Cristóbal, when Dalton planned to rob the bank. We were drinking. We were all very drunk, talking about what we would do with the money after the robbery. Dalton told me he would do what he always said he would do and he would make the villa his own."

Virgil shook his head some and walked out of the room.

"When were you last there?" I said.

"I have been near there many times, but not back to the hacienda."

"Why have you come back?" I said.

"I told you. Alejandro has many friends. The captain, for one. Captain Chapa is my friend, and I like the ocean . . . The ocean is very beautiful."

"Where is this Captain Chapa?"

"The same place. His fishing boat. He is older now, he drinks too much, but he is still fisherman and Alejandro's friend."

"And this villa," I said, looking at the map. "It is here, in Veracruz?"

"Near Veracruz, but not easy to find."

"We best not get there and you say we need to go someplace else."

"It is there, it is most beautiful place. You will see, most beautiful."

62

⁓

THE SUN WAS SETTING WHEN I WENT OUT INTO the busy plaza to get us some food. In a small café I got us *mole carnitas* with *frijoles*, fruit, and goat cheese, and brought the food back to the room. After we ate, Virgil and I played blackjack for a spell. Later, I walked Alejandro to and from the privy, then locked him back to his bed.

"Alejandro is not going anywhere, Everett," he said, not wanting to be locked up.

"I know."

He continued to complain as I closed the door between him and the main room. I joined Virgil sitting on the balcony. He was smoking a cigar and sipping some tequila.

After a long silence I said, "Here we are."

Virgil smiled and poured me some tequila.

"Long way," I said.

"Damn sure is."

Virgil took a long pull on his cigar. He lifted his head and blew the smoke up.

"You don't think this is some ruse here, do you, Virgil?"

Virgil thought for a moment, then shook his head some.

"The captain is a lot of things," Virgil said. "But I don't think concocting something like this would play in his favor."

I nodded.

"That story he was telling us about looking for his father, what happened in the barn with the pitchfork, the fights, the games, the sweetheart in Silver City, this place," I said. "Seems pretty fertile makings for what has got us down here."

"Does."

"No matter now," I said. "It's what we're doing."

"We are."

"Like Alejandro said himself, though," I said. "There's no guarantee."

Virgil shook his head a little.

"And like you always say," I said. "There never is."

"No, there's not, Everett."

"I reckon it's the best bet," I said.

Virgil smiled.

"I keep telling myself that."

We thought about that as we sat for a bit in the dark, drinking tequila and watching the people in the plaza.

"What do you think about those Federales?" I said.

"Unexpected."

"Was."

"They don't seem to care for Alejandro."

"They don't."

"They don't seem to care for us none, either," I said.

"Don't seem like it."

"The Americano law officials," I said.

"We are."

"Don't like us Americano law officials traipsing around on their Córdoba soil."

"No," Virgil said. "They don't."

"Think they're gonna be a problem for us?" I said.

"Could be," Virgil said.

"The lieutenant speaks good English."

"He does."

"Might prove to be a help, though."

"Might."

"You think he's got other ideas?" I said.

"I do."

"Like what?"

"He thinks two Americanos mean money."

"In exchange for the woman?"

"First thing the lieutenant asked about," Virgil said.

"It was."

Virgil nodded.

"You want to try and get on outta here?" I said. "Slip out tonight without them knowing?"

"Don't," Virgil said. "Don't want to get the whole Mexican police force on our ass. The fewer we got to deal with, the better."

We stopped talking for a bit. Virgil smoked his cigar, and we drank, thinking about the prospect of the situation.

"Regardless," I said. "I hope for the woman's sake we're not pissing in that wind you were talking about."

"Me, too."

"Can't be too pleasant for her," I said.

"No," Virgil said. "Don't imagine it is."

63

THE FOLLOWING MORNING I CAME DOWNSTAIRS an hour before sunrise. The two Federales that had been left to watch us were sleeping when I entered the lobby. I figured, like Virgil said, it best not to try and slip out on them and then find ourselves in a sling with the whole force of Federales. I kicked the boot of the sergeant major a little harder than needed.

"Wake up!" I said.

He looked at me through his dark slits for eyes, and even though he was startled by being abruptly awakened, he showed little sign of concern.

I spoke to him in English but made sure my tone of voice expressed what I was getting at, whether he understood me or not.

"We'll be leaving here in one hour. If your lieutenant and any of the Federales are interested in joining us on the journey, they should get ready right now."

I walked out.

After getting our horses saddled, I brought them to the front of the hotel. Virgil came downstairs, and we drank some coffee in the lobby of the hotel as we waited on the lieutenant.

An hour past sunup we climbed into our saddles when we saw the lieutenant with five of his Federales trotting across the plaza.

"Lieutenant's got him a handful," Virgil said.

"He does," I said.

"Let's keep them in front of us, Everett," Virgil said.

Included in the group were the surly sergeant major, a big heavyset hombre with a few stripes on his shoulder and a grin of silver teeth, and three younger stocky privates that looked like they were brothers. All five were riding dark bay horses that looked fit.

The lieutenant and his men pulled up next to us.

"We don't need to be waiting on you, Lieutenant," Virgil said as he turned Cortez. "We won't do so again."

Before the lieutenant could reply, Virgil clicked Cortez around in a circle behind the lieutenant.

"Lead the way, Lieutenant," Virgil said.

With that we were off, headed for Veracruz.

We traveled up a narrow road leaving Córdoba. It was an old, well-traveled thoroughfare with turns weaving through homes and farms in the hills. By midday we started downhill. We stopped at a small village and rested our horses some. The Federales settled on one side of the road. Virgil, Alejandro, and I settled on the other. Virgil, Alejandro, and I took shade next to an old church. We sat with our backs to the wall. Alejandro poked at some dirt with a stick as he looked to the Federales across the road under the side awning of a feed store.

"Look at them," Alejandro said. "They are like vultures."

"Who did you rob?" I said.

"Alejandro?" he said incredulously.

"*Sí*, Alejandro," I said. "High-profile robbery, the lieutenant said."

"Ah," he said. "The lieutenant is full of shit, simple *exagerando*."

"Simple *exagerando* enough to have him wanting your hide."

"I stole some supplies from one of Maximilian's many leftover conservatives," Alejandro said. "I only took what belong to my people."

"What did you steal?" I said. "What kind of supplies?"

"Everything I could carry that was worth some value."

"How'd the Federales know you?" I said. "Why the warrant?"

"I sold what I took to the wrong person," he said. "Also a conservative."

"Bad move on Alejandro's part," I said.

"*Sí,*" he said. "Alejandro did not know!"

I looked at the Federales. They were eating jerky and drinking from canteens and paying no attention to us.

"When you found out Jedediah was posing as a banker in San Cristóbal," Virgil said, "how did you know to send a wire to Dalton in La Mesilla? How did you know he was there?"

"Before San Cristóbal, I was with Dalton there in La Mesilla."

"And you left him?" Virgil said.

"*Sí,*" he said. "I did not like his shit amigos in La Mesilla."

"Why did you send the wire?" I said.

"I told you," he said. "For years Dalton was looking for Jedediah."

"But why send the wire?" Virgil pressed.

"After everything, all the so many years, we were brothers," Alejandro said. "Jedediah, Dalton, Alejandro were all brothers . . . In San Cristóbal, Jedediah did not even want to know me. This was no *bueno* to act as if he did not recognize me, like he was better than Alejandro."

ROBERT KNOTT

"But why contact Dalton?" I said.

Alejandro poked around in the dirt with a stick.

"I thought it was a good idea to rob the fucking bank," he said as he looked up to us from under his sombrero.

"Why'd Dalton want to cut you out?" Virgil said.

"I don't know. He was bad to many, but not me. He turned on me."

"Thought you were brothers?" I said.

"So did Alejandro. Maybe he turned on me because I left him, I guess. Maybe greed. Maybe gringo amigos, they did not care for the Mexican Alejandro . . . Maybe everything."

"How was it you got into a shootout with them?" Virgil said.

"The night, Christmas, we were drinking, Dalton's amigos point guns at me, laugh, tell me to leave saloon. I left, and they followed me."

"Dalton did not stop them?" I said.

"No," Alejandro said, without looking at us.

"Why?" I said.

"I don't know," Alejandro said with a shrug.

"And that's when you shot them?" Virgil said.

"The bastards tell me to get on my horse. They shot at me. At first I think to scare me. But then they shot close. I shot back. Alejandro is a good shot. Better. Steady. Not scared. And Alejandro hit them both."

"You said Dalton shot at you?"

Alejandro nodded as he poked in the dirt.

"He damn sure did. He come out and shot at me . . . tried to kill me. I already tell you, Dalton is most likely the Diablo himself."

250

64

WE LEFT THE SMALL VILLAGE AND RODE ON TO
Veracruz. We passed farms, ranches, and homes along the road. It
was dark as we neared the city. The breeze in our faces carried the
salty smell of the ocean, and the air was getting cooler as we rode.
We were moving slowly, approaching the city, and began to see the
lights below. Alejandro rode his tall tricolored medicine-hat gelding with the one blue eye twenty feet in front of Virgil and me as
we descended the narrow road and the Federales led the way.

The lieutenant dropped back from the Federales and sidled up
next to Virgil and me.

"We will be into Veracruz central very soon," he said.

Virgil didn't say anything.

"This is a long way you have traveled," the lieutenant said.

"Is," Virgil said.

"Who are these hombres you are after?"

Virgil said, "Abductors."

"And this a wealthy woman they abducted?"

"She's a wife," Virgil said. "A daughter."

"This wife, this daughter, must be very special?"

"She is."

"Worth a lot of money?"

Virgil didn't say anything.

"Why did you say there is no price for her return?"

"I told you, Lieutenant, no price. No ransom."

"You said that, but I'd expect you'd have mention of a reward."

"Hard to know what you'd expect," Virgil said politely.

"I'm disappointed in you, Marshal."

"What's your disappointment, Lieutenant?"

"Marshal, you should disclose all the necessary information."

"Told you all there is concerning this matter, Lieutenant."

"Yes, with no mention of the money," the lieutenant said.

"It's against the law to take somebody that don't want to be took," Virgil said. "We are here to enforce the law, to find this woman."

"Every woman has a price," he said. "Every father, too."

Virgil didn't reply.

We rode in silence for a bit.

"So you know from your prisoner," the lieutenant said, "where we are to find these hombres and this woman?"

"We do," Virgil said.

"Where?"

"We'll know when we get there."

"Tonight?"

"No."

"Why not tonight?"

"Not a good idea," I said.

"It's not," Virgil said.

"Why?"

"Don't know the lay of the land," Virgil said.

"Would it not be wise to have the element of surprise in our favor?" the lieutenant said.

"Need to know what we are getting into," Virgil said. "In the light of day. You know that, Lieutenant."

"Of course," he said.

We rode for a bit before the lieutenant felt the need to apply his authority.

"You need to know. I mean no disrespect to you, but this is my jurisdiction."

"Point being?" Virgil said.

"What I say goes."

"What would you say?" Virgil said.

"This is not America."

"We're fully aware of where we are, Lieutenant," Virgil said.

"I just would not want you to get the wrong idea."

"Never do," Virgil said.

"Then we will proceed as I command."

"What would you command?"

"*Mañana*, once I have assessed the situation, I will let you know."

"You do that," Virgil said. "Just make sure you don't get in our way of doing what we came down here to do."

"Just remember where you are, Marshal."

"That's real easy, Lieutenant."

"Good," the lieutenant said.

The lieutenant pulled out a piece of paper from his pocket. He unfolded it and handed it to Virgil.

"This wire, from a Mr. Jantz Wainwright, you may find helpful."

65

⁓

"I KNOW IT IS DARK," THE LIEUTENANT SAID. "I don't expect you to be able to see this notice, but I know you will find it interesting. Perhaps you already know of this notice from Mr. Jantz Wainwright? It is an offer of a reward for the return of this woman, Catherine."

We did not reply as we rode for a bit.

"The wire was sent to a Mexico wire service," the lieutenant said. "It's from her father, of course, this Mr. Jantz Wainwright, offering a generous reward for the return of his daughter. It provides her description and all the necessary information. There is more detail, something about a bank robbery. All this you, of course, know, but I thought you might want to see this, no matter. Such a crime, *mis amigos*, such a terrible crime, but not to worry, we will help you find her."

"We appreciate your help, Lieutenant," Virgil said.

"Mexico is here to help you."

The lieutenant spurred his mount and moved on. He passed Alejandro and rode to the front and led the way with the other Federales.

Alejandro was well ahead of us and heard nothing of the exchange with the lieutenant.

"Goddamn," Virgil said.

"This is not good, Virgil."

"No," he said. "Don't think it is."

"Not only do they think we're carrying ransom money, now they have the prospect of a reward and potential robbery money to boot."

"They do."

"Now we know if the Federales are help or trouble," I said.

"Thanks to Jantz Wainwright," Virgil said.

"You called it," I said.

"Didn't expect this, though," Virgil said.

"Me, neither."

"Wainwright fucked up."

"Wonder why the lieutenant went this long with us?" I said. "Not saying anything?"

"Don't know."

"He could have just carried on with Alejandro searching for her."

"He could."

"Could want to make sure we don't know something he don't."

"Could be."

"Maybe he's thinking there's too much work left to be done."

"Gun work?" Virgil said.

"Yep. If there is a fight with Dalton, it makes better sense for them to wait and let us do the fighting."

"It does, but sense and this bunch don't go hand in hand."

"One way or the other, they'll not want us around for the tally."

"No," Virgil said. "I don't think they will."

"Then they don't need us."

"They don't."

"Won't need Alejandro, either," I said.

"No, after the ball drops, they won't," Virgil said.

"If by chance they were to come out on top when all this is all over, they might want to take Alejandro in for pride's sake."

"Don't think they'd go to the fucking trouble," Virgil said.

"Probably just kill him."

"Along with us," Virgil said.

"What do you figure we do?"

"Don't let 'em," Virgil said.

66

〜

WHEN WE ARRIVED IN VERACRUZ IT WAS NINE IN the evening. Once again we boarded in a hotel; it was a small single-story wooden place by the Plaza de la Aduana on the docks, and the place smelled of fish. We'd had no more conversation with the lieutenant or any of his Federales. We kept a close eye on them as we boarded the horses and got squared away.

After we got into a room, I watched the Federales from the window as they gathered across from the hotel on the porch of a dock cantina. They took seats around an oval table under a tiled awning.

The room we settled in was not large. It was full of narrow bunks, and from the smell of the place, it most likely was a shacking room for itinerant sailors.

In case we needed to move quickly, I let Alejandro sit on one of the bunks without being shackled to anything. Alejandro looked at me with gratitude, but I didn't say anything to satisfy his appreciation.

Virgil and I sat at a table near the window, where I had a clear view of the Federales at the cantina. Virgil lit a cigar, and after he got it going good, he opened up the telegram the lieutenant had handed to him. It was in Spanish. He read it a bit, then looked at me.

"Fifty thousand," he said, shaking his head slightly.

"Not good," I said.

"Lot of money."

"Is."

Virgil slid the telegram across the table to me.

"Your Spanish is better," he said.

I picked up the note and read it out loud.

" 'Fifty-thousand-dollar reward for the return of an American woman from San Cristóbal.' "

"*What?*" Alejandro said with a surprised tone of voice. "What? What's this?"

We looked to Alejandro.

"*This, this is no good!*" Alejandro said excitedly. "This is no good at all, Virgil Cole."

Virgil looked at me. It was clear he agreed with Alejandro.

"All of Mexico will kill for this," Alejandro said.

He gestured to the Federales.

"Especially the fucking Federales. They will kill you, too."

"Nobody is killing anybody," Virgil said. "Not at the moment they are not, so don't go acting like it."

"Virgil Cole," Alejandro said, shaking his head, "if I show Federales where to go, they will kill Alejandro *un minuto después*. If Alejandro does not find them, they will also kill him. Alejandro will be dead, no matter!"

"Go on, Everett," Virgil said.

I continued reading: " 'Dateline Mexico. June fifth notice: attention all news agencies and law authorities. Abducted American woman is believed to be in Mexico, near Mexico City.' "

Alejandro sat on the bunk with his elbows on his knees. He was shaking his head, looking at the floor as I continued to read.

" 'Be on the lookout for Catherine Wainwright Strode, twenty-five, five-foot-three, strawberry-blond hair, green eyes, and pale complexion. U.S. authorities, led by Marshal Virgil Cole and Deputy Marshal Everett Hitch, are in pursuit of Mrs. Strode. Her abductor is Dalton McCord, thirty-five, six feet, dark brown hair, blue eyes.' "

"Virgil Cole," Alejandro said, looking up. "This is very bad."

I looked to Virgil.

"The worst part is yet to come."

"The bank?" Virgil said.

I nodded.

"Get to it," Virgil said.

" 'Dalton is also wanted for the robbery of the Comstock Bank located in San Cristóbal in the New Mexico Territories.' "

"That it?" Virgil said.

"Yep," I said.

"Holy hell, this is very stupid," Alejandro said. "We will all die."

"Ellsworth, Everett," Virgil said. "He must have played his hand in orchestrating this reward business with Wainwright."

"Providing the description of Dalton?" I said.

"Yeah," Virgil said. "Ellsworth said he saw Catherine talking to a man on the street."

"He did."

"They thought they're doing the right thing," Virgil said.

"Well," Alejandro said with a huff. "Whoever you are speaking of, they do not know Mexicans. Now the whole of Mexico will be looking! All this money! It will be like hunting for treasure."

67

"HOW FAR, ALEJANDRO?" VIRGIL SAID. "TO this villa where we're headed?"

"What does not matter? How will we get out of this alive?"

"How far?" Virgil said.

"Not far," Alejandro said, shaking his head. "Two-hour ride, maybe a little more."

I pulled the map out and spread it on the table.

"Now is the time, Captain," Virgil said. "Where is this place?"

"I know what you are thinking," Alejandro said. "They will kill me, and then you and Everett will need to know."

"Right now," Virgil said, "they need you more than they need us."

"If they kill us, then it's just you and them," I said.

"I believe what you said is right, Alejandro," Virgil said. "After they find out what they need from you, they will no longer need you."

I nodded.

"Virgil and I are your best bet for getting out of this alive."

"So let's not fuck around here anymore," Virgil said. "Where, Alejandro?"

Alejandro looked back and forth between Virgil and me for a moment. Then he lifted off the bunk and moved close to the map. He leaned over, looking carefully at the map for a moment.

"I told you. This is on no map . . . but it is near here . . ."

He pointed to an island.

"This should be the Isla del Toro, here," Alejandro said, cocking his head slightly. "Across from the island, right here, there is a point, cliffs, not on this map, but here, I think this is it, here."

"You think?"

"Yes, Everett, that is what I think from looking at this worthless map. Where Alejandro goes is where he knows to go, and it is not on any map. But there is a point here, a large bluff into the ocean. This side of that bluff there is a river that flows from the mountains to the ocean here. Up this winding river there will be a place for us to cross. Then we go up a ways, this is where we are going. This is where the villa is. It is Villa del Toro."

"Villa del Toro?" I said.

"*Sí.*"

"How many roads into this villa?" Virgil said.

Alejandro shook his head.

"From this side, there are no roads. The entrance to the villa hacienda comes from the opposite side. The road in is a coast road south," Alejandro said, pointing to the map. "You will see this bluff I am telling you about—it is a wall that runs from the ocean up the south side of this river."

Virgil pointed to the map on the south side.

"Why don't we come in this way and miss the river and bluff altogether," Virgil said.

"This is a mountain here," Alejandro said. "To travel around this

261

and come in from the road would take weeks. Where Alejandro say we come into the hacienda, from the river is the only way in, and it is a narrow way in. Us three boys never traveled that road south. We came from this way I'm telling you."

"Is there another way in from here?" Virgil said, pointing to the shoreline. "Across the river, coming up from the coast?"

"No, there is the cliff. It rises from the ocean and follows the river on the south. It's too high, too rough. There is just this, the river that comes from the mountains. When we *muchachos* went there the first time, the water was low. But it rained while we were there and the river got difficult to cross. It could be like that now. This is how we would come and go when we moved about. We were never even on the road south into the hacienda. I don't even know where that goes. It connects to a city on the other side of the mountain. A city I've never even been. We three would leave before it was light and cross the river and return after dark."

"Where would you go?" I said.

Alejandro shrugged.

"Everywhere . . . nowhere. Looking for food."

We stayed, looking at the map some.

"We are here?" I said, pointing to the docks.

"*Sí,* and Rio Toro is close to here, Villa del Toro is here."

"You are sure?"

"*Sí.* As sure as I can be looking at this, Everett, but Alejandro knows where we are going."

"Villa del Toro," I said.

"*Sí.*"

"Bull Villa."

"*Sí.*"

"And up through here runs Bull River," I said.

"*Sí.* It can very much be a bull, too. If not for Jedediah, Alejandro would have drown in Bull River, but he catch me."

Alejandro shook his head some.

"And who would ever know, many years later, Jedediah would never remember Alejandro."

"Everything looked well watered, riding from Córdoba," Virgil said.

"Did," I said. "Looks like there's been plenty of rain in this country. Might be full."

"*Sí.* Bull River can be furious mad and very hard to cross, but Alejandro knows how."

"How far up before we cross?" I said.

"A few miles maybe," Alejandro said, "there we will find is the best place to cross. It might be easy, it might not be easy."

I sat back in my chair as Virgil looked at the map more closely. I'd been keeping an eye out the window, watching the Federales across the way on the porch of the cantina. One of them pulled away from the others and started walking toward our room.

"Here we go, Virgil," I said.

Virgil looked out the window.

"We got company," I said.

"Oh, shit," Alejandro said quietly. "Oooh, shit."

68

········· ᵔᵔ ·········

I KEPT AN EYE ON THE FEDERAL AS HE WALKED
closer to the hotel.

"That Federal don't got a pistol in his hand, does he, Everett?"

I shook my head, and then we heard the Federal's boots on the hotel room porch followed by a knock on our door.

Virgil opened the door.

"Buenas tardes," the Federal said politely.

"What can I do for you?" Virgil said.

"Lieutenant, he tell me, he like for you and your deputy to join with him," the Federal said.

"Join with him for what?"

"He would like to purchase you and your deputy refreshment."

"All six of you over there?" Virgil said.

"Perdóneme?" he said.

"All your *compadres* at that table?" Virgil said, then called quickly to me. "Count them, Everett."

I looked out the window and counted the heads of the Federales.

"Six total, including the hombre standing in front of you," I said.

"Good," Virgil said. "Tell the lieutenant we'll be right over."

Virgil closed the door.

"The invitation is for you and Everett," Alejandro said. "It is okay, Alejandro will just stay here."

"Think they're calling us out?" I said.

"Could be," Virgil said.

"One thing is for certain," Virgil said. "So far, we've not given them a chance to get the jump on us."

"Think this is it?" I said.

"Don't think so," Virgil said, "but no reason not to be ready."

"They could pull on us."

"They could at that," Virgil said.

"Maybe they want to try and get us over there so they can come and get Alejandro," I said.

"Very well could be," Virgil said. "They could pull on us and grab Alejandro."

"Maybe Alejandro should have refreshments with you and Everett," Alejandro said.

"Not just Alejandro they are interested in," I said. "They'd like to scour our belongings, too."

"Yep," Virgil said.

"They think we got ransom money," I said.

"They do."

"What do you think is their best option?" I said. "Now, tonight, tomorrow?"

"This might well be it," Virgil said.

"They could wait until the middle of the night and try to ambush us."

"They'd risk killing Alejandro," Virgil said, "if they unloaded on us here in a dark room."

"Might be like we were thinking, though," I said. "Maybe they want to let us sort things out with Dalton. Let us do the fighting."

Virgil thought for a moment, then nodded.

"I do think that," Virgil said.

"I think at the center, they are a lazy bunch," I said.

"I think that, too," Virgil said. "Just need to keep in mind lazy dogs can bite."

"Yep, and there's every reason not to think this refreshment invitation is entirely social," I said.

"There's every reason and then some."

"Get ready?" I said.

"We do," Virgil said.

Virgil pulled his second Colt from his saddlebag and loaded it.

"Leave the eight-gauge," Virgil said. "No reason to bait the situation, but do get your second behind you."

I nodded and got my second Colt and cartridges from my saddlebag and started loading it.

Alejandro looked back and forth between Virgil and me as we loaded our second pistols.

"What about me?"

"You're coming with us," Virgil said.

"Mother Mary. Perhaps Alejandro should just stay?"

"Perhaps not," Virgil said.

"But Virgil Cole, there are six *hombres Federales* over there," Alejandro said.

"There are," Virgil said.

"You cannot go against six hombres alone!"

"I'm not alone. Everett is with me, and you will be, too."

"What about a *pistola* for Alejandro. I cannot be of any help with these."

Alejandro held up his shackles.

"Sure you will," Virgil said. "They will be less likely to pull on us with you in the middle."

"The middle?" Alejandro said.

"*Sí,*" Virgil said. "We'll stay close together and walk over there with you in the middle."

Alejandro shook his head.

"Better than you staying here and them coming to get you," I said.

"'Sides," Virgil said, "if they do want to share refreshments, it'd be best if you don't have no *pistola* in your hand."

Virgil secured his second Colt behind his back, and I did the same with my second Colt.

"How do you want to go about this?" I said.

"You stay on the right," Virgil said. "Alejandro in the middle. I'll be on the left. If we find ourselves in a have-to situation, I will take the three on the left, you take the three on the right."

"Mother Mary, sweet Jesus," Alejandro said.

"Let's go," Virgil said.

"What if they only want to drink?" Alejandro said.

Virgil took a final pull of his cigar, then placed it in the seashell ashtray sitting on the table.

"We will drink," Virgil said. "Friendly-like."

69

〜〜

I OPENED THE DOOR AND WE WALKED OUT OF THE
room. As Virgil instructed, I was on the right, Alejandro was in the
middle, and Virgil was on the left. One hundred feet away, the six
Federales huddled around the table on the cantina porch. As we got
closer, it sounded as if they were talking quietly, then the Federales
laughed loudly as we neared.

"Be ready," Virgil said quietly.

"Oh, shit," Alejandro said under his breath.

The lieutenant turned, smiling at us. He stood, and instead of
pulling on us, he held out his arms like he was a welcoming relative.

"Welcome, Marshal Cole. Deputy," he said loudly. "Good of you
to join us. And look! You brought the prisoner. I'm glad you
brought the prisoner, too. Please sit."

The lieutenant barked at a few Federales to get us chairs. They
did, and we sat. He barked at another to get glasses and pour us
some rum. The heavyset silver-toothed Federal sat with his arms
crossed on one side of the lieutenant, and the slit-eyed sergeant
major sat on the other.

"I know you think I'm interested in the money and that is all,
but I assure you that is not the case," the lieutenant said, smiling.

Virgil didn't say anything.

"How many hombres are with this bank robber, Dalton McCord?"

"Don't know for sure," Virgil said.

"You asked me not to get in your way."

"I did."

"That is what we will do."

"Good."

"Marshal, what I said about remembering where you are is just that we, too, have law, and it is my responsibility to enforce the law here, just as you enforce the law in America. As I mentioned before, this is my jurisdiction, so I ask you to please be respectful of my authority."

"Will do," Virgil said.

"Do you have a strategy for tomorrow?"

"Not much to strategize," Virgil said.

"But you have some kind of plan?"

"Do," Virgil said. "What to expect is, of course, unknown. We'll let you know how it shakes out."

"Oh," the lieutenant said with a smile, "we won't just sit here and wait on you. We will be there with you, Marshal, every step of the way."

"All right," Virgil said.

The lieutenant took a sip of his rum and smiled.

"I did some investigating of my own," the lieutenant said.

"What sort of investigating?" Virgil said.

"The bank robbery in America," the lieutenant said, "in San Cristóbal."

"What of it?"

"It seems this Dalton McCord got away with a very large sum of money."

Virgil didn't say anything.

"So why did he also take the woman?" the lieutenant said.

"Wouldn't know," Virgil said.

"If he robbed so much money," the lieutenant said, "why the risk of ransom?"

"Told you," Virgil said. "There is no ransom."

"Yes," the lieutenant said. "I'm sorry, I forgot."

Virgil nodded.

"Then why did he take the woman if there is no ransom?"

"Hard to know that, Lieutenant."

"Her father, this Mr. Wainwright, has also offered a big reward," the lieutenant said.

Virgil nodded some.

"Read about that," Virgil said.

"Just know, Marshal, money or no money, we are only here to help you find this woman."

"Mr. Wainwright will be grateful," Virgil said. "Me, too."

The lieutenant smiled some as he turned his glass of rum. Then he leveled a friendly gaze at Virgil.

"So," he said, "where will we be traveling tomorrow?"

"Alejandro here is the pathfinder," Virgil said. "He will lead the way."

The lieutenant looked to Alejandro but spoke to Virgil.

"Has he provided you a map, directions, et cetera?"

"We know where we are going," Virgil said.

"What if something unfortunate were to happen to your prisoner?" the lieutenant said.

"Like what?" Virgil said.

"I don't know," the lieutenant said. "I just want to be cautious and respectful of this young woman's life, that's all."

"I don't intend for nothing unfortunate to happen to Alejandro," Virgil said.

The lieutenant took a sip of rum and looked at Alejandro for a long moment.

"So he's provided some details?"

Virgil looked to Alejandro.

"Oh, he's said some, but he's not provided the necessary details," said Virgil.

Alejandro smiled.

The lieutenant looked back to Virgil.

"I want you to know, Marshal. My hombres and me know our people and this country, so we will be an asset in every respect."

"Good," Virgil said.

"I want us to be helpful for each other," the lieutenant said.

He held up his glass.

Virgil lifted his up some, and I did, too. We took a sip.

"More rum," the lieutenant said to one of his men.

"Might have us another nudge," Virgil said, "but seeing how this is your jurisdiction, I should make you aware of one thing."

"What is that, Marshal?"

"We'll be leaving two hours before sunrise," Virgil said, "so you might want to go easy on the rum."

The lieutenant laughed. The heavyset silver-toothed Federal laughed, and the slit-eyed sergeant major did not so much as grin.

70

AFTER SOME TIME IN THE CANTINA IT WAS CLEAR what the lieutenant's coyote-like intentions were. He was more interested in his evening rum and the prospect of us doing any gun work that needed to be done. It was obvious to us the lieutenant wanted to reassure us of his authority and his utmost interest in helping us find Catherine, but there was no doubt in our minds he was as untrustworthy as the day was long.

The next morning, two hours before sunrise, we tended to the horses and got ready to ride. The animals were in a corral divided by a long open shed. Virgil, Alejandro, and I had our horses on one side, and the Federales had theirs on the other.

The lieutenant and his men were slowly getting up and readying themselves to ride. It was certain they hadn't heeded Virgil's warning. They sounded rum rough. I was watching one of the hands. He was moving unsteadily, and I heard another one of them somewhere coughing up a gulletful of last night's libation.

We were not the only ones up at this early hour. In the distance down the dock from the hotel I could see lanterns moving and hear the echoing voices of the fishermen as they readied their boats.

Alejandro placed the saddle blankets on his medicine-hat as he eyed the Federales on the other side of the shed.

"Once Alejandro leads us to where we are going," Alejandro said, "what will make them not just kill me then and there?"

"Me," Virgil said, "and Everett."

"You will try."

"More than try."

"There are six."

"I know."

Alejandro picked up his saddle.

"And why would you do that, Virgil Cole? Why try and save Alejandro?"

"Our arrangement," Virgil said.

Alejandro put the saddle on his medicine-hat.

"You remember our arrangement, don't you, Alejandro?"

"*Sí*," he said. "Proof."

Alejandro situated the saddle where he wanted it.

"That's right, prove yourself," Virgil said. "Dalton proved himself to be a no-good. Your chance to prove yourself *not* to be a no-good is why you are here with Everett and me. You do that, you prove yourself, then we've both honored our arrangement."

"*Sí,* honor," he said, "arrangement."

Alejandro flipped the left stirrup into the saddled seat, reached under the hat horse, got the cinch, looped it, and started snugging it tight.

Since the day we'd left San Cristóbal, Alejandro managed his own horse business, and he did so without complaint. He took good care of his tack and his medicine-hat with the blue eye. The hat's name was Comanche, but Alejandro called him Man or Hombre

273

when the hat was acting up or when Comanche didn't want to do something Alejandro wanted him to do. Alejandro had gotten to be a pretty good hand at managing his business while wearing shackles.

"Arrangement or not," Alejandro said, tilting his head toward the Federales, "they will honor nothing."

"The Federales got one thing on their mind at the moment," Virgil said. "You just do what you come down here to do, and me and Everett will do everything we can to square up the rest."

Alejandro looked across the back of Comanche to Virgil.

"Virgil Cole, I told you what I believe, where Dalton said he would go, what he would do. Dalton told me more than once. Jedediah will know this, too. I did not tell Jedediah, but he knows. How he knows, I'm not sure—maybe this wife told him, maybe Dalton baited him like pork for crawfish, maybe he just knows. But I am sure of one thing: they have done this, they have been nose to nose with each other every day of their life, no matter if they are face-to-face or not. Like scorpion and fiddler. You said you want Alejandro to prove himself."

Alejandro pulled a rosary from his pocket and pitched it in the dirt at Virgil's feet.

"My mother's. I took this from her as she was dying on the floor . . . Alejandro is here to do what you asked, and I'm shackled like a slave, a target for Federales, for everyone, anyone, without defense."

Virgil did not reply, and Alejandro talked no more as we continued to ready ourselves to ride.

Virgil scooped the rosary out of the dirt and climbed atop Cortez. He rode to the opposite side of the shed and spoke to the Federales.

"Let's get mounted, Lieutenant, hombres," Virgil said. "Ready to ride."

Virgil rode back around to our side, where Alejandro and I were finishing up with our horses.

"Everett," Virgil said quietly and with a matter-of-fact tone, "get them shackles off Alejandro and give him your dingus."

"Will do."

I unlocked the irons from Alejandro's wrists.

"Don't make you a free man, Captain," Virgil said as he pitched the rosary back to Alejandro, "but it makes you a whole lot closer to being so, providing you don't fuck up."

I pulled my derringer from my breast vest pocket and handed it to Alejandro.

"Do not under any circumstances pull that out unless you have to use it," Virgil said. "You *comprende?*"

"*Sí.*"

"You try and use it on me or Everett," Virgil said, "you will most assuredly be killed by me or Everett."

"*Comprendo*, Virgil Cole," Alejandro said as he stuffed the derringer into the pocket of his jacket.

Virgil turned Cortez for the gate.

"Virgil Cole? Alejandro has much respect for you and Everett Hitch. You are *mis amigos*. I will do my best for you."

Virgil rode Cortez to the gate of the corral. He reached down, lifted the chain loop from the gate, and swung the gate open. Within a few minutes, and just as Virgil had proclaimed, we took off, two hours before sunup, and were headed for Bull River.

71

⌒⌒

ALEJANDRO LED THE WAY AS WE RODE SOUTH through the narrow streets of Veracruz until we were out of the town and clear of structures. The temperature was pleasant, the air crisp, and the crescent moon provided us with enough light to make our way. We worked the horses down a rocky road toward the ocean and turned onto a well-traveled path that followed the water's edge.

We rode the winding trail for almost an hour before the morning began to show light and the Gulf shoreline started coming to life.

It had been a long time since I'd seen the ocean. It was an impressive sight, and we watched the gathering light across the water as the sun made its way over the surface.

The sea was calm, and it was very quiet except for the calls of the gulls and the every-so-often wave that dropped with a thud on the sandy shore. Up ahead in the far distance it appeared the beach ended in a massive wall of rock that rose out of the ocean.

We continued on the path, riding for about thirty minutes, when the lieutenant held up, waiting for Virgil and me.

Virgil was riding just behind me, the last of the line of horsemen.

"Why is the prisoner no longer shackled?" the lieutenant said.

"Took them off," Virgil said.

"I can see that," the lieutenant said. "Why?"

"We need him," Virgil said.

"For what?"

"For leading us to where we need to go."

"I'm fully aware of that, Marshal," the lieutenant said with a smile, "but there is no need for him not to be shackled."

"There is," Virgil said. "Don't want him getting into a situation where he could no longer be alive to assist us."

"What sort of a situation are you referring to, Marshal?"

"For one," Virgil said, "we're going to cross a river."

"He's nothing but a desperado, interested in getting away."

"I know who he is."

"My concern is he will lead us into a situation and will try to run."

"Understand your concern," Virgil said, "but I don't think that."

"Have you thought maybe this is a trap?"

"I think things through, and I think it best he's not ironed."

"Well," the lieutenant said. "You don't want him getting away."

"He won't."

"What makes you so sure?"

"We got five Federales, six counting you, on fine, fleet-looking horses that won't let him get away," Virgil said.

"Let me remind you. Not only is he wanted in America, he is wanted in Mexico, and after this is over, he will be in my custody."

"Appreciate it."

"What?"

"Reminding me."

"Don't push your luck with me, Marshal."

"Luck don't got nothing to do with this," Virgil said.

The lieutenant shook his head.

"We are here for one reason—a woman's life is in danger, Marshal."

He gaffed his bay horse and rode ahead.

"Likes to puff up his feathers, don't he?" I said.

"He does."

"Exercise his authority."

"Yep."

"He's not very good at it."

"No, he's not."

"One minute seems like he's got a play, next he acts like he don't."

"If I was to bet on the come, I'd say he's got a play."

The wall ahead of us we had been riding toward was now in clear view. It was a massive rock bluff, and just this side of the bluff were washed sections of shoreline where river waters spread out into small streams that spilled into the ocean.

Alejandro stopped. He looked back to us, pointed west, and turned Comanche inland.

The southern side of the river was as Alejandro said: a rock wall that looked to be fifty feet high. We trailed out behind Alejandro as he rode west up the northern bank of the river. We rode for a ways and eventually the waters narrowed as we gradually made our way upgrade. It was not a long ride before we found the river to be full and swift. We followed the edge as the river continued to narrow even more. We wound our way through rocky hills, and after a while we were in forest. The river was not wide, but it was full of powerful swift-moving water.

"Bull River," I said.

"Looks like a goddamn bull."

"Does," I said.

72

⁓

WE CONTINUED ON FOR A WAYS, FOLLOWING THE wild whitewater river, then stopped when Alejandro stopped.

"A ways ahead will be the best place to cross," Alejandro said.

The sun was fully up now. I could feel the heat from it shining through the trees. It hovered above the ocean to our left as we edged our way close to the narrow and loud river. The place in the river Alejandro had approached was wide, and the water appeared to be deep.

Alejandro turned Comanche to face us.

"Be best to swim them here," Alejandro said.

"Swim them?" the lieutenant said.

"*Sí,*" Alejandro said.

"There have been plenty of low-water crossing we have passed," the silver-toothed Federal said with a rough voice and thick Latino accent. "We will be best to find footing at a wide ford and walk them."

"Go ahead," Alejandro said.

Alejandro walked Comanche to where Virgil and I sat our horses.

"This is best here," Alejandro said. "Put in here in the high section of full water. The water is moving fast, we need to be fast across. Across before we get pushed downriver to the white rocks. I can go first."

"No," the lieutenant said.

"Okay," Alejandro said. "After you."

"There has to be a better crossing," the lieutenant said.

"I'll go first," I said. "Alejandro, you come behind me."

I removed my bandana, tucked it under my hat, and nudged my horse to the water's edge at the top of the full water section. He was resistant, but I stayed persistent, and within moments we were in the water. The water was cold and moving fast. I hung on to my saddle horn, urging him insistently, and within a minute of time we emerged out of the water on the opposite side.

I looked back, and Alejandro and Comanche were already in the water. Virgil followed on Cortez with no problem, and the first of the six Federales, the big silver-toothed hombre, was right behind him. He, too, made it. The others followed, including the lieutenant, and within a short time we were all now on the south bank of Bull River.

We took time to shed as much water as we could. We shook our firearms, exposing them in the breeze, blew out the chambers, and dried them with the bandanas we'd tucked inside our hats. After we got situated, we mounted up and continued our way to the Villa del Toro.

We weaved our way south some, through tall trees full of loud and exotic birds. They were squawking and crying as they darted around above us in the shining sun of the new day. The wind was picking up as we rode uphill. When we got near the top of the rise it was blowing strong coming up off the ocean.

Alejandro stopped Comanche and looked back to Virgil.

"This is it. Just over this hill here."

"What is it that is just over?" the lieutenant said.

Alejandro did not answer the lieutenant. He turned Comanche and maneuvered him next to Virgil.

"The barn is just there, Virgil Cole," Alejandro said with a point. "The casa is this way, toward the ocean."

"Let's tie up here," Virgil said. "Lieutenant, be better than a good idea not to have everyone in this party come along."

The lieutenant looked up the rise and shook his head.

"No," the lieutenant said. "It will be best we stay together."

Virgil didn't say anything. He checked his Colt and started walking up. The Federales readied their pistols, I pulled my eight-gauge from the scabbard, and we all started up. Virgil stopped and turned to everyone.

"Silencio," Virgil said. "Silencio."

The men nodded. Virgil turned and continued walking up.

We walked up through dense vanilla with wide, waxy leaves that supported clumps of fragrant long beans and soon began to reach the top of the rise.

We could see through the trees a clearing ahead where the sun shone fully, and Alejandro and Virgil were the first of our party to crest the rise. They stopped, and in a moment all of us were looking to the open area where the sun shone brightly.

"¡Ay!" Alejandro said quietly. "This cannot be."

"This is it?" the lieutenant said under his breath. "This? This is the destination? You have come this far to find this woman here?"

"You sure we crossed at the right place?" I said. "This is it?"

"*Sí,* Virgil Cole. Alejandro does not know what to say."

"I do," the lieutenant said. "In America, Marshal, I believe the proper phrase is *railroaded*. We have been railroaded."

73

A HUNDRED YARDS AWAY, ALEJANDRO AND THE rest of us were looking at nothing but ruins of an old home place. What most likely was once a beautiful hacienda was now a long-forgotten overgrown acreage with dilapidated structures.

"Virgil Cole," Alejandro said. "I am very sorry."

"Some Mexicans give my country a bad name," the lieutenant said with a snarl.

Alejandro just shook his head, looking out at the hacienda.

"You do not fool me," the lieutenant said.

The rock walls of the huge main house were still standing, but from what we could see, they were covered with overgrowing ivy and the roof was gone. It appeared the place had burnt. Next to the main house was a carriage house. It still had its roof, but its insides brimmed with weeds that filled the windows and entrance.

"I warned you, Marshal," the lieutenant said with a low, groaning voice, "your pathfinder is no pathfinder. He is a common desperado and no more."

The lieutenant looked to Alejandro.

"You brought these lawmen to Mexico all this way for this?" the lieutenant said, shaking his head. "You will most certainly regret what you have done here."

Virgil stepped out a ways.

"Let's stay quiet," Virgil said. "Everyone, stay quiet."

"For what purpose?" the lieutenant said with an obliged low growl. "There is nothing here. What do you expect to find out here, Marshal?"

"Don't know."

In the distance, beyond the big house, stood a tall-gated entrance. The gates were missing, but the arch over the road leading to the house was still intact.

The large sloping acreage was bordered with a low rock wall, and within it there were weed-covered stone paths that probably once bordered gardens and orchards, but now only tall weeds and crippled fruit trees remained.

We could see the ocean, the curve of the earth, even from where we were, but this property that once had life and beauty was no longer.

The wooden barn was close to us, just to our right. It was upright, but it, too, was in bad shape, with missing doors and sections of its roof.

"Just follow me," Virgil said quietly. "Let's just have us a proper look-see."

Virgil moved slowly, walking toward the barn. Everyone followed him across the weeded corral and into the wide opening of the back side of the barn.

I looked at Alejandro. He was looking around the barn, shaking his head a little.

I thought of the story he had told us about the proprietor

beating young Jedediah in this barn, wanting to do bad things to him, and thought maybe this was a fitting end for this estate. Then again, I thought, maybe the lieutenant was correct. What if this whole thing was just concocted by Alejandro? Either way, we were here, and for the moment it seemed this whole endeavor was for naught and a waste of time.

With the exception of rusted farming tools and pigeons nesting in the rafters, the barn was empty.

The loft posts were missing, most likely rummaged at some point, and the whole top loft section bowed like an eroded hillside, making the barn's sides fold as if they were being pulled by a giant corset.

"So, Marshal Cole," the lieutenant said, with continued heed for Virgil's request for quiet. "Like my cousin, I am much smarter than I look."

"That's good," Virgil said without looking at the lieutenant.

The lieutenant looked to Alejandro.

"You do not expect me to fall for what Mr. Vasquez has done here, do you?"

Virgil was looking toward the big house and did not glance to the lieutenant as he answered.

"Right now, I don't expect much of anything out of you, Lieutenant."

Virgil remained looking toward the house as he stepped out the front side of the barn.

"Virgil?" I said.

"Yep."

Virgil looked back to me.

"You see what I see?"

"I do."

"What?" the lieutenant said. "What do you see?"

"Might not be now," I said, "but not long ago, there was some-body in here."

The lieutenant looked around.

"What are you talking about?" the lieutenant said. "How do you know?"

I pointed to the ground.

"Broken grass," I said. "Footprints. Might have been some time pass, but somebody was here."

There was an overgrown path from the barn that went past a water well and then traversed down to the back side of the house.

Virgil started off down the long path toward the house, and we followed. We passed the water well and continued down some steps and followed the weed-covered rocks toward the house.

The wind was in our face as we walked the long path. When we got close to the house, Virgil held up his hand, and everyone, in-cluding the lieutenant, stopped.

Virgil moved closer, looking in through a side window. He looked at me and tilted his head in the direction of the house. I moved near Virgil to see what he was looking at.

We could see through the window that the entire front part of the house was missing and the ocean was visible. There was also a small table we could see through the window, and next to the table, looking out toward the front gates and the sea beyond, sat a man.

74

VIRGIL MOTIONED TO THE LIEUTENANT. THE LIEU-
tenant moved up, seeing the man.

Virgil pointed for the lieutenant, the silver-toothed man, and
the sergeant major to go around one side of the house and he'd go
around the other with the other three Federales.

The lieutenant nodded.

Virgil grabbed Alejandro and moved him off around the far side
of the house with him.

I crept up on the other side with the lieutenant and his two
Federales behind me.

The wind was in our favor, blowing directly in the face of the
seated man, concealing the sound of our movement as we approached.

I could see Virgil and Alejandro and the three Federales on the
opposite side of the structure through the window. They were moving slowly as we proceeded toward the front of the house.

Soon I saw the man at the table through another opening. He
was a large man with no hat and long sandy-blond hair. His hair
was blowing with the ocean breeze, but he was not moving. I could

tell right away when I saw the side of the big fella's face that he was not alive.

From his body position it seemed he might have died of natural causes, but the pitchfork planted just under his rib cage suggested otherwise. The fork's handle extended downward and rested on the big man's knee.

Virgil and Alejandro were positioned at an opening just opposite me, and they were looking at the man, too.

We looked through the openings, surveying the cavernous room, and saw no one else. The entire house consisted of three two-story-high walls, the back of the house and two side walls, and with the exception of the table and chair, the place was completely empty.

The fire that took the house looked to have been twenty years past. The wooden table and the chair the man was sitting on obviously had been placed there at a later time.

We stepped into the interior of the structure. The small table the dead man was sitting at was cluttered and positioned in the center of the room close to what used to be the front wall of the building.

The big fella was sitting to one side of the table. His legs were crossed, and one of his large arms was resting on the table. He was a tall white man, clean-shaven, and looked to be in his late twenties.

"Goddamn fishhook," I said.

A fishhook was hooked in the man's upper lip like he was a fish that went for the bait.

"By God," Virgil said, shaking his head.

"What is the meaning of this?" the lieutenant said.

Virgil didn't say anything.

I looked at the pitchfork plunged into his body.

"Fork's in him deep," I said.

Virgil nodded.

The tines of the pitchfork were completely submerged in the man's sternum. There were four trails of dried blood coming from the pitchfork holes, which had puddled and soaked into the lap of his trousers.

"Who is this hombre?" the lieutenant said.

Virgil and I looked at the dead man closely. He lifeless pale blue eyes were open, as if he were staring out at the distant ocean.

"Don't know," Virgil said. "Alejandro?"

"Sí."

"You know this big hombre?"

Alejandro looked at him closely and shook his head.

"No, Virgil Cole."

"You sure?"

"Sí."

I put my hand to the big man's forehead.

"How long, you figure?" Virgil said.

"He's been dead awhile," I said, "but from the looks of the blood, not that long, I say, day maybe."

There was a newspaper under the big man's arm that rested on the table. Virgil pulled the newspaper free and looked at it.

"This is day before yesterday's paper," Virgil said, looking at the date on the newspaper. "Veracruz."

Virgil looked through the paper a bit, then dropped it on the table.

Sitting on the table were various odds and ends—a few large broken seashells, a busted oar, and an empty rum bottle—and curled in the huge man's large fist was a can of empty peaches with a spoon resting in the can.

75

I **LOOKED AT VIRGIL AND HE LOOKED AT ME WHEN** we noticed the can.

"What is the meaning of this?" the lieutenant said again, impatiently.

Virgil shook his head as he looked around the room.

"Hard to say, Lieutenant," Virgil said.

The lieutenant watched Virgil as he moved around the large area of the burnt-out structure, looking at everything and nothing.

"Well, you have to know something."

"Don't," Virgil said.

The lieutenant moved to the dead man and looked at him closely.

Virgil stepped out across what used to be the front porch and looked to the ground. He looked toward the hacienda gate twenty yards away. He walked in that direction some as he stayed looking at the ground.

The lieutenant started to pace.

"What is happening here, Marshal?"

Virgil looked at the ground a bit more, then looked toward the house. He walked back near the dead man at the table before he answered.

"Well, Lieutenant," Virgil said. "It's clear somebody killed this hombre. By my account, I'd say this was yesterday sometime."

The lieutenant was clearly irritated. He shook his head and looked to Virgil with his chin up high.

"What is it that you're not telling me, Marshal?"

Virgil was thinking the same thing I was thinking. This might be it. He looked to the other Federales—the burly slit-eyed sergeant major, the heavyset silver-toothed fella with two stripes, and the three stocky hombres that looked like brothers.

They were all looking at Virgil, and each still had their *pistolas* out. My eight-gauge was cocked and ready to go if need be.

"Don't know what you are talking about, Lieutenant."

"What are you not telling me?" the lieutenant said.

Virgil looked at me, then looked back to the lieutenant.

"Telling you what I know, Lieutenant," Virgil said. "Been some people in front here. Looks like a few. It's been a while, though, and with the wind, it makes it hard to know just what we're dealing with."

"Your pathfinder," the lieutenant said, looking at Alejandro, "has led us here, and he knows more than what he has told us."

"I do not," Alejandro said.

"Shut up," the lieutenant said.

Virgil didn't say anything.

"This is a gruesome display," the lieutenant said.

"Is," Virgil said.

"This man was, of course, killed with this pitchfork," the lieutenant said, "and then put into a chair as if this were a casual *escenario*."

Virgil nodded.

"I will not fall for this," the lieutenant said as he removed his hat.

"You are in our sights!" a rough voice called loudly.

At the rear of the house, three other Federales stepped in with rifles trained on us. They'd obviously been out of sight on our trip to Veracruz but had been on our trail the whole way. The one talking was the man with the pockmarked face who we'd met on our journey to Córdoba.

The lieutenant replaced his hat as the Federales moved closer.

"You remember my cousin," the lieutenant said.

The pockmarked cousin smiled.

"This idiot game is over, Marshal," the lieutenant said.

Virgil didn't say anything.

"Did you think I would walk away and forget about this?"

"Don't know what you'd think."

"If you thought you'd have this common piece of trash lead us up here in an attempt to make me believe this was the conclusion and we would leave you alone," the lieutenant said, "you are mistaken."

"Good," Virgil said. "It's relieving to know I did not make that mistake, Lieutenant."

The lieutenant grabbed Alejandro by the hair and put his pistol to Alejandro's head.

"Now we will go about this my way," the lieutenant said.

"*Hombre!*" a voice called out loudly. "I have a rifle aimed at the back of your head. Tell your men to drop their guns or you will be dead!"

I could see a rifle poking out of the overgrown weeds inside the window of the carriage house, fifteen feet from the big house.

The lieutenant froze. He squinted, curious where the voice had come from.

"Who are you?" the lieutenant said without moving.

"Do it!" the voice said. "Or you will die!"

But the lieutenant had another idea. In an instant, he turned with Alejandro in front of him and fired in the direction of the carriage house, and when he did, all hell broke loose.

76

THE RIFLE SHOT FROM INSIDE THE CARRIAGE
house missed the lieutenant but hit Alejandro as the lieutenant
went to the ground.

A rapid follow-up shot from the carriage house caught the
heavyset hombre with the silver teeth square in the head, and he
dropped.

As per our usual protocol, Virgil took the men to the left, I took
the ones to the right.

Virgil shot the three brother-like hombres and one Federal
behind them with a rifle before they got off a shot.

The burly slit-eyed sergeant major got a shot off at me, but I was
moving.

I let one barrel of the eight-gauge go as I went to the ground,
and it hit the sergeant major, knocking him back hard. My next
shot hit the pockmarked cousin, who was firing at me but missed.

The last two Federales ran out the back, and two shots rang out
from the carriage house.

The lieutenant still had hold of Alejandro's hair. He held Alejandro in front of him, back to the wall, and had his pistol to Alejandro's head.

"I will kill him!" the lieutenant shouted. "You say you need him? Drop your pistols!"

Alejandro's head was slumped forward. He was moaning from the gunshot wound.

"Do it!" the lieutenant shouted again.

Alejandro's hand was in the pocket of his captain's jacket, and in one swift, simple move, he brought the pocket up underneath the lieutenant's chin and pulled the trigger of my dingus. A single shot went up through the jacket's pocket, and blood kicked up out of the back of the lieutenant's head and splattered across the rock wall of the once beautiful Villa del Toro.

The lieutenant's legs stiffened for a moment and then went slack.

Virgil and I looked to all the Federales as the gun smoke moved away with the breeze. None of them showed any sign of life.

I broke open my big gun on the move fast toward the rear of the house as I reloaded. Virgil moved toward the rear of the house, too. We had heard the two shots of the rifle after the two Federales had run but did not know if they'd been hit, were on the run, or ready for volley.

Virgil stayed out of the open doorway on one side of the rear of the house as he reloaded. I was to the opposite side of the house, staying out of the window. I crossed the opening quickly. From the opposite side of the window I could see the two Federales. They were both on the ground. One was facedown and the other was on his side. The Federal on his side was moving slightly.

"Both down," I said. "One's still showing."

I kept my eight-gauge pointed at him as I stepped out the window opening and moved to him. When I got over him I could see he was shot in the side just under his arm. He looked up at me. His eyes were wide with fear, and then he did what I had seen happen to other dying men before. He tried to speak. He uttered something, but blood came up in his mouth and he died staring at me. I stepped back through the window.

"All dead."

Virgil nodded, and we moved back quickly toward Alejandro.

"You out there, doing the shooting, we are marshals from the USA," Virgil said. "This is played out!"

Jedediah McCord, alias Henry Strode, stepped out of the weed-filled doorway of the carriage house carrying a Spencer rifle. He limped slightly as he walked to the big house. He was trying to move with pace, but his injuries from the beating by his brother Dalton made it difficult. Jedediah was anxious. He knew he'd just shot Alejandro.

"Alejandro," Jedediah called as he walked. "Alejandro!"

Jedediah had shaped up considerably from the last time we saw him unconscious and badly beaten at Doc Mayfair's office in San Cristóbal. The swelling of his face was gone and the lacerations on his face had healed up significantly. Jedediah was taller and stronger-looking than I remembered him, and though he was tired and ragged, he was handsome, with a strong face, blue eyes, and thick, dark hair. He entered the house through the wide opening and looked to Alejandro.

"Damn," Jedediah said as he moved to Alejandro. "Aw . . . hell . . ."

Alejandro was sitting slumped over between the legs of the dead lieutenant. Virgil and I got to each side of Alejandro and lifted him away from the lieutenant. We laid him on his back to look at his wound. I pulled back his captain's jacket. He'd been shot in the shoulder just below his left collarbone.

"You never were much of a shot," Alejandro said to Jedediah.

77

WE GOT ALEJANDRO'S CAPTAIN'S JACKET AND shirt off. The bullet had exited out the back of his shoulder. Alejandro was bleeding heavily from the front and back. We turned him slightly so to put pressure on both the entrance and exit wound. Virgil placed his bandana on the front wound. I gave Virgil my bandana, and he put vise-like pressure on the back and front wound.

"I'll get a fire," I said.

Virgil nodded and looked to Jedediah.

"Let's get the cleanest strips of cloth you can off these dead men," Virgil said. "Get my knife."

Jedediah pulled Virgil's knife from its belt sheath. He moved to the nearest Federal and went about cutting away his trousers.

In short order I gathered dried twigs, leaves, and grass and moved to a corner out of the breeze and got a fire going. I kept stoking the fire, and once it was hot I laid the blade of my knife in the flame. I removed my belt and wrapped the knife handle so to withstand the blade's growing heat. When the knife blade was red-hot, I nodded to Virgil and moved to Alejandro. Alejandro was looking at me.

"This is gonna hurt, Alejandro," Virgil said.

Virgil let off the pressure on the front wound and I laid the hot knife blade to Alejandro's chest, cauterizing the entrance hole. Alejandro remained looking in my eyes. He did not flinch, but his eyes filled with water. Then Virgil lifted Alejandro up slightly and I laid the hot blade to the exit wound on his back.

For the moment, the cauterizing stopped the bleeding. Jedediah came with strips of cloth. Virgil rolled two strips and put one over the front wound and one over the back, and I helped Virgil wrap Alejandro's shoulder from front to back. Alejandro looked to Virgil like a boy watching his father do what he did best.

"This bullet was a long way from your heart, son," Virgil said, then glanced to Jedediah. "No matter what this Mexican fella here says about you, for a banker, you're a fair hand with that Spencer."

"You know me?" Jedediah said.

"Course we do," Virgil said.

Jedediah was clearly trying to piece together what was happening and what had just happened. He looked back and forth between Virgil and me. He looked at the ground for a moment, then to the Federales.

"These Federales here?" Jedediah said, shaking his head, "They . . . ?"

"Bad hombres," Virgil said. "With bad intentions."

"And you are marshals?"

"We are," Virgil said. "I'm Marshal Virgil Cole, this is my deputy marshal, Everett Hitch."

Jedediah offered a slight nod to Virgil and then me.

We finished wrapping Alejandro's shoulder. He was in a great deal of pain, but he was tough as hell and was doing a good job of not showing how bad he hurt.

"Not only do we know you," Virgil said, "we know you ain't who you claimed to be."

Jedediah looked to Alejandro.

"We know you're Jedediah McCord," Virgil said. "We know you got a brother, Dalton, that led you here. Been following you for a long way."

Jedediah looked to Alejandro, shaking his head, confused.

"Why? And Alejandro? You are here?" Jedediah said.

"*Sí,*" Alejandro said. "Alejandro is here."

"How did you . . . why did you come? How did you know?"

"Alejandro led us here. We've been trailing you," Virgil said, "trailing you and your brother all the way from San Cristóbal."

"I saw you walking down here to this house," Jedediah said, "with Alejandro and the Federales and I, I was . . . We were here, so long ago . . ." Jedediah trailed off, turning to Alejandro.

"*Sí.*"

"I wasn't sure I would remember how to get here," Jedediah said.

Jedediah didn't know what else to say. He was confused and at a loss for words. He stared at Alejandro.

"Damn good of you to throw in with us here," Virgil said.

Jedediah looked to the dead men, then looked back to Virgil.

"You know about the robbery?" Jedediah said.

"We do."

"Then you know it was not me," Jedediah said.

"Know that, too."

Jedediah shook his head a little.

"And . . . you know about my . . ."

Jedediah went silent, but it was clear what was on his mind. Words he could not get out easily.

"We know some about your wife, too," Virgil said.

78

JEDEDIAH LOOKED AT VIRGIL FOR A LONG MO-ment and didn't say anything.

"We're here to find her," Virgil said, nodding toward me a bit.

"Thank you . . ." he said. "He's insane, you know?"

"Seems," Virgil said.

"The crazy, out-of-his-mind sonofabitch," Jedediah said.

Virgil didn't say anything.

"I didn't know what to expect when I got here," Jedediah said. "I thought about it the whole way down here."

Jedediah looked around at the dead Federales.

"I didn't expect this. I expected this place would look like it looked when we were kids. I envisioned finding my killer brother here, getting rid of him once and for all," Jedediah said. "And I'd hoped, I wished, and I prayed I would find my, my wife, but now this . . . What now?"

"We keep looking," Virgil said.

"Where, Marshal?" Jedediah said.

"You've not laid eyes on him at all?" I said.

"No."

He looked to the pitchfork in the man's gut, then to Alejandro.

"He's damn sure here, though."

"Know him?" Virgil said, looking at the big dead man.

"Yes," Jedediah said. "His name is Drummer. He's one of Dalton's men. He was at my house the night before the robbery."

"What was he doing at your house?"

"Holding us hostage."

Virgil looked to me, then back to Jedediah.

"How'd this robbery of the Comstock Bank go down?" Virgil said.

He pointed with the Spencer rifle to the big dead man in the chair.

"This man, and another man," Jedediah said. "They held my wife."

"Demanded you get the money?" Virgil said.

Jedediah nodded.

"My wife Catherine and I went out to a café for supper," Jedediah said. "When we returned, this man Drummer and another man, his name was EG. They were in our home. They held us at gunpoint through the evening and in the morning told me to clear out the vault or they would kill her."

"Dalton was not there at your house with the men?" Virgil said.

"No," Jedediah said. "But they're his men, and this was Dalton's plan."

"Why not rob the bank that night," Virgil said. "Why in the morning?"

"That's Dalton," Jedediah said. "Wanted to make sure it was me, people saw me taking the money."

"Then what?"

"They wanted me to meet them south of town and give them the money in exchange for my wife."

"Why didn't you alert Sheriff Hawkins?"

"Bad idea when you're dealing with Dalton," Jedediah said. "I could not take the chance."

Jedediah looked to Alejandro.

Alejandro nodded a bit, agreeing.

"I got to where I was to meet them with the money, and Dalton was there with Catherine and the two men," Jedediah said with a crack in his voice. "She was scared to death. I told Dalton to take the money and leave, but he had other ideas."

"Beat the hell out of you?" Virgil said. "And take your wife."

Jedediah nodded.

"How did you know to go to La Mesilla to look for them?"

"I knew Dalton had been in La Mesilla for a long time," he said.

"How?"

"I had a man come into the bank I'd known from my younger days. Like Alejandro, he recognized me, and told me my brother was in La Mesilla. I knew it was just a matter of time before Dalton found me."

Alejandro tossed his bloody white shirt aside and put on his jacket.

"Maybe if you knew me," Alejandro said, getting slowly to his feet. "If you had not acted like you were someone else, pretending not to know Alejandro, maybe this would never have happened."

Jedediah looked to Alejandro and nodded slowly.

"Maybe."

"We were together for such a long time," Alejandro said. "We were brothers, here, so many years ago. We did so many things."

"So many things I needed to get away from, Alejandro," Jedediah said. "I needed to forget."

Alejandro shook his head.

"Everyone has things they want to forget," Alejandro said, "things they want to get away from, but that is not how life goes, Henry Strode. You cannot escape."

79

"**WHEN DID YOU ARRIVE HERE, AT THIS HACI-**enda?" Virgil said.

"This morning," Jedediah said. "Not long before you."

"You had a day's jump on us," Virgil said. "What took you?"

"I've been moving as fast as I could," he said. "Train broke down, horse went lame. It has not been without incident getting here."

"Where is your horse?" I said.

Jedediah pointed away from the river.

"I heard you coming," he said. "He's over there in the trees."

"Dalton tell you he was coming down here?" Virgil said.

Jedediah looked to Alejandro, then back to Virgil.

"No," Jedediah said. "He would not do that."

"How did you know, then?" Virgil said.

"He told my wife about this place," Jedediah said as he looked to Alejandro. "He charmed her. That is his way of getting to me. Hints, clues, signs. Life between us was nothing but a mean and dangerous game to Dalton. The more mean, the more dangerous, the better."

"*Sí,*" Alejandro said.

"He told her about this place. The sonofabitch. He told her it was the most beautiful place and that she should see it someday," Jedediah said. "Dalton knew she would tell me. But hell, now . . ."

Jedediah looked around the burnt-out shell of the building.

"Not so beautiful anymore, is it?"

Jedediah shook his head and walked toward the front of the structure and looked out to the ocean.

"And now what?" Jedediah said dejectedly. "God only knows . . ."

"Bullshit," Alejandro said.

Jedediah looked back to Alejandro.

"God has nothing to do with this," Alejandro said. "Don't be a stupid ass. Banking has made this Henry Strode soft, wearing fancy suits and sitting on polished pews . . . God helps those who help themselves."

Alejandro moved toward Jedediah.

"Dalton did not get you down here for you to give up," Alejandro said. "This is about him winning. You know that. He does not give a care about your beautiful wife. She is bait. He got you down here for one *razón* and one *razón* only, and that is for you to lose and for him to win."

Alejandro walked close to the big dead man now known to us as Drummer.

"Right now, Drummer is God," Alejandro said. "This dead fucker here, with the *horca* up in his gut and the fishhook in his lip, he is talking to you. He will tell you what to do and where to go."

Jedediah was listening. He moved a few steps toward Alejandro and looked to Drummer.

"You did not come this far to give up, did you?" Alejandro said. "He wants you to find him. He's got you just where he wants you."

"Where is that?" Jedediah said.

"Where you are ready," Alejandro said.

"Ready?"

"*Sí.*"

"Ready for what?"

"To kill or be killed."

80

⁓

A WISH TO DIE BY THE SWORD OF YOUR BROTHER, a grim tale, it seemed; a Cain and Abel legend, brothers united by loss and separated by envy and greed, and ultimately driven to revenge and murder. Following Alejandro's theory, the only way for Jedediah to win in the eyes of his brother Dalton was to walk away from killing him.

"This is no longer a stolen horse with a bridle left tied to a tree," Alejandro said.

Alejandro looked to the big hombre, Drummer, and the table strewn with the various items.

"This," Alejandro said, "all this, is a path to a story that means something absolute. You kill him or he kills you."

Jedediah looked at Drummer, with the pitchfork in his gut and the fishhook in his lip.

"The cruel pitchfork," Jedediah said. "A blatant reminder of Dalton's youth."

"Of *our* youth," Alejandro said.

"Of his sacrifice," Jedediah said.

Jedediah walked near Drummer and looked at him. Then walked

around the table, looking at the items littered across its top, the seashells, the busted oar, the can of peaches.

"This can," he said, shaking his head. "These peaches are from my home."

Jedediah looked at the seashells, then picked up the newspaper. He turned a few pages, stopped, and turned the page back. He squinted some, looking at the page. He turned the page, looking at it from the front and then from the back.

"This article is cut out," Jedediah said. "The headline is still here, but the story is missing, been cut out."

Jedediah held up the paper. There was a square cut from it.

He handed Alejandro the paper.

"What does this say?" Jedediah said.

"This story about fishing," Alejandro said. "It has been cut away carefully to leave the heading, but no story."

Alejandro handed the paper to me.

I read it once through.

"The basic grind of it says," I said, "the first great northern of the year blew down the coast, bringing strong winds, rains with rough seas, but the aftermath brought fish?"

Nobody said anything for a moment, then Jedediah spoke up.

"He's the great northern, no doubt," Jedediah said without looking at us.

His comment was followed by another moment of silence, then: "And you," Alejandro said, "the *pescado*."

"Yes," Jedediah said, "me, the fish."

"And him the shark!" Alejandro said with some urgency to his voice. "The great northern!"

"What?" Jedediah said.

Alejandro looked quickly to Virgil, then to me, then back to Jedediah.

"You remember the captain?" Alejandro said.

"Captain?" Jedediah said with a frown.

"Yes! Captain Chapa! Something I always remember," Alejandro said. "Dalton remembered it, too! When we were in prison he said to me what the captain said."

Virgil looked to me.

"If you are not the shark," Alejandro said, "you are the fish."

Alejandro looked at us and nodded.

"Dalton," Alejandro said. "He said when he got out, he would never be the fish."

"So you think this is where?" Jedediah said. "You think this is what this means? All this?"

"Yes!" Alejandro said. "Must be!"

Jedediah looked to the table.

"It was a place where Dalton knows!" Alejandro said.

"All this," Jedediah said. "The oar, the hook, the fish story . . . you think that is what this is, what he is trying to say?"

"It makes the most sense to me!" Alejandro said, looking back and forth between the three of us. "Virgil Cole?"

Virgil thought for a second as he looked to Alejandro.

"And you know where this is?"

"¡Sí!"

"Captain got a home," Virgil said. "Or does he live on his boat?"

"Boat," Alejandro said. "That is the fisherman's life. Boat to cantina, no more."

"Worth a try," I said.

"By God," Virgil said.

81

‌

WE LEFT THE DEAD FEDERALES AND DRUMMER gutted with the pitchfork in Villa del Toro just past noon, a fitting requiem for the conspirators. We took four of the best horses the Federales were riding, stripped the others of their saddles and set them free.

We crossed Bull River without any trouble and rode west. As we journeyed down toward the coast, a layer of warm rain rolled in off the ocean. The rain was light but steady by the time we turned north back to Veracruz.

When we arrived back to the city, Alejandro led us to a mooring area that was on the opposite side from the waterfront where we'd hoteled and sat in the cantina with the now dead and gone Federales.

The dock where Captain Chapa had a slip was at a smaller port on the opposite side of the bay. By the time we neared the dock, the rain had let up some, but there was a layer of fog hovering low above the coastline.

We tied the horses behind a tall old church made of pink stone that looked to have been riddled with old lead ball pockets from a fight centuries ago.

"How do you want to go about this, Virgil?" I said.

"How far to the dock, Alejandro?" Virgil said.

"Not far," he said, "just through the work yard here."

"Let's get down there," Virgil said. "See what we can see, figure out our options."

We walked through the misty fog, making our way through the dockyards, where the salty sea air mixed with smoke from the drying houses, curing fish. We made our way though some dockworkers going about their chores of repairing dry-docked vessels.

"Hold up," Virgil said.

We stopped just before we got to the waterside. A few men working on the hull of a schooner watched us.

No doubt we were an unusual sight on the wharf, three tall gringos and equally tall Alejandro with his naval jacket, concho breeches, and fancy sombrero, and all of us carrying weapons.

"This the dock here?" Virgil said.

"Sí," Alejandro said. "Captain Chapa's boat is on the far end of this landing ramp just ahead of us here."

"Everett?" Virgil said. "What do you figure?"

"Well, it's not too foggy," I said, "and in this particular instance, I'd say that's a bad thing."

"It is," Virgil said.

"Why?" Jedediah said.

"Not a good idea the four of us just go waltzing down there to the boat," I said.

"It's not," Virgil said.

"Night would be better," I said.

"It would," Virgil said.

"What do you propose, Marshal?" Jedediah said. "We wait?"

"Alejandro, that dock over there," Virgil said with a point. "Is there a way to have a look at the captain's boat from that dock?"

"Maybe," Alejandro said. "I would think so, but with this weather it might be hard to see the boat from there. We can try."

Virgil nodded.

"Let's do," Virgil said. "Everett, why don't you and Alejandro get to that other dock."

The dock looked to be more than a hundred yards from where we were standing.

"See what you can see," Virgil said. "See if the boat is even there. See if you see any people. Be better if just the two of you moved about. Don't want to appear like a herd around here. Jedediah and me will stay right here, near the end of this dock."

"Let me say one thing, Marshal," Jedediah said.

"Go ahead."

"My brother is vicious," Jedediah said. "He is a shark, and he will attack, will come from behind, from anywhere."

82

~~

THOUGH THERE WAS STEADY DRIZZLE COMING DOWN and it was foggy, Alejandro spotted Captain Chapa's schooner from where we were positioned on the neighboring dock.

"That brigantine just there," Alejandro said. "On the other side of the dock, near the end."

"You sure?"

"*Sí.*"

Alejandro removed his sombrero, pulled his mother's rosary from his pocket, and slipped it over his head. He held the cross.

"I wish for Captain Chapa's safety," Alejandro said. "He is a good man, a *borracho*, but a good man."

Captain Chapa's schooner was a far distance from us. It was backed into the slip on the far side of the dock, but we could see it clearly. It was a long and wide gaff-rig schooner with a low aft cabin, and compared to most of the rigs around the marina, it looked like a well-kept vessel.

"Thought the captain's boat was a fishing rig," I said.

"It is," Alejandro said.

"Big boat for fishing."

"It is also for shipping goods."

"What kind of goods?"

"Not to worry, amigo, nothing illegal," Alejandro said with a grimace and then lowered his chin to his chest.

Alejandro was still holding the rosary.

"You all right?"

Alejandro kept his head lowered for a moment longer, then looked up and nodded with grim determination.

"*Sí.*"

"Let me see."

"Alejandro is okay, amigo," he said.

"Alejandro, open."

Alejandro reluctantly opened his jacket, showing me his bandaged shoulder. Blood was showing solidly on the outside of the bandage.

"Have to tend to that."

"I will be okay."

He pulled his jacket back up on his shoulder as he looked toward Captain Chapa's schooner.

"Right now we have el Diablo to reckon with."

Alejandro was tough as they come, I thought as I looked back to the schooner.

"Reckon with him if he's here," I said.

"*Sí,*" Alejandro said. "If he is here."

The dock was quiet, and there was no one moving about in the misty weather. We were in a good spot behind a moored rig, where we could watch the captain's boat without being spotted.

"If el Diablo is on this boat," Alejandro said, "he is in one way, in a good way, and in another way, in a bad way."

"How's that?" I said.

"Well," Alejandro said. "There is only one way in and one way out on the dock—that is the bad way."

"The good way?"

"They could sail away," Alejandro said.

"He would need the captain."

"Maybe."

"You'd know how to operate that rig?"

"*Sí,*" he said. "Well, I have been out before, for a short time. It was a time ago. Alejandro remembers. I have spent much time, too, watching them, the sailors."

I looked to Alejandro in his naval jacket and thought maybe he was right, maybe he could operate the schooner on the sea.

"Well," I said, "if what you were saying before is right, if Dalton wants a final showdown with his brother, sailing away would be fishy and not sharklike."

"Maybe even more sharklike," Alejandro said. "Torment."

"Don't think so," I said.

"Why do you not think so?"

"Be the end of the trail," I said.

Alejandro thought about that some.

"Maybe, Everett," Alejandro said. "Maybe, *mi amigo.*"

"Here we go," I said.

I saw movement on Captain Chapa's schooner. Then we saw clearly it was a man moving about.

"That's not Captain Chapa, is it?" I said.

"No," Alejandro said.

"And you're certain that schooner we are looking at is Captain Chapa's."

"*Sí.*"

"That Dalton?"

"No."

"Gotta be the other fella Jedediah was talking about," I said.

"EG," Alejandro said.

"Yep."

We watched him for a while moving about the schooner. He stopped and looked around as if he was looking for somebody.

"It's him all right," I said. "Gotta be."

He went back to busying himself with something, but I couldn't tell what he was doing. After a moment he ducked back into the cabin.

"Let's move," I said.

Alejandro had been on one knee, and he was slow to rise. I took his good side and helped him, and we started up the ramp toward shore.

I glanced back, and I saw the man again out on the schooner deck. We stopped and hunkered down behind another boat and watched. I couldn't tell clearly, but it looked as though he was putting on a jacket.

"Maybe he's about to take that bad way I was talking about, Everett?"

We watched a little more.

"Might be," I said. "Let's move."

I kept looking back as we walked up the dock for the shore.

"If he does," I said, "it'd be a good idea to welcome him."

83

～

ALEJANDRO AND I WENT QUICKLY BACK TO WHERE we left Virgil and Jedediah on the shoreline, halfway between the two docks.

"It's them," I said. "One of them, anyway."

"My wife?" Jedediah said. "Did you see my wife?"

"No," I said.

"He might be coming," I said, pointing to the ramp leading to Captain Chapa's slip.

"What'd you see?" Virgil said.

"Big gringo," I said. "Long black beard."

"That's him," Jedediah said, looking in the direction of the ramp. "That's EG, the other sonofabitch was in our house."

Jedediah started to move, but Virgil stopped him.

"Don't want to confront him here," Virgil said. "If he is leaving this dock. He's of course going somewhere. There is no telling where your brother and wife are, if they are even on that boat, so let's see what this EG fella reveals to us."

"He's got his razor sharp," I said. "He was expectant, it seemed, bird necking, scanning about."

Virgil turned around, looking behind us, and pointed to a big shop with an open door and a schooner inside resting on its side.

"Over there," Virgil said.

We moved as fast as we could with both injured Alejandro and recovering Jedediah to the shop and positioned ourselves behind the far side of the building. There was a window on that side of the shop where we could look out the shop's open door to the dock.

We waited.

Alejandro leaned against the shop with his back to the wall and looked to the ground.

I motioned to Virgil.

"Losing blood," I said.

Alejandro looked up at me.

"I have had bigger cuts in my eye, amigo," Alejandro said as he moved away from the wall of support.

"No matter," I said. "We don't get you cared for, it will be the last cut you ever have."

"That's him," Jedediah said softly. "You were damn sure right about this, Alejandro. Damn sure."

EG was walking up the dock toward the shore.

"By God," Virgil said. "Got himself healed."

"He does," I said.

He had a bone-grip pistol on his hip and was carrying a long-barrel rifle with a brass-capped Swiss butt in one hand and a big canvas bag in the other.

"Looks like he might be going somewhere," Virgil said.

"Does."

EG was big, not much over six feet, but bulky and tough-looking. He looked like a mountain man with his long beard, huge chest, and arms. He held his bulky arms away from his body with his shoulders back, but he was for sure on guard as he moved.

We watched him walk away from the dock, then moved to the opposite end of the building to see where he was heading. We kept him in sight as he walked up the narrow dockyard road in the mist and fog.

Virgil removed his hat.

"Everett, let me get almost where he is there now before you follow me. Don't want to walk on after him like pack dogs."

I nodded.

Virgil pulled the collar of his coat up. He placed his hat in front of him and waited for EG to get on a ways farther, then followed him. There were other people on the road, workers going about their business, a few oxen with pull carts, as Virgil did his best to blend in.

We waited like Virgil said, and then after a moment we followed, walking through the foggy dockside, past salt-packing fish shacks and up the road toward the church, where we tied our horses.

Virgil turned up a road just before the church. By the time we got to the road Virgil was under the awning of a big stone building.

"He went into a tavern," Virgil said. "A ways ahead here."

Jedediah cocked his Spencer.

"Good time to do that waltzing Everett was talking about, don't you think, Marshal," Jedediah said. "Walk in there and find out from the goddamn sonofabitch where my wife is."

"I do," Virgil said.

"And while we are at it," Jedediah said, "there is no telling what might happen to EG."

Virgil looked to me, then back to Jedediah.

"No telling," Virgil said.

84

JEDEDIAH MIGHT HAVE CHANGED HIS WAYS, LIV-ing the high life of the banker Henry Strode, with his good business acumen, customer friendliness, and mild manners, but he still had that hair trigger, that snap that so many away from the simple life carry with them on the makeshift road to redemption.

We started walking to the tavern.

Virgil stopped twenty paces from the door.

"Everett and me will walk in first," Virgil said. "Don't want to be too gun-ready. Don't want him jerking and ending up dead, and no telling what he might do when he sees you, Jedediah. Don't want to have to kill him first order."

"How much time?" Jedediah said.

"A minute," Virgil said.

Jedediah nodded.

The four of us walked toward the tavern, and as we neared we heard the voices of the patrons talking and laughing.

"Might be crowded," I said.

"Might," Virgil said.

Virgil held up his hand, stopping Alejandro and Jedediah. They stayed back, and in a steady move Virgil and I entered the tavern.

It was a small place. There was a bar to the right, and to the left the room was half full of fishermen and dockworkers sitting at small tables, telling their tales.

EG was sitting at the end of the bar with a glass of beer in one hand and a chicken leg in the other. He stopped eating when he saw us.

His long rifle was leaning on the wall next to him, and in his gun hand he had a greasy leg of chicken.

"I'll be goddamned," EG said as he sat back on his bar stool, looking at us.

"Where are they?" Virgil said.

The room of people felt something; three gringos with guns was enough to silence their lively talk. A few went out the door as Jedediah entered, followed by Alejandro.

EG leaned back, looking past Virgil and me, and rested his eyes on Jedediah.

"Might have expected you," EG said, looking at Jedediah, "but not you two. You are them marshals come down to Mexico looking for the girl, ain't you?"

Jedediah raised the Spencer rifle and pointed it at EG's head.

"Where's my wife?"

"Whoa there, boy," EG said, raising his hands in the air. "He fucked us both."

"Where?" Jedediah prodded.

"On that goddamn boat," EG said.

"You're lying," Jedediah said.

"No, boy," EG said. "I ain't, and if you want to ever see her again you might want to get yourself back over there before they debark or embark or whatever the fuck you call it—leave."

"Why would they be leaving now?" Jedediah said fiercely. "Why?"

"Easy, son," EG said. "Your brother paid some damn Mexican kids to wait on that beach over yonder and, when you showed, for them little shits to come tell him you were here. There was a whole passel of them. They come back and was talking that Mexico to your brother and told your brother what they'd seen. I don't speak no Mexico. Your goddamn brother told me it was just you on his trail."

EG looked to Virgil and me.

"Never said a goddamn thing about nobody else," EG said. "He told me they was gonna take off, and I told him I wasn't about to go sailing off on no goddamn boat in no fucking ocean."

Virgil looked to Jedediah.

"He told me," EG said, "if I saw you, to be sure and tell you some good news."

"What?" Jedediah said.

"So far he ain't fucked her," EG said.

I looked to Jedediah, and his bottom lip began to quiver.

"But no telling how long that will last," EG said, "with them being out there on that ocean. He also said to tell you he'd send you a letter where they ended up and, bomb voyage."

Jedediah lowered the Spencer rifle and turned for the door. When he did, EG dropped the chicken leg and—thinking this was the moment to get the jump on Virgil and me—went for his bone handle. But Virgil pulled, smoke kicked from his Colt, and the lead hit EG in his chest before he touched leather.

85

⌒

THE FOG AND MIST WERE HEAVIER AS WE GOT
closer to the marina. Alejandro was slowing significantly and having a hard time keeping up, but we hustled as best we could back to the dock.

"Stay back," I said to Alejandro.

"No, amigo," Alejandro said. "We have come this far."

I thought about that, about all that had happened, all that led us to this mysterious world of Veracruz and Bull River with its storied history of the orphaned boys in their youth. As Constable Holly had put it, this whole saga has been quite the ordeal.

I was piecing everything together as we walked. This journey we'd been on was all about feelings. I thought about what Virgil always said: *Feelings get you killed.* And in this case he was damn sure right about that.

Feelings. This whole goddamn saga started with Alejandro having hurt feelings when he saw Jedediah on the street and Jedediah acting as if he were someone else, someone Alejandro could not know.

I thought about how Alejandro must have felt when someone he knew so well, so thoroughly, disowned him by assuming another man's identity and living the life of the happily married bank president in San Cristóbal. It must have made Alejandro feel small.

Alejandro was right, he would have most likely never thought of contacting Dalton in La Mesilla if Jedediah would have acknowledged him and not rejected him. Alejandro would have never had that shoot-out with the two bandits in cahoots with Dalton, who tried to cut him out of the first robbery attempt last Christmas, if it weren't for feelings.

Us tracking Alejandro down, then him escaping, and us finding him again in El Encanto would not have happened if it weren't for feelings.

Dalton's men hold Jedediah's wife hostage, threaten to kill her unless Jedediah cleans out the vault. Dalton and Jedediah fight and Dalton severely beats Jedediah and runs off with the bank's money and Jedediah's wife.

None of this would have ever happened; Slingshot Clark would not have found Jedediah unconscious on the porch of her Cottonwood brothel.

Or Jedediah escaping from Doc Mayfair's office and following the trail left by his brother. Or us tracking Dalton to La Mesilla, where Sheriff Talmadge was killed by Dalton's men, and Virgil then gunning down two of them who tried to test their mettle. Then we discover Jedediah had been in La Mesilla but was now headed to Mexico in pursuit of his brother and his wife, Catherine. Getting Alejandro out of jail in hopes we could find the *especial* place Dalton knew about from their childhood. Jantz Wainwright offering a reward for the return of his daughter that pitted Virgil and me up against a renegade band of Federales that goddamn near got us killed. This all was connected to one simple thing: feelings.

And now, after all that, here we were on the docks of Veracruz. How this would play out, I had no idea, as the four of us walked down the dock toward Captain Chapa's schooner.

Jedediah was ahead of us some. He was charged with a composed combination of fear, anger, and rage as we walked through the fog toward the schooner.

"Let's not just run down there," Virgil said. "Ease into this, Jedediah."

Jedediah slowed and looked back to Virgil.

"Everett, you and Alejandro walk that side of the dock and Jedediah and I will be on this side. Let's take it steady."

We did just that. Alejandro and I moved to the left side and Virgil and Jedediah stayed on the right. Alejandro and I were separated from Virgil and Jedediah by about fifteen feet as we approached Captain Chapa's schooner.

The first image we saw through the fog as we neared Captain Chapa's slip was that the schooner's sails were hoisted but were luffing with the light breeze. The long boat looked ghostly in the misty fog, and EG was right: the schooner was preparing to set sail.

We heard Dalton before we saw him.

"Ahoy, little brother!"

Dalton's voice was deep and raspy.

Virgil held up his hand for us to stop, and we stopped.

"I was hoping we could have seen each other on Bull River," Dalton said from somewhere in the fog. "I was disappointed. So many memories, but as you could see, that place went to shit."

"Let her go, Dalton!" Jedediah shouted. "Just let her go!"

"She's tied up at the moment," Dalton said. "Besides, that would spoil this adventure."

Virgil moved up a bit, and we all eased a little closer. Then we saw Dalton.

He was positioned closest to us on the port side of the schooner. He had one foot up on the gunwale. He had a pistol in one hand and a rope wrapped around the other.

86

❧

DALTON MCCORD, THERE HE WAS, AFTER ALL
this time, after all this bloodshed and heartache, there he was,
standing proudly on the side of Captain Chapa's schooner.

"The rope wrapped around my hand here is connected to Captain Chapa's Greener harpoon gun," Dalton said, "and that harpoon
with its razor-sharp arrowhead is aimed at your wife's heart, little
brother."

Dalton was taller and more rugged-looking than his brother,
but they had very similar features. He wore no hat. His hair was
thick and dark. Like Jedediah, he was handsome. His face was
strong and golden-colored from the sun, with high cheekbones and
deep-set eyes.

"You make a move, if I go down for any reason and this rope is
pulled, there she goes," Dalton said. "Boom goes the harpoon and,
well, that would be tragic."

Dalton was standing in a position as if he wanted to be remembered in a painting. He wore a long blue gentlemen's coat with a
white open shirt. He had a second pistol on his hip with the butt
forward and wore striped pants tucked into tall military boots.

We moved up a bit more and then we saw Catherine. She was not crying, but she looked like she was in shock. She was tied to the main mast, and just as Dalton had explained, the Greener harpoon launcher was secured atop a barrel, between Catherine and the cabin. The launcher was a large-bore rifle fixed with a harpoon protruding from the barrel. The point of the harpoon was aimed directly at her chest, and the rope wrapped in Dalton's hand was rigged through a block and through the trigger guard of the Greener.

"Captain Alejandro," Dalton said with a smile, "good of you to come, it's been awhile, and marshals, it's good of you, too, to come and see us off."

"Dalton," Jedediah said. "No, brother, no."

Dalton ignored Jedediah and looked to Captain Chapa, who was slightly shaking his head.

"You remember Captain Chapa here," Dalton said.

Captain Chapa was a wiry old fella with weathered dark skin and cropped white hair. He was small and tough-looking for his age, and even though this was a tense situation, he seemed relaxed and unafraid.

"The captain is now the first mate," Dalton said with a smile. "Right, Captain Chapa?"

Captain Chapa said nothing. He just stared at Dalton.

Dalton looked back to us.

"I am the captain now, though, I'm afraid," Dalton said. "And Señor Chapa here is, yes, my first mate, and a damn good first mate he is."

"Dalton?" Jedediah said. "Please . . ."

"He will be steering us on this journey," Dalton said, ignoring Jedediah. "Once I say the word, he will set us off out to sea."

"Dalton," Jedediah said calmly again. "Enough."

Dalton went on as if Jedediah had said nothing.

"It's a long journey where we are headed, but like I told EG, I will send you a letter, little brother," Dalton said. "And if you're still interested, who knows, maybe you will seek us out . . . hope so."

"Dalton," Jedediah said. "I'm sor—"

"Catherine?" Dalton said without looking back to her. "Before we sail away, do you have any parting words you want to say to Jedediah? Oh, sorry, correction, I meant Henry, yes, Henry Strode?"

Catherine's head was slumped forward a bit, and her hair was in her eyes.

"Don't worry, little brother, I told her who you really are," Dalton said. "At first she didn't believe me, but I'm pretty certain she's convinced of it now."

"Dalton," Jedediah said. "Stop this."

"Catherine?" Dalton prodded again.

She lifted her head and looked at Jedediah.

Jedediah took a step toward her.

"Nothing to say, Catherine?" Dalton said.

Catherine's face contorted and she started to weep.

"No?" Dalton said to Catherine. "Well, all right, then." Dalton looked directly at Jedediah but called loudly, "First Mate Chapa?"

Captain Chapa did not reply.

"First Mate Chapa?" he said even louder.

"*Sí,*" Captain Chapa said quietly.

"Drop the lines!" Dalton said, never taking his eyes off of Jedediah.

Captain Chapa did as he was told.

"Dalton," Jedediah said. "I'm sorry . . ."

"First Mate Chapa!" Dalton said sternly as he remained staring at his brother. "Set sail!"

"Aye, aye," Captain Chapa said.

Captain Chapa moved up the starboard side and trimmed the main sheet. The air was very slight coming in off the foggy ocean, but the sail slowly began to fill with the wind.

Dalton was staring at Jedediah as the schooner slowly began to move away. He smiled.

"And remember, little brother," Dalton said. "What the good captain, now first mate, always said . . ."

Captain Chapa was making his way back to the helm, and when he did he turned the Greener harpoon gun at Dalton.

"If you are not the shark," Dalton said. "You are the . . ."

"Nooo . . ." Jedediah said as he charged toward Dalton.

Dalton jerked the rope tied to the trigger of the Greener as he raised his pistol at Jedediah.

The large-bore Greener gun exploded loudly. The harpoon rifled from its barrel, hitting Dalton square in the back just as Dalton fired his pistol.

The bullet missed Jedediah, but the sharp-tipped harpoon went through Dalton and stuck six inches out of his chest.

Dalton's arm dropped to his side, and his pistol fell from his grip.

He looked down at the tip of the harpoon sticking out from his chest. He looked back up to Jedediah. He smiled a little, and then toppled over the gunwale.

Jedediah took off running and leapt from the dock and onto the moving schooner.

Captain Chapa quickly released the sail, stopping the schooner's motion, as Jedediah moved to untie Catherine from the mast.

Captain Chapa pitched a cleated line around one of the dock bollards and slowed the schooner's forward movement.

We moved to the schooner and helped the captain with securing the lines to the docks.

We got the schooner tied off just as Jedediah freed Catherine from the mast.

She was trembling and crying. She burst into tears even more as she reached for her husband. She clutched onto him, clinging to him tightly.

"My God, Henry. Thank God!" Catherine said. "Oh, my . . . my husband . . . my Jedediah, my . . . Jedediah . . . my God, my husband . . . my, my life, you're here, you are here . . . oh . . ."

Catherine buried her head into Jedediah's chest as he held her.

"Yes, dear," Jedediah said. "I'm here now. I'm here. It's all over. I'm here, Catherine . . . I'm here."

Catherine pulled back from him, looking up at him. She put her hands on each side of his face and kissed him gently.

I looked to Alejandro. He was looking at Jedediah and Catherine. He smiled a little, and then his legs gave away and he dropped facefirst on the dock.

87

Loss is never easy, not even for killers and thieves. We'd been in Veracruz for a week since Dalton yanked the rope that fired the harpoon he thought was aimed at Catherine's heart. A fortuitous end for Dalton and his evil, tormenting ways to die by his own hand, triggering a shark-killing harpoon. *If you are not the shark, you're the fish.*

The majority of the money Dalton stole was recovered from Captain Chapa's schooner, and Jedediah worked out the necessary details with the Veracruz Bank for the transfer of the capital back to the Comstock Bank in San Cristóbal.

The weather was pleasant now; there was not a cloud in the sky as Virgil and I walked Jedediah and Catherine to the L. C. Garcia & Company steamer destined for Matamoros. There they'd catch a river steamer up the Rio Grande to Juárez, then take the train back to San Cristóbal, a quicker and less arduous method of travel.

When we got to the gangway, Virgil looked to Catherine.

"Ma'am," Virgil said. "Mind if I have a word with your husband?"

She smiled and looked to Jedediah.

"Give us just a minute, dear," Jedediah said.

"Certainly, darling," she said.

She turned to us and smiled her fetching smile. Even though Catherine had been through a hellish experience, she maintained a particular radiance. She had a stimulating quality I could see maybe concerned some people and got others' attention, but it was obvious to Virgil and me she loved her husband—no matter what his name was.

"Gentlemen," Catherine said. "I thank you from the bottom of my heart for being here with us, for us, for finding me and rescuing me."

"Believe your husband had a big hand in you being rescued," Virgil said.

She smiled and looked to Jedediah. She kissed him on the cheek.

"Yes, indeed, I believe he did," she said. "Gentlemen."

We tipped our hats and said good-bye.

Catherine turned on her heel and walked up the gangway.

We watched her for a moment.

"Lovely lady," Virgil said.

"Thank you," Jedediah said, "and I wanted to just say thank you to the two of you and how grateful I am to the both of you. You two men are . . . well, goddamn brave."

Virgil pulled a cigar from his pocket as he looked out over the bay.

"Been meaning to ask you something, Jedediah."

"Marshal?"

Virgil bit the tip of the cigar. He spit it away.

"Tell me about Henry Strode."

Jedediah looked at Virgil, squinting a little, but didn't say anything.

Virgil dragged the tip of a match on the bone handle of his Colt, cupped it, and lit the cigar.

"Who was he?" Virgil said. "Me and Everett are curious."

"A good friend," Jedediah said.

Virgil puffed on the cigar to get it going as he looked to Jedediah.

"What happened to him?"

"He died."

"You kill him?" Virgil said as he flicked the match away.

Jedediah looked at Virgil, then me, then back to Virgil.

"Galloping consumption killed him," he said.

Virgil nodded a bit, working on the cigar.

"Why'd you take his name?" Virgil said. "His identity?"

"It was his idea," Jedediah said. "I had no credentials, I'd never been to school, nothing. He saw it as an opportunity for me, and so did I."

"So how'd you learn to do the business stuff," Virgil said. "Banking business and so forth?"

"Henry taught me a lot before he died," Jedediah said. "I worked for him, taking care of his horses. He had no family but had some money, and when he died he left what he had to me. I did the best I could with it and what I learned from him. He was a good man. A real brother to me."

Virgil nodded a little, looking at Jedediah as he puffed on the cigar.

"We supposed to believe that?" Virgil said.

Jedediah looked to me, then back to Virgil, and smiled.

"You don't have a choice," he said.

The steamer's whistle blew loudly. Virgil looked up the gangway, then back to Jedediah. He puffed on his cigar, looking at Jedediah some.

"Have a good trip, Jedediah," Virgil said.

Jedediah looked to me. I tipped my hat. He looked back to Virgil.

"Thank you," he said, then turned and walked off up the gangway.

"You believe him?" I said.

"Like he said . . . We don't have a choice."

88

VIRGIL AND I WATCHED AS THE STEAMER LEFT the dock, then we walked back to where we'd tied our horses. We mounted up and trotted up a road that traveled above the town and arrived at a large two-story stone building with three flags on tall flagpoles in the front.

We tied our horses on a hitch under the flags, entered the building, and made our way up to the second floor. We walked down the hall and came to a room with an open door, where Alejandro was sitting in a bed next to a vase of flowers.

"¡Hola, amigos!" Alejandro said.

"Better?" I said.

"Sí," Alejandro said. *"Mucho."*

Virgil looked around the room a little, then looked to Alejandro.

"You did all right with our arrangement," Virgil said, "but you know you are still my prisoner. Don't you, Alejandro?"

"Sí, Virgil Cole."

Virgil nodded a little and walked to a window and looked out toward the ocean.

"Been taking good care of you here, it looks like?" Virgil said.

"*Sí,*" Alejandro said, looking around the room. "Alejandro is fortunate. This place, this Veracruz naval infirmary, is the same place where my father, he died. He was not as fortunate as Alejandro."

Alejandro looked to the flowers.

"Look at the beautiful flowers! I have never had anyone ever give me flowers. Jedediah and his lovely wife, they brought them for Alejandro. Are they not so very beautiful?"

"They are," I said.

A pretty young nurse wearing a crisp uniform came into the room to check on Alejandro. She smiled at us sweetly, then tended to Alejandro. She touched his head, feeling his temperature, then held his wrist as she looked to a clock, checking his pulse.

"This is Maria," Alejandro said as he smiled at her. "She does not know our Americano language and she does also not know one day when I am free I will come back here and she will be Alejandro's wife."

Alejandro grinned at her just as Captain Chapa rapped his knuckles on the doorjamb.

"Captain!" Alejandro said excitedly. "*Bienvenido!*"

"*¿Te sientes mejor?*" Captain Chapa said.

"*Sí,*" Alejandro said as he grinned to Maria. "Who would not feel better with this beautiful woman to look after me."

"I wanted to check on you before I left," Captain Chapa said.

"*¿Dónde vas?*" Alejandro said.

"Vanilla run up the coast," Captain Chapa said.

Alejandro nodded a little.

"One day I will return to see you," Alejandro said.

"When do you depart?" Virgil said.

"Mañana," Captain Chapa said.

"You need a first mate?" Virgil said.

"¿Quién?" Captain Chapa said.

Virgil pointed to Alejandro.

"What about him?" Virgil said.

Alejandro looked to Virgil with a curious expression on his face. Virgil met his look.

"You think you got enough good in you to make a hand?" Virgil said to Alejandro.

"Virgil Cole . . ." Alejandro said. "I . . . I do not know what to say."

"Tell me," Virgil said.

Alejandro's eyes filled with water.

"Alejandro has enough good in him to make a hand," Alejandro said.

Virgil nodded a bit.

"Good," Virgil said.

Virgil looked to Captain Chapa.

"Think one day," Virgil said, "you might be able to make a real captain out of him?"

Captain Chapa looked to Alejandro and smiled.

"Sí," he said.

"Good," Virgil said.

Maria fluffed Alejandro's pillow, smiled at us, and left the room.

Virgil looked to Alejandro.

"This is your chance to be a hero, Alejandro," Virgil said sternly. "Don't mess it up."

"I won't, Virgil Cole," Alejandro said.

"I see you up America way," Virgil said, "I will arrest you for trespassing. *Comprende?*"

"*Comprendo,*" Alejandro said.

Virgil nodded a bit. He looked around the room, then looked back to Alejandro.

"Good," Virgil said.

Virgil and I bid Alejandro and the captain farewell. We left Alejandro's room and walked down the hall. When we started down the steps, Maria was on the landing between the floors. We tipped our hats and continued on down the steps.

"Thank you," Maria said.

We stopped, turned to her.

"For?" Virgil said.

"For giving him a second chance," she said.

Virgil looked at me, then Maria.

"My father is a navy captain," she said. "Alejandro will, of course, have to ask my father for my hand, and I can assure you my father will make certain any husband of mine will have to run a tidy ship."

Virgil looked at me and smiled.

"Good," he said.

She smiled and walked up the steps.

Virgil and I left the naval infirmary. We mounted up and turned our horses toward the ocean and started back down the road.

"What do you want to do now?" I said.

Virgil eased Cortez on a bit before he answered.

"Why don't we get out of Mexico," Virgil said.

"Why not," I said.

ACKNOWLEDGMENTS

Bull River was chock-full of notorious outlaws who took to task providing their well-oiled weapons and bottled remedies—they all played a hand in helping sort out the unexpected turns this twisting river took. Real desperadoes and rabble-rousers like tracker Jamie "Whatnot" Whitcomb, sultry chanteuse Julie Rose, mountain guide Rob Wood of Rancho Roberto, duelist Allison Binder, clairvoyant Jayne Amelia Larson, Rex "Hook 'em" Linn, the flamenco trilling provocateur Christine "Sevillanas" Champion and the Wild Bunch: Josh Kesselman, Steve Fisher, Jack Leighton, Chris Ridenhour, and Will Lowery.

A big thanks to Ed Harris, the extraordinary man who so expertly brought Robert B. Parker's Virgil Cole to life on the silver screen: "Feelings get you killed." And Viggo Mortensen for his continued inspiration as the man of reasoning, Everett Hitch. I'd also like to tip my hat to the whitewater team Helen Brann, Chris Pepe, and Meaghan Wagner. Importantly, I'd also like to acknowledge Joan Parker for her inspiration. Her profound, frank, and perceptive take on the work was intoxicating, and she will forever be truly missed.